He opened his mouth, but his breath was gone.

In the last second of his life he realized he had failed. It was over for him; in the short space of one second of consciousness, his mind raced over the things he had wanted to do, things he would not get the chance to do. His vision dimmed and narrowed to a small dark, blurred spot. His face clouded as his paralyzed mind seemed unable to visualize the inevitable.

When the back of his head hit the pavement, he was already dead. . . .

LIFE FORM

"In the tradition of *The Andromeda Strain* . . . an engrossing and well-written first novel."
—John David Connor, author of *Contagion*

Life Form

KEITH WILSON, M.D.

BERKLEY BOOKS, NEW YORK

LIFE FORM

A Berkley Book / published by arrangement with
the author

Berkley edition / August 1992

Copyright © 1992 by Keith D. Wilson.
This book may not be reproduced in whole or in part,
by mimeograph or any other means, without permission.
For information address: The Berkley Publishing Group,
200 Madison Avenue, New York, New York 10016.

A BERKLEY BOOK ® TM 757,375
Berkley Books are published by The Berkley Publishing Group,
200 Madison Avenue, New York, New York 10016.
The name ''BERKLEY'' and the ''B'' logo
are trademarks belonging to Berkley Publishing Corporation.

PRINTED IN THE UNITED STATES OF AMERICA

10 9 8 7 6 5 4 3 2 1

Acknowledgments

First, a special thanks to my dear friend and greatest teacher, Gary Provost, for his help in seeing this book through to its completion.

To the various assistant secretaries of defense at the Pentagon for their kindness and generous supply of information.

To Don Bottles of the Federal Bureau of Investigation.

To Barbara Norville, Dennis Hensley, and Nan Shram Williams for their fine editing of a cumbersome beginning.

To Anne LeClaire for her kindness and advice at the beginning. To Frank Strunk for his encouragement and to Lori Strong for her review.

A very special thanks to Cathy for hours of rewriting, editing, suggestions, and constant support.

And finally to Lori Perkins and Andrew Zack for making it happen.

K.D.W.

To Cathy—
my friend, editor, and wife

1

Vicki James tossed and turned during the night as she fought with the blankets, first burning up and sweating, then shaking with chills. When the first pale shaft of sunlight streamed through the windows, she threw back the damp blanket and rolled upright on the cot. Squinting against a painful knot in her stomach, she forced herself to get up. She wasn't about to stay in bed on the biggest day of her life.

Declining a room in the guest house with the other riders, Vicki had chosen to sleep in the stable on a cot to be near her horse. She always slept in the stables when they were on the road.

Vicki peered across the stable in the direction of the big chestnut stallion but couldn't see him through the dust-choked air. But she could hear the spirited, temperamental stallion snorting and banging his powerful body against the stall.

Vicki pulled her straw-colored disheveled hair away from her face. She was a thin, delicate-appearing twelve-year-old; her large gray-blue eyes added a sense of frailty. But first impressions were deceiving. Her small, wiry frame possessed great stamina; months of hard training had produced legs like strong springs and a back that held its posture after hours in the saddle. The quiet, intelligent girl was driven by a stubborn determination. Her relentless pursuit of the Cup would shortly be tested against the best riders in the nation.

Vicki went into the tack room and gathered her clothes and overnight case. She needed a hot shower. As she started to leave she clutched her stomach and vomited a small amount of bitter clear mucus. A churning nausea moved through her belly and she retched again, bent over with painful dry heaves. She felt shaky and broke into a cold, clammy sweat as she held on to the door frame to steady herself. She'd been sick for two days and knew she was coming down with the flu.

After a minute the bone-melting weakness receded, and Vicki wiped sweat from her forehead with a towel. She picked up her duffel bag and headed for the shower.

She paused in front of the stallion's stall. Diablo stretched his neck toward her and shook his head violently, throwing his black mane out in a wide arc. With ears back flat against his head and eyes wide, showing white, he gave a loud shrill neigh. His muscles twitched, and he stomped the ground impatiently.

She slapped his thick, muscular neck. "Morning, you rascal. You're sure perky. I'm glad one of us had a good night."

A massive stallion possessing great strength, Diablo stood almost eighteen hands high. His bloodline was unique. He inherited muscle and raw strength from his dam, a tall, powerful Hanoverian; his fiery temperament came from his Arabian sire. The combination was a unique genetic blend creating the ultimate jumper. Vicki was the master of the stallion who was too spirited for most men to ride. There was a special bond between her and the great animal.

"Just wait, Diablo. Patience. Today's our day. We can do it." With a final quieting pat, she rubbed his soft muzzle and moved on.

Vicki was lightheaded and dizzy as she walked along the stalls. Her joints ached, her head throbbed, and her eyes burned. Wishing she had gotten more sleep, she wondered how she would make it through the day.

"Are you feeling all right, squirt? You look a little pale." A figure stepping from the shadows startled her.

"Oh! Morning, George."

"You don't look too good," he said, studying her. "You sure you can go through with it today?" Seventy-year-old George Martin had been training horses on the James ranch forever; what he didn't know about horses wasn't worth knowing. His wide-brimmed Stetson and bowed legs were his trademarks.

"We'll do fine, George. Quit worrying." Her smile showed braces.

George stepped up closer. "I'm not talking about Diablo, I'm talking about you." He placed his hand on her forehead. "Gotta fever, don't you?"

She pushed his hand away. "Nah, I'm okay. Are Mom and Dad here yet?"

"No, they just called from Boston to say their plane's been delayed," he said. "But don't you worry," he said when her shoulders sagged in disappointment, "they'll make it. Get some rest this morning and let me exercise Diablo. You just take it easy." George gave her an assuring hug and walked away.

Vicki's parents owned a large horse farm on the outskirts of Loudonville, a remote picturesque town in the White Mountains of New Hampshire. She had been around horses even before she could walk; the love of horses was in her blood, more natural to her than bicycles or roller skates.

She and Diablo had compiled an impressive record of three consecutive Grand Prix victories, including the President's Cup in Washington, D.C., a week earlier. Today's National Invitational in Lexington, Kentucky, was the final event of the summer.

One more victory and she would be in the World Cup competition.

Horse Park Stadium reverberated with the tension of the thousands of spectators and reporters jamming the stands. Only forty-five horses and riders out of a field of three hundred had qualified for the season's final event. The trophy was the American Cup. The winner would qualify for the World Cup competition in Sheffield, England.

The grass sparkled in the bright sunlight, and the temperature was a perfect seventy-two degrees, with just enough breeze to keep the flags rippling slowly overhead. The field smelled of cut grass, fresh paint, and sawdust, mixed with a faint hint of leather and horse.

The championship course had fifteen difficult gates. During the first round, twenty-three horses were knocked out of the competition solely because of fence number eleven—a treacherous triple combination. It started with a small knoll that required just enough effort to make the first five-foot rail a cumbersome uphill jump that strained both horse and rider. Before regaining full strides, two short strides brought the horse to a six-foot wall and pole, followed immediately by another rail, then a drop back down the knoll. Even if the horse made the jump without a fault, considerable time could be lost in a timed event.

Only nine horses had survived the first round without a fault, and they were now facing a jump-off round to determine the winner of the Cup. It would be a timed event; the rider who finished in the shortest time without a fault would be the winner. Tension spread through the crowd as it waited for the drama to begin.

The timed round would be brutal. Rider and horse would be testing the limits of their skill and endurance.

The first two horses in the final jump-off had completed perfect rounds, with only seven seconds separating them. The horse just finishing the course had been an Olympic finalist and a previous Cup winner, but it had knocked down a rail at gate fourteen, an automatic elimination in a jump-off. Seeing the horse ahead of her fault at post fourteen unnerved Vicki.

"Don't push Diablo too fast on the turns. Keep him reined tight." George looked up at her and winked. His thick gnarled fingers checked the buckle on the cinch for the third time. "Go get 'em, fella," he said, slapping the stallion on the rump before he left to join her parents in the grandstands. He turned back toward her and gestured a thumbs-up, then continued on, his old stained Stetson soon lost among the crowd.

Vicki sat high and straight on the massive chestnut stallion as they waited their turn to enter the arena. They were beautifully matched for color and grace and were always favorites with the crowds. Her straw-colored hair flowed over the shoulders of her crimson jacket, and her black, polished boots gleamed in the sunlight. George had groomed Diablo's coat to perfection, and the stallion looked magnificent with his black saddle and contrasting red girth. The awesome size of the horse demanded attention.

A tangled network of black cables fed into a large truck bearing the ABC SPORTS logo that housed the control center for a bank of cameras. A man with a portable camcorder moved beside Vicki for a close-up shot. She looked up into the crowded stands; George and her parents were somewhere among the sea of faces. Her parents had arrived an hour ago and had just had time to give Vicki a quick kiss and a hug before the event started.

Diablo ground the bit in his teeth, threw his head up, and snorted. She felt the stallion tremble and he pawed at the ground. The noise of the packed stadium excited him. His sides flared as he gulped air through his nostrils and his powerful shoulder muscles twitched nervously. She needed to maintain absolute control of her horse to achieve the critical timing necessary at the start of each jump, or the large horse could become too feisty even for her. The stallion's ribs strained against the tight cinch of the saddle as Vicki fought to subdue two thousand pounds of raw nerve and muscle. She jerked on his reins, her own nerves frayed. The stallion neighed back in protest and snapped his head down.

Vicki leaned forward and grabbed a handful of thick mane and forced a firm "Diablo!"

A wave of nausea hit her again. Vicki shivered. Cold sweat soaked her back. She had vomited several times during the morning and gulped down enough Pepto-Bismol to turn pink.

A skull-crushing headache made her wince in pain. Vicki reached up and loosened the hard hunting cap and wiped her forehead with the back of her glove.

She placed her hands on either side of her head and tried to squeeze the pain into submission. Weak and dehydrated from vomiting, she prayed for relief, just for a little while. The nausea ebbed a little.

Why did everything have to come at the same time? Her first National Invitational event, the flu, and a jump-off round for the championship. The illness that now threatened to undo her months of disciplined training angered her.

"Number thirty-seven, Miss Vicki James riding Diablo."

That was her cue. She adjusted her cap and nudged Diablo with her knee. He turned sideways, jerked against the reins, then trotted into the arena.

She eased Diablo into a progressively faster gallop. His powerful body moved effortlessly toward the first jump, his thick muscles rippling in the sun. Vicki's hair streamed out as she leaned low on his back, her arms stretched forward in perfect form.

The first jump was a five-foot gate and Vicki pressed her knees tightly and moved up on the pommel of the saddle. She stretched low over the Hanoverian's thick neck as he bolted easily over the obstacle. Rhythm and balance were essential between horse and rider. They moved through the air as one and landed smoothly.

She felt dizzy again. Her eyes watered. She squinted against the stinging wind and turned Diablo to face the second jump, a six-foot rail that he took with ease. Time was the only thing separating the winner from the losers and Vicki let Diablo go. The fiery horse sensed the free rein and steel muscles responded as he accelerated, a faint layer of foamy sweat forming on his withers as long legs ate up the ground. The unchecked horse moved like a demon possessed, nostrils flaring and ears back.

Charging at the gates with pure instinct, the stallion jumped the next seven gates effortlessly, his stride never faltering, never pausing. Vicki struggled to keep her balance as Diablo gained momentum for the jump at gate ten, a wall and pole combination. He lunged upward, and she found herself sliding up onto his withers as she struggled to hang on. Again, he cleared it easily.

Everything dimmed and Vicki thought she was going to faint. What was happening to her? Her ashen-gray face was beaded with a cold sweat. She didn't dare stop now; she couldn't do that to Diablo when they were so close to victory. They had worked so hard and had come too far.

They arrived at the ultimate challenge, gate eleven—the feared triple combination obstacle on the steep knoll. She should have reined Diablo in a bit, but she didn't. His powerful legs could easily carry them over the jumps, and she planned to do it quickly to put time between them and the other horses. When Diablo ran with free rein, nobody could catch him.

Vicki nudged him on. Her head pounded with each stride and she grew sicker by the minute. Unable to focus on anything ahead of her, she followed through the jumps by feeling his cues beneath her. She felt his muscles pull as he climbed the knoll and jumped the first rail.

When he took the second jump, she was too far forward on his neck, which would have prevented most horses from even starting the jump. But Diablo's great size and strength kept him in stride and he cleared it. The jump threw Vicki wildly off balance. She grabbed his sweaty neck and dug her fingers into his mane to hang on, but she couldn't recover in time for the third jump. She went flying over Diablo's head.

She slammed into the ground with a thud and didn't move. Diablo tore off at a full gallop, circling the area with reins flailing behind. The crowd's moan was followed by an unsettling quiet.

Diablo walked back to her and nudged her body firmly with his nose. Vicki didn't move. Her mother stood and screamed.

2

Methodist Hospital
Lexington, Kentucky

"CODE THREE ARRIVING!"

Emergency. Red lights and siren. The nurse made sure the two doctors—a second-year emergency-room resident busy reading an article on brown recluse spider bites and a senior surgery resident on the phone trying to arrange a date with a pediatric nurse with a wild reputation—had heard her.

They both looked up and nodded.

The pneumatic doors hissed open and the lifesquad paramedics wheeled Vicki James into the emergency room. Overhead bright surgical lights blazed on and Trauma Room Number 3 came to life. The two residents and three nurses swarmed over Vicki, checking pupils, respirations, and blood pressure. Fingers probed and penlights clicked on as they searched for injuries. An ugly purple bruise covered her right shoulder where she had landed.

A nurse looked up from the monitor. "Blood pressure is eighty over forty. Pulse fifty-two." She checked her watch and recorded her findings and time on the ER sheet.

The surgery resident checking Vicki for fractures nodded. "She's got to be losing blood somewhere. Maybe a ruptured spleen. Get an IV going and hang a liter of Ringer's lactate. Piggyback two ampules of Dopamine in five hundred cc's of D5W." He pulled out his stethoscope and listened to her lungs. Loud moist rales crackled with each labored breath.

He looked over at the ER resident. He was worried about

her slow heart rate, afraid that her lung was punctured. "I don't know what's going on here. Why does she have bradycardia? Maybe a pneumothorax?"

The ER resident nodded and turned to a nurse. "Get an oxygen mask on her, six liters per minute. Order a portable chest x-ray stat, then call the lab and get a stat type and cross-match. Hang two units of O-negative now. And monitor that blood pressure."

Using large bandage scissors, the nurses cut away her clothes and put a clean light blue hospital gown on her. They glued monitor patches to her chest and snapped leads in place, then threaded an eighteen-gauge angio-cath needle into a vein in her elbow.

Vicki remained unresponsive. Technologists from the laboratory and radiology arrived.

"Get a neurologist down here," the surgery resident ordered, not happy with the way things were going. A slow heart rate with hypotension suggested brain damage, and a neurologist would be much better prepared to handle that.

Dr. Jim Eller, neurologist, was making rounds on the eighth floor when his beeper went off for the hundredth time, this time sending him to the ER. He went to the elevator and punched the "down" button several times. He'd never finish rounds at this rate. Eller sported thinning blond hair and stood six-feet-three with broad shoulders and thick fingers more suited to being a linebacker, which he had been at Ohio State.

Ten hours into his twenty-four-hour shift, Eller had already consumed seven cups of coffee, but he hadn't eaten yet. He had learned long ago how to doze ten minutes at a time between calls. Wired on stale coffee and craving a Rolaids to quell the acidic eruption in his stomach, Eller stared down at the bitter grounds at the bottom of his cup, the last dregs left in the pot after the day shift.

Within minutes Eller arrived and performed a quick but thorough neurological examination. Vicki was unresponsive even to painful stimuli, and his examination suggested that the meningeal tissues that covered her brain and spinal cord were inflamed. Her respirations were shallow and labored.

Eller snapped on his penlight and did a quick neuro-ophthalmic assessment. Vicki's dilated left pupil showed no reaction to light stimulation. "She's burning up. Looks more like sepsis than a head injury. Somebody read me her sheet."

A nurse picked up the clipboard: "Twelve-year-old female sustained undetermined injury after being thrown from a horse. Suspect head and internal injuries. She has remained unresponsive and hypotensive with bradycardia. Blood pressure seventy over forty, pulse fifty-two. She's from New Hampshire. Her parents are in the waiting area."

Eller's hands probed around her neck. His penlight darted around, looking for blood in the ear, behind the eardrums, in the eyes and nose, but there was no evidence of external bleeding from a skull fracture. He turned to the two residents: "Could be a brainstem hemorrhage. Call radiology and get a CT scan." Eller was perplexed; everything pointed more to infection with sepsis rather than shock from blood loss. And that didn't fit with her history of a fall.

Vicki's breathing became progressively more labored with deep wheezing sounds, her lips drawn tight.

Eller grabbed the chart and read it again. "I want blood gases and electrolytes drawn, stat! And get a tray out for intubation."

The surgical resident took a stainless-steel instrument from the tray and slid it down the back of her throat. He fed the curved polystyrene endotracheal tube over the metal guide into her trachea and inflated the cuff. Vicki coughed and turned a cyanotic dusky blue. He suctioned her through the tube, then snaked a nasogastric tube through her nose and down into her stomach.

A nurse stabbed another needle into her elbow, and the IV tubing fed dark red O-negative into her veins. Less than an hour after arriving at the hospital, a tangled network of tubes, catheters, and IVs had invaded her body, robbing her of dignity.

Portable x-rays taken in the trauma room revealed a broken right shoulder and two broken ribs and her chest x-ray showed dense infiltrates in both lungs. Eller decided to perform a spinal tap. After scrubbing her back with Betadine antiseptic he carefully guided the long shiny needle into her lumber spinal canal between the fourth and fifth vertebrae. Dirty yellow cloudy cerebral spinal fluid dripped out. He withdrew enough fluid to culture, then pulled the needle out.

"Start IV Keflin," Eller blurted out as he scribbled in the chart. He decided Keflin was probably the best antibiotic to start her on until the cultures came back. He wanted her moved to the intensive care unit as soon as possible. "Give her two grams over the first hour, then six grams divided over three doses. Get blood cultures hourly times three."

He knew he was dealing with an overwhelming infection. This was not just a straightforward trauma case. He couldn't put it all together. He jotted a quick progress note in the chart, tossed the foam cup in the trash, and left to finish rounds.

Eller checked in on her shortly after midnight, but there had been no change. He staggered back to bed.

At 3:58 A.M. Dr. Eller's phone rang.

"Dr. Eller, ICU stat!"

Weary from lack of sleep, he scrambled over to the intensive care unit. Vicki James had had a seizure, followed by a life-threatening crisis of vascular collapse with a dangerously low blood pressure. Dr. Eller ordered an ampule of Isuprel bolus to get her blood pressure up fast, and a phenobarbital drip to control her seizures.

The infection was causing the brain to swell, and the cerebral edema drove her brain into a deeper coma, slowly and methodically shutting down all of her vital function centers. All voluntary movement was absent and she could no longer struggle; her only movements now were reflexes.

The blood gases were worse than before. Pneumonia choked her lungs and robbed them of air.

Eller wrote orders for Decadron IV every four hours and a mannitol infusion to decrease her intracranial pressure, and tagged the order sheet "stat." The Decadron and mannitol would ease the swelling of her brain.

He should have signed off this case earlier. It sure as hell wasn't neuro, and he was too busy to get involved in some damned complicated infectious disease case. But now he was too involved to drop it. Eller went back to bed to catch up on some much needed sleep.

During the dark early hours on Sunday, Vicki's condition deteriorated. The slow, regular *beep . . . beep . . . beep* of the cardiac monitor stopped, followed by a high-pitched alarm. The nurse shot a glance at the monitor and spun around. "Code in bed three! Get Dr. Eller over here."

"CODE 99—INTENSIVE CARE! CODE 99—INTENSIVE CARE!"

Eller leaped out of bed and grabbed his coat just as his own beeper went off. He tore through the door and sprinted the short distance to intensive care. The ER resident was already there, and the code team was on Eller's heels.

"She's in v-fib!" Ventricular fibrillation, a useless quivering motion of the heart that produced no pulse. The nurse pulled the crash cart over to the bed as another nurse injected a 50mg bolus of lidocaine through the IV line, a drug that would make the heart beat normally.

"Defibrillation paddles," he bellowed out. After a quick glance at control settings on the machine, Eller placed one under her left breast, the other behind her shoulder. "Everybody clear."

Electric defibrillators sent a short 400-watt charge through her chest. Her arms and legs jerked from the jolt, then dropped lifeless.

A nurse looked up at the flat tracing on the monitor.

"Asystole." Vicki's heart had stopped.

Eller glanced at the straight line tracing. He was going to

lose her—from pneumonia. What the hell was going on? He ripped open the front of her gown and exposed her chest, and his fingers found the lower end of her sternum.

"Intracardiac epinephrine." Eller took the syringe with its three-inch needle and guided it between her breasts into the left ventricle of her heart, drawing back dark venous blood to check his position, then injected three cc's of 1:10,000 dilution of adrenaline directly into the heart.

Sweat beaded his forehead and soaked his day-old scrub shirt. The muscles in his temple twitched.

Things were going to hell in a hurry.

"Two ampules of sodium bicarb! And another bolus of seventy-five milligrams lidocaine!" The sodium bicarbonate would neutralize the toxic buildup of acid caused by a heart that had stopped pumping.

For one desperate hour the unit became a scene of frantic scrambling as the doctors and nurses on the code team tried everything, alternating drugs, electrical conversion, and mechanical cardiac compression.

Vicki did not respond. Eller looked up at the monitor, defeat carved in his tired face. The cardiac monitor buzzed a flat tracing. He snapped on his penlight and forced himself to look into the empty eyes of the young girl. Dull, glazed eyes stared out at nothing, the pupils dilated and unable to respond to the light.

"Cancel the code. We've lost her." A tearful, bleary-eyed Eller buried his head in his hands.

Vicki James was pronounced dead at 5:45 A.M. on the morning of July twenty-eighth. Tubes and catheters were removed, a starched white sheet was pulled over her body, and the cart wheeled away to the morgue.

Bed three in intensive care stood empty.

Eller slammed his fist on the table, then left the unit. It didn't make any sense!

3

Desolation Peak
New Hampshire

MATT STRONG CLUNG to the rock by his fingertips as his body dangled eight hundred feet above the ground. He hung from a vertical face with only a sliver of ledge to grip. Sliding his hands along the groove, he inched his way across the granite slab. Fingers that were nearly useless from fatigue felt like they were being pulled from their sockets by the weight of his body. His foot kicked against the rock, searching for a hold.

Matt's six-foot two-inch frame was trim and firm, but his arms ached and tired muscles cried out for a break. He had been hanging by just his fingertips for more than ten minutes. The pain that burned through his fingers demanded that he find a foothold and give his hands a rest.

He couldn't see his best friend, Jeff Stockwell, waiting seventy feet below him; Matt's face was pressed flat against the rock as he struggled to hang on, unable to look down. The granite was cold against his cheek, lifeless and impersonal. Jeff, a precise technical climber, with every move calculated, had suggested taking an easier route to avoid the dangerous rock face.

But Matt, a daring climber whose moves bordered on recklessness, relying more on instinct than standard technique, had ignored him. He wanted to *conquer* Desolation Peak, not walk around on it. So he had led them up the most challenging route. Now, Matt was hanging like a piece of laundry as he tried to traverse the vertical slab. Doubts began to crowd into his mind. Maybe he'd pushed himself too far this time, maybe he'd been too reckless.

Matt's boot knocked loose a melon-sized chunk of rock that clunked once against the face, then ricocheted into space.

"Rock!" he yelled down to Jeff.

The rock fell silently, then smashed into the boulders eight hundred feet below with a sickening crunch. His foot explored again and the edge of his boot caught a piece of rock. Matt tested it with a little weight. His boot slipped and the sudden jerk sent pain coursing through his exhausted shoulders, biceps, and into the ends of his cramped fingers.

Sucking in a lungful of air and gritting his teeth against the pain, he stretched his foot out even farther and tried again; the lug of his boot found another edge. It held. He moved his hand out along the rock, but the groove disappeared and he palmed only smooth lifeless granite. Out of options and his energy drained, it seemed the rock face was about to defeat him. His right hand could find no hold on the rock and if his boot slipped, he would fall.

Eight feet to his right he spotted a long jagged fissure in the rock that would hold a piton—if he could reach it. But eight feet seemed like a mile when hanging by only the fingers of one hand and the tip of a boot.

"Slack!" he called down. Sweat beaded his face and he tried to ignore the blinding pain that threatened to paralyze his already spent fingers. The braided nylon rope around his waist went slack. It was the worst possible time to go off belay, but he had eight feet of rock to cover.

Fatigue oozed from every pore of his body. Using only a shaving of a foothold, he called up the last bit of strength from deep inside himself and lunged for the fissure. Fingertips clawed at the rock and found a hold, then he deftly brought up a piton and jammed it home, snapped a carabiner through the eye of the piton, and secured the rope.

"Tension!" he called. The rope drew tight and Matt eased his weight down to test the piton. His arms dropped to his sides and he worked to loosen tight, cramped muscles. That hellish prehistoric piece of granite hadn't defeated him yet, he thought with growing satisfaction. Swaying from the rope tied around his waist, he pounded a Phillips bolt into the rock for added security and snapped on another carabiner. He flexed and extended his hands, trying to restore life into his nearly useless fingers.

He still had to get off the slab.

Leaning back to get a better view, he studied the rock face. The easy, unassisted class three free climb on granite had deteriorated into a dangerous class five technical climb on low-grade metamorphic junk. Crumbly and unreliable.

The cut to his right that snaked upward along the contour of the mountain would lead them to the top. It had large boulders, deep fissures—good granite rock with secure holds. Easy class three stuff from there.

He took a deep breath and stretched his leg out for a new footing, extended his arm and found a groove in the rock. Swinging up and grabbing another outcrop of rock, he was finally on his way. He climbed with his eyes now, studying ahead and memorizing the rock. With catlike agility he followed ridges and cracks with pure body balance, smooth motion of hands and feet using three-point support. Foot up, test the hold, pull up and over the rock, jam fingers into a new crack, and move higher.

Deftly and with assurance he found routes over the rock where none seemed to exist. This was climbing. No more crude fingernail holds. He pushed with his feet, pulled up with his hands, and nimbly crawled over the rock, now eighty feet above the smooth rock face he had traversed.

Matt anchored himself for a belay. Jeff would swing across the slab on the rope like a pendulum, then follow Matt's route to the cut on the right and take the lead. Except for the most difficult and challenging sections of a climb, Jeff, the technical purist, always took lead point.

Matt wedged himself between two boulders, wrapped the rope around his hand, then secured the nylon rope with a turn around a boulder. He wiped sweat from his forehead with the back of his hand. It was the heart of summer, and the afternoon sun beat down without a breath of wind to counter its relentless, building heat. "Secured!" he yelled down to Jeff.

"On belay." Jeff leaped from his position a hundred feet below and swung across the vertical face. The winding on the rock took the strain, and all Matt had to do was keep the line tight. Jeff completed the traverse and started up the cut. Matt freed the line from the boulder and started taking up slack.

Then it happened.

Jeff shouted an obscenity through the sound of crashing rock and scree. Matt grabbed a fistful of rope and braced himself as the line snapped taut with the full weight of Jeff's falling body. Pain erupted as the knot around Matt's waist jerked and the rope dug in—seeking a weak spot to tear out his guts. His right hand dug into the rock for a grip while his left hand held the rope. His fingers burned with pain as he struggled to keep his grip. Agonized sweat beaded his face. It lasted all of thirty seconds but felt like an hour.

"Off belay," Jeff finally called from below and the rope went slack. His voice was strained as he fought for breath.

Matt adjusted his hold on the line and kept tension, prepared to take hold for another emergency belay. "Hey, Jeff, what the hell you doing down there? You nearly cut me in half. Are you okay?"

Without answering, Jeff moved to the left and took the lead up the cut, avoiding the dangerous scree that filled the fall line. He moved toward the summit, pulling the braided nylon rope after him. Matt saw that the fall had torn Jeff's sleeve, and his arm was soaked with blood.

With the safety rope stretched between them the two men climbed. The summit of Desolation Peak rose two hundred feet above them, the rest of the climb to the top mostly class three. The New Hampshire cliffs were different from the peaks they had scaled together in Colorado. Climbing the eastern peaks was usually a mechanical process. Careful attention to technique and sound climbing skills would generally get you to the top.

But there were no hundred-mile scenic views from the summit to reward climbers. Desolation Peak was only 4,270 feet high. Mount Washington was the "king" of the Appalachians even though it stood only 6,288 feet—freezing, windy, and unpredictable as hell, but it offered no real excitement.

But the Rockies were majestic; dangerous with jagged peaks, granite canyons, craggy walls of hundred-ton boulders. To conquer them required imagination, pitting strength of body and mind against the mountain. At the top the air was crisp and thin, the winds powerful, and the view extended a hundred miles in every direction. The climbs in Boulder and Eldorado Canyons were always class fives on nearly perfect granite.

Matt and Jeff—"Mutt and Jeff" to their friends—had been close friends ever since they moved into the cramped quarters of room 637 at Smith Hall their junior year. Matt and Jeff roomed together their last two years at the University of Colorado, climbed mountains together, biked together, and once even dated the same girl.

In many ways, however, they were opposites. Jeff Stockwell was fair-skinned with brown hair showing a few strands of gray. He had a thick stout body on a five-foot nine-inch frame. Jeff, the pragmatic and organized one, had majored in math.

Matt was taller, a ruggedly handsome man with pale blue eyes that contrasted a tan face and thick, black hair. Angular cheekbones molded a sensuous face, accentuated by a generous mouth and a disarming smile. Matt was the idealistic one, often impetuous, but always rebellious, shunning rules and conformity. He had majored in biology.

They were the same age and as close as brothers. They shared a zest for life that pushed them to their limits; danger and excitement was the common thread and cementing force of their friendship. They had scaled dozens of peaks together and experienced that special bond that comes from hanging roped together two thousand feet above the ground.

Smith Hall's room 637 saw the birth of dozens of crazy stunts and practical jokes. At Jeff's urging Matt joined the University of Colorado's bicycle team and together they led the Colorado Buffaloes to an NCAA championship season their senior year.

The nylon rope pulled taut and Matt followed Jeff's lead, finally pulling himself over the top. It had been a difficult climb. A dirty, dangerous, scrappy climb up crumbly rock and scree.

Jeff had already taken off his shirt and was wrapping his arm with gauze from the emergency kit. After quickly dropping his pack and coil of nylon rope to the ground, Matt took the gauze and finished dressing Jeff's wound. Blood was already starting to soak through the dressing. Matt watched the gauze turn red as he put strips of adhesive over it. "You should have let me take a look at it before you wrapped it up. How bad is it?"

"Just a scrape," Jeff said. "It's nothing. I wasn't paying close enough attention to the rock."

"Seems like a lot of blood for just a scrape." Matt ripped off the end of the tape and secured it. Then he took trail mix from his pack and sat down against a rock.

Jeff pulled an apple out of his pack and bit into it. "Well—I've made a decision."

"About what?"

"I've decided I'm not going to teach next year. I quit."

"What? You quit? What are you talking about?"

"I've joined the Special Forces. As an instructor. After basics and boot camp I'll be promoted to second lieutenant."

"You're joking. You actually joined the army?"

"Special Forces. I can't take being inside four walls all the time. I've got to try something different."

"Wasn't there anything you could think of doing other

than joining the army?'' Matt asked. Jeff had talked about doing something different, but Matt always assumed it was just the kind of daydreaming that everybody did, like saying you wished you'd become a cowboy or a forest ranger. But people just talked about it; no one ever actually quit their job and tried to do it.

A feeling of indignation began welling up inside him because Jeff hadn't told him about his plans until now. "You're crazy. You're too old," Matt said. "You won't be able to keep up with them."

"What, those pimply adolescents we have in class? You've got to be kidding. We're in better shape than any of them."

Matt shook his head as he looked at his friend in disbelief. "What do you think you're doing? You're twenty-nine years old. The army wants younger men to do that. That's what this whole thing is about, isn't it? Turning thirty next month."

"No, that's not what this is about. I just don't want to wake up some morning and realize that I didn't live my life the way I wanted to, that I'd wasted it." He looked at Matt. "That's why I joined. I don't want to miss anything."

Matt looked down at the ground, still unable to believe what he'd heard. "How soon do you leave?"

"Not till after Labor Day," Jeff said and glanced down at the bloodstained bandage. "I'll be stationed full-time at Fort Carson to teach mountaineering. Jennifer and I have moved our wedding plans up, probably November." Jennifer had taken a job in Denver after graduating from college, and Matt knew the long-distance relationship was a growing problem for Jeff.

"You're just going to leave everything you worked for behind? You're crazy, you know that?"

"Yeah, maybe—but I had to do it or hate myself forever for not trying," Jeff said. "I want to go back to Colorado, marry Jennifer, and settle down."

"Settle down? Stagnate is more like it. You'll spend your weekends cutting the lawn and washing the station wagon."

Jeff looked at him and shaded his eyes from the sun, a smile on his face for the first time. "When are you going to get married? You're not getting any younger."

"Probably never. I'd make a lousy husband." Matt was fiercely independent. Although he had a great passion for sports and women and pursued them both with vigor, he could never commit himself to marriage or the responsibility of raising children. His heart had been broken once and he didn't want that to happen again.

A red-tailed hawk glided through the sky at eye level, and screamed a cry of defiance at the forest while they sat in silence under the hot sun, staring out over the New Hampshire hills from their lofty perch.

Jeff finished his apple. "Hey, we've still got the rest of the summer."

Matt stood and prepared to rappel down. "Last one down buys the pizza and beer."

Jeff threw his apple core at him and sprang to his feet. Ropes flew over the side and the two leaped into space. The rope burned through their gloves and their feet kicked them away from the rock as they dropped.

The ground moved up to greet the winner.

4

Fort Carson Army Base
Colorado Springs, Colorado

THE FIERCE SUN baked the vast silence with a heat so intense
it was tangible. The air shimmered above the parched,
cracked dirt. Heavy combat boots pounded the rutted road
as sixty figures bobbed in unison through the blurring heat.
Not a breath of wind stirred; the yucca and sagebrush that
dotted the plains stood motionless as the troops passed.

Private First Class Jeff Stockwell knew he still had three
miles to go, and he was feeling worse by the minute. His
soaked T-shirt clung to his back like a soggy rag, and goose
bumps dotted his clammy skin. He swatted at tiny annoying
insects that darted around his face.

An errant puff of breeze brought no relief, only a brief
gust of oven-hot air.

Jeff and the other sweating "grunts" were about to finish
their third week of basic training. They looked homoge-
neous; heads shaved, white T-shirts, olive-drab fatigues,
black boots. They marched, ate slop from the mess, endured
daily ten-mile runs, fired their M-16s, learned hand-to-hand
combat, slithered on their bellies through black mud. Then
they started over again. They marched at night, in the rain,
chin up, chest out, eyes forward. They hadn't read a
newspaper or seen television since they had arrived. The
army owned them.

Jeff had been in Colorado only three weeks and wondered
whether his weariness was due to the higher altitude's thin
atmosphere. The afternoon sun burned relentlessly as rivers

of sweat blurred his vision. Each step became more difficult as the heat drained energy from his body.

Jeff possessed a solid muscular body that moved with the agility of a cat. He was a superb athlete and couldn't understand why today's run was so difficult. He knew he was in better condition that any of the younger recruits around him.

He had been fighting a cold for the past two days but until now thought the worst of it was over. Waves of stomach cramps churned in his guts, and his joints ached. Pain knifed through his lungs and he labored for every breath.

He pushed on.

Two miles to go. Determined to make it, Jeff focused on the road ahead and kept cadence with the others, refusing to fall behind and ignoring the protests of his body.

At the top of the ridge, the front range of the Rockies came into view. Even in July snow clung stubbornly to the highest peaks. The faded barracks of Fort Carson, spreading in white lines across the ravine below, marked the end of the agonizing ten miles. Thunder rumbled from the artillery field and blended with the muffled engines of jeeps and troop trucks that crisscrossed the base.

The base was in a flurry of activity preparing for the arrival of a new base commander, some young gung ho two-star general. High-ranking military brass had arrived throughout the week. Polished jeeps and 109mm howitzers had been moved into position around the parade grounds; flags fluttered over the freshly painted reviewing stands, and units marched in formation on the open drill fields. The army loved parades; it thrived on them. Parades symbolized what the army was all about: absolute discipline and order.

Jeff wondered if maybe he should have stayed in New Hampshire and continued teaching. He and Jennifer could have had a good life. He pushed the thoughts from his mind. It was just the inevitable expected feelings of insecurity about facing the unknown, along with a gnawing homesickness for familiar surroundings and the friends he'd left behind.

Less than a mile to go, all downhill. He was hot. He was thirsty. And he was exhausted. Jeff began to wonder if he could finish the full ten miles. Cold sweat ran down the small of his back and a shiver rippled through him. His hands were ice-cold, despite the searing heat.

The sandy-haired grunt in front of him glanced back. "Hey, Jeff—you look like shit. You gonna make it? What you say we tell that motherfucking sergeant up there to stuff this and get you back to the clinic?"

"Nah. I'll make it, Rusty. I might puke on your ass if you don't pick up the pace, but I'll make it." But he wasn't sure he could.

The road dropped down a steep ravine toward the barracks. His vision blurred. A wave of nausea turned his stomach sour. Damned heat! His limbs were heavy, his strength drained, and cold sweat dripped from his ashen skin.

Grabbing at his gut as it tightened with cramps, he staggered from the formation. His knees turned to rubber, and he tumbled forward into the dirt with a weighty thud.

Trembling hands spread out on the ground for support as the world spun wildly out of focus, his consciousness hazy. In agonizing slow motion he tried to sit up, then slumped back. He looked up at the fiery sun that seared into his eyes for a final, brief moment, then darkness closed over him.

Major Raymond Yost opened the door and started down the dark corridor. Yost had hated the morgue ever since medical school. The smell of a dead body with its belly gaping open to expose intestines and the pungent odor of formaldehyde nauseated him.

The sudden death of the young man sent ripples of alarm through the base. Yost and his staff feared an outbreak of meningitis. Within the close confines of a training base, the lethal bacteria Neisseria could spread through the barracks in hours, with heavy mortality.

Private Jeff Stockwell never regained consciousness, and he died less than twenty-four hours after collapsing on the road. While still on the ridge he had had a seizure, vomited, and sucked acidic gastric contents into his lungs. His condition deteriorated rapidly after his arrival at the base hospital.

Platoon Drill Sergeant Jones reported that Private Stockwell had been sick for two days and had requested aspirin because of a severe headache. But on the morning of the ten-mile run he seemed better.

In the emergency room an examination revealed no motor movement, and no response to painful stimuli. A pinpoint left pupil and retinal bleeding suggested a diagnosis of intracranial hemorrhage with increased pressure. An emergency brain CT scan showed a mass within the right temporal lobe of the brain that the radiologist thought might be a large abscess. The scan showed evidence of increased intracranial pressure, brain edema, and compression of the brain stem against the skull.

A portable chest x-ray showed dense infiltrates in both lungs. Yost thought it probably represented both aspiration and pneumonia.

Yost admitted Stockwell directly to the intensive care unit and put him on a ventilator. His lungs were stiff and useless, unable to move air. Blood gases had shown an alarming drop in the p02 blood oxygen saturation to just thirty-five percent, dangerously low. The ventilator forced air into the lungs, but the effort was futile.

Bacteria and inflammation spread through the alveolar air spaces with the speed and tenacity of a windblown fire, choking off his lungs and suffocating him by degrees as organ systems failed. Finally, his oxygen-starved brain ceased to function and death followed.

The autopsy room was cold. Like death. Air-conditioning

hummed from the ceiling. Torrents of icy air poured out of large vents onto the scene below.

Colonel Myers was a spooky little man, and the role of pathologist seemed to suit him well. He sat hunched over his microscope and muttered rapidly into a microphone clipped to his jacket. A cigarette was smoldering away in the ashtray already piled high with butts and ashes. His nicotine-stained fingers trembled slightly as he fumbled with the focusing knob.

"What the hell did you guys do to this young man?" he asked harshly, without looking up.

Yost ignored the remark. "What have you found so far, Colonel?"

"Sepsis. Goddamned abscesses everywhere. Liver, kidneys, brain. Especially in the brain." His smudged glasses clicked against the eyepieces as he squinted into them, moving slides under the high-power field with the agility of a dealer shuffling cards.

Myers took a long deep drag from his filtered Winston and spoke through a growing blue cloud. "The lungs probably did him in, though." After snapping on a pair of gloves, he held up a lung, glistening and engorged a deep red, and pressed his finger against it. "Stiff as oak," he said, the cigarette bobbing up and down as he spoke, sending flakes of ash down.

Yost glimpsed over at the waxy pale body; naked, lifeless gray, and already transformed from a human into just pieces of muscle, bones, and organs. The belly gaped open to reveal an empty cavity, already having been completely gutted through one massive ventral incision extending from the top of the sternum to the pelvis. The lungs, heart, intestines, and liver had all been removed. Glistening white bone of the lumbar spine showed through the thin fascia at the back.

The deener was the assistant to the pathologist. His job was to prepare the body for gross examination by first sawing off the top of the skull and removing the brain, then systematically cutting out all the major organs. He stood at a long stainless-steel sink, weighing and measuring each organ before he placed it in a metal tray for examination by the pathologist. A stream of cold water running from a nozzle washed the blood down the drain.

The casual manner in which this morbid ritual of death was being carried out made Yost uncomfortable. This was not his territory. He did not belong here. His place was with the living, not with the dead.

"Any evidence of meningitis?"

"Nothing fancy like Neisseria if that's what you mean. Meningitis for sure . . . but just shit bugs. E. coli, staph, clumped cocci, and all kinds of gram negative rods. But no meningococci. The brain's over there if you care to examine it."

The brain lay in a shiny metal tray on the table, coldly illuminated by an overhead fluorescent light. Yost felt a wave of revulsion but walked over to steal a quick glance at it. Thick, purulent fluid covered the meninges and filled the deep furrows of the brain. A swollen, infected brain oozing pus.

Yost swallowed back the bile taste in his mouth. "When will the slides be finished?"

"Tomorrow, with any luck."

With a preliminary pathology report under his arm, Major Yost returned to his office.

Yost pulled the chest x-ray from the pile of other x-ray film folders on his chair and held it up to the light. He had looked at it a dozen times already. In ten years of military medicine, as chief of the Internal Medicine Department, he'd never seen such rampant infection by normal flora in a previously healthy individual.

The autopsy report described massive, overwhelming infection and sepsis, with brain abscesses and pneumonia as a complication. But the cultures were only garden-variety bacteria, staph aureus, E. coli, and *Bacillus subutlus*, all normal flora and not considered dangerous. Just skin and fecal contaminants—"shit bugs" as hard-assed Myers had called them.

"Shit bugs, my ass!" Yost mumbled in disgust and dropped Stockwell's chest x-ray back on the pile. He had been at the desk in his small office for over an hour, quietly contemplating the puzzling case. The blood smears had shown only a minimal leukocytosis, and the bone-marrow biopsy was normal.

Yost had systematically ruled out every possibility. He looked for drug reaction, leukemia, bone-marrow suppression, Mycoplasma organisms, even the plague. HIV antibody for AIDS was negative. He ran a toxin battery profile. He ran virus serum titers. The staff even searched for spider or snake bites. Everything. Something. Anything.

The body simply had not fought back. No immunity. But why not? Yost wondered. He made a note to himself to order a serum immunologic electrophoresis and to review all the viral serologies when they were finished.

The case had already ruined a weekend fishing trip in the mountains that he had been planning for weeks with his nine-year-old son. Top brass continued to demand information about the nature of the recruit's death. The pressure was unrelenting. They wanted answers now. What measures would they have to take to prevent an outbreak of meningitis?

Yost dropped the three-inch-thick, eight-pound *Darnoff's Immunology* textbook onto the desk and rubbed his eyes. He was tired and frustrated. It was late evening, and the sound of a lawn sprinkler mixed with the smell of the freshly cut grass drifted in through the open screened window. The streetlamp outside cast a faint light onto his desk. A radio on the bookshelf appropriately was playing "Solitary Man" by Neil Diamond. Everything had returned to normal at the base.

The report in front of him was both unrevealing and alarming. What had happened was evident:

Final Diagnosis:
1. Cerebral hemorrhage
2. Multiple abscesses
3. Necrotizing lobar pneumonia
4. Respiratory and renal failure

But something was missing. Why had it happened? What had suppressed the young man's immune system so suddenly?

Something different, something terribly out of the ordinary had happened to Jeffrey Stockwell. Yost guessed that there must be a clue somewhere in this whole mess, a clue that would have revealed the secret of this mysterious death.

But they hadn't found it, and the real diagnosis would be buried with the young soldier.

He opened the medical chart and under CAUSE OF DEATH he wrote. "Code 64.903, Pneumonia."

Like hell, pneumonia, he thought. He knew that wasn't the real problem—but he had to complete the chart. After stapling the folder closed, he jammed it in among the hundreds of routine medical records that filled the large, gray-metal file cabinet. The drawer shut with a thud, and the case was closed.

The phone on his desk rang. It was Myers.

"Get down here. I want you to see this."

Yost went down to the lab and Myers motioned him over to the microscope.

"This is a blood smear on Stockwell. Take a look at the leukocytes, Major," Myers said, smoke curling out of his mouth and nostrils as if a fire were smoldering inside of him. "The damn white blood cells are falling apart!"

5

Loudonville, New Hampshire

FALL CREPT QUIETLY into the woods of New England, marking each tree in crimson, rust, amber, and bronze. A chilled northern breeze gave a hint of winter. The days were shorter and the late-afternoon sun cast an orange hue over the hills.

A sudden gust whipped through the leaves that had piled against the high-school building and scattered them over the lawn. A spider making a web on the outside window frame was momentarily disrupted by a leaf that blew onto its web's sticky fiber.

Matt Strong didn't see the transformation of autumn as he stared out the window. His mind was drifting, confused and unfocused. The telegram had been brutally brief. He had not been prepared for this harsh jolt into reality. It had happened too suddenly, totally without warning. He pounded his fist in frustration against the windowsill.

The last bell of the day jarred him out of his trance. He moved from the window to his paper-strewn desk, which was as disorganized as his life seemed to be lately. The noise from slamming lockers and the loud voices in the hall echoed more loudly than usual because of the football game just a few hours away.

Homecoming, the biggest weekend of the season; the big football game and dance. The pep rally had just ended and an occasional horn blast or drum roll in the hall could be heard above the rest of the commotion as the marching band dispersed.

The noise created an uneasiness spiced with irritation inside him. It seemed inappropriate. Jeff was dead!

His mind reeled; his hands clenched into fists, knuckles white. He wadded up the telegram and threw it against the wall.

Jeff dead? Not possible!

Matt felt hollow and a gnawing resentment swept over him. How could Jeff die!

He gathered up papers that needed grading over the weekend and stuffed them into his backpack, along with two biology books. After taking a thick wool sweater from its hook on the wall and slipping it on, he picked up the backpack and pulled the straps over his shoulders. He lifted his sleek black Italian Cinelli bicycle from the corner of his office and wheeled it outside into the sunshine.

The community of Loudonville stretched across a wide valley in the White Mountain range of New Hampshire. Agriculture and forestry sustained the small town that bordered the White Mountain National Forest. Matt rode through the old section of town where tall oaks lined the winding streets. A stiff breeze brought the leaves down in golden torrents and blew them across the street in swirling patterns.

Matt's powerful legs bore down on the pedals like pistons. The wind stung his face and whipped through his hair. In a desperate attempt to outrun his grief, he dropped low over the handlebars and shifted into a higher gear. His legs kept pumping, pounding like the beat of his heart in unison with the gears and the chain as he pushed the black Cinelli harder. Like a machine, he thought. Only machines don't grieve.

Pneumonia. The message said pneumonia.

Pneumonia?

People didn't die of pneumonia, not someone as healthy as Jeff. It was too absurd, too final.

Driving himself even harder, Matt recklessly forced his bike too fast into a turn. Suddenly a blurred figure appeared directly in front of him in the middle of the crosswalk. He squeezed the brakes and yanked the handlebars to swerve, but it was too late. A cry was cut short by the force of the impact. He felt a thud, the bike went down, and the ground slammed into him. His body slid against the pavement and he skidded to a stop, still clinging to his bicycle.

He jumped to his feet, trembling and shaken. The torn elbow from his sweater revealed an ugly abrasion caked with dirt and blood. After leaning over a second to catch his breath, he walked toward the crumpled form on the curb and saw that it was a young woman.

"I'm sorry!" he said, leaning over her. "Are you all right?"

He glanced down at her as she still lay curled on her side. The front of her trench coat was open and revealed long bare legs. At first Matt thought she was naked under her coat, but when she sat up, he saw she wore dance tights.

"Let me help you," he urged.

She shook leaves from her hair and stood up. "No second shoots—that was a take, right?" she said, an eyebrow raised in amused contempt.

As soon as she stood, Matt recognized her as one of the new teachers he had caught a glimpse of once in the hall. Several of the men teachers had talked about a great looker, but until now Matt had never really *seen* her. She was tall and graceful with long, lithe thighs. The dark blue Danskin displayed every contour of her drop-dead figure. She shaded her eyes from the sun as she studied him with sparkling hazel-colored eyes. There was a wild beauty about her, accentuated by long cinnamon-colored hair hanging loosely over her shoulders.

"Are you all right?" Matt asked. "I'm so sorry! I didn't see you."

She looked down at her spilled bags of groceries. "Anyone for fresh omelettes?" she laughed. Her infectious smile set the tone and put him at ease once he knew she wasn't hurt.

Matt looked down at the mess. An unmistakable thick viscous river of broken eggs oozed out from the bottom of a torn grocery bag. A half-dozen oranges lay scattered across the street.

"Let me help," he said, leaning forward to pick up the bag. The last orange fell through the bottom of the egg-sodden sack, bounced once on the pavement, then rolled down the street and disappeared in the leaves. She bit her lip to stifle a grin and brushed leaves off her coat.

Matt felt the heat stealing into his face as it flushed a deep crimson. He held his hand out to her. "I'm Matt Strong. Please forgive me."

"Danielle Carter—and you'd better have that arm looked at," she said. She leaned over to retrieve her purse. She wrapped the coat back around her.

"Those bags were probably . . ."

"Yeah, tonight's supper," she said, and shook her head at the mess.

He stammered for a moment. "Look, let me buy dinner tonight. It's the least I can do."

"Thank you, but you don't have to do that. I'll just order a pizza."

"Let me try that again," Matt said sheepishly. "I'd like it very much if you'd have dinner with me tonight."

She studied him for a moment, then smiled. "All right."

On the day following the fall equinox, ducks began to gather by the tens of thousands on the large Niwot marshland in New Hampshire, just as they had done for thousands of years. Their arrival marked the final passage of summer and the splendid arrival of autumn in New England.

The gathering grew larger daily with the arrival of canvasback, mallard, eider, ring-neck, and teal. Late arrivals of pintail, redhead, and merganser filled the sky with a frantic beating of wings and guttural quacking as they settled in among the marsh grass and reeds.

The ducks had remained at the protective marsh for two

weeks preparing for their mass migration southward, feeding on the cattails, wild orchids, and swamp candles along the banks or the water grass pulled from the muddy bottom.

On this particular afternoon there was an unusual silence of anticipation, of watching. The sky was clear, and the northern marsh baked under the autumn sun in a strange silence. Perhaps on a given signal, or maybe merely by chance, thousands of birds suddenly took off amid a flurry of beating wings to start their long journey.

The sky turned black as thousands of ducks joined others in low growing lines. They flew together at first in great huge flocks—teal mixed among mallard, eider, and ringnecks. And for the first few hundred miles they would stay together in a single dense flock that snaked through the sky for miles, until they broke away to follow their own particular flyway that led them southward.

The great migrations from the northern marsh had happened thousands of times, over many centuries, following well-established flyways.

But on this October afternoon, as the ducks left the Niwot marshland with a great loud quacking and furious beating of wings, the migration would be different.

6

A DOGWOOD TREE laden with crimson berries marked the edge of his lawn, and behind it stood the small, white frame house with its inviting front porch. Overhead a cacophony of quacking and the sound of beating wings grew louder as thousands of ducks cut through the sky in long lines, skimming over the trees moving southward. Matt looked up and shaded his eyes from the sun. The lines seemed endless. The great migration of northern ducks had started.

He pulled the bike onto the porch, went through the house to the kitchen, and dropped the backpack onto the table.

He filled the copper kettle and clanged it down onto the front burner. He knew he drank too much coffee; hell—he was addicted to the damned beans. But he couldn't think clearly without coffee, and right now he had a lot of thinking to do.

Matt paced back and forth in the kitchen waiting for the water to heat, his mind spinning. The message on the telegram kept haunting him. For a moment he couldn't remember the sound of Jeff's voice. Why was he trying to remember that? Jeff was *dead*.

Matt went to the sink and washed off his elbow and winced when the water ran over the open wound. He held a wet washcloth to his elbow to stop the bleeding, then remembered the cut on Jeff's elbow when they climbed Desolation Peak. It was the last climb they had done together. They had planned to do several more before Jeff moved, but there hadn't been time.

He dropped the washcloth on the counter and went into his bedroom, took a picture off the wall, and brought it back into the kitchen. It was a photograph of Jeff and him, leaning on each other's shoulders, laughing back at the camera after winning a race.

Studying the picture, he slowly submerged into a distant memory. Jeff had been more than his closest friend, he had become family, the brother that Matt never had. Matt was an only child, good at sports, but in high school was too independent and headstrong for any sport except track and swimming. He could never be just another conforming cog on a team, huddled around a coach taking orders.

His father, an accountant, was tragically killed when Matt was only fourteen, shot to death in a convenience store while trying to talk a nervous gunman into turning over the gun. Matt took over the role of "man of the house." Impetuous and fearless, much like his father had been, Matt never avoided confrontation and never hesitated to get involved when he felt it was necessary to do so.

Matt dated a few girls while in high school, but was never romantically head-over-heels with any of them. He first learned about sex his senior year from a college girl two years older than he.

The following fall he entered the University of Colorado in Boulder. During his first two years in college he dated several girls, with a few brief affairs, but was never really serious about any of them.

Not until his junior year when he met Christine at a party, a gorgeous senior with thick, luxuriant black hair, large dark eyes, and a disarming smile. They immediately became an item and spent every spare moment together. Sex was natural with them, always fresh and exciting. Matt intended to marry her.

But just before her graduation, Christine suddenly broke off the relationship and began dating "a more serious man,'' someone with a future in law. The breakup devastated Matt and it was a year before he would ask out another girl.

Athletics became an important part of his life. One cold Saturday morning while riding his bicycle along the foothills outside of Boulder on highway 36, the University of Colorado bicycle team came storming past him. Matt saw a challenge, dropped low over his handlebars, and bore down on the pedals. After three grueling miles he caught up with the pack and, using every bit of energy reserve he could muster, moved toward the front.

By now everyone was sprinting in response to his challenge. Matt had moved ahead of everyone except the leader. For another three miles Matt stayed behind him, not losing ground, but not gaining on him either.

Back on the campus, Matt stood beside his bicycle, huffing for breath, his legs burning and his body drenched in sweat. The man who had beaten him walked over to Matt and slapped him on the shoulder. "Good ride. Have you ever ridden in competition?''

"No. Just riding for exercise.''

"I'm Jeff Stockwell," he said and extended his hand. "How would you like to ride on the team?''

By spring semester he and Jeff were best friends.

Matt looked at the photograph again. Realizing he was shaking uncontrollably, like an old man with tremors, he struggled to remain calm and turned the picture facedown on the table. Lightheaded, his hands turning numb, he realized he was hyperventilating. He forced himself to take long, slow breaths, to relax.

A shrill whistle from the kettle on the stove made him jump and pulled him out of the haunting past. He poured a cup of boiling water and stirred in a heaping spoonful of his own special blend—half Folgers, half dark British Royal Blend. Tart black coffee with a bite. Matt felt the warm steam on his face as he sipped the strong coffee.

He sat in the kitchen, lost in thought and unaware of the

time. It was nearly dark. He tried to focus on the day's events, but the memories came crowding back like a hidden current. Matt leaned forward, his legs wrapped around the rungs of his stool, and occasionally blew on coffee that had long since turned cold in the mug.

Glancing around the room, he suddenly became aware of the time. Damn! He was going to be late.

He decided to call off his dinner plans with Danielle. Going out for the evening and making small talk was not what he felt like doing tonight. He wanted to be alone. But her phone number was unlisted, and after debating with himself, he finally decided he'd go through with it. He at least owed her dinner, and maybe it would do him some good to get out.

He was in and out of the shower in less than a minute, quickly put on a pair of slacks, an oxford shirt, navy-blue knit tie, and a corduroy jacket, and left. He walked past his bike, and went around the side of the house to his 1969 blue Nova. He had always marveled at the ingenuous, magnificent engineering of a bicycle—a noble machine of efficiency and design. But his old two-door Nova sedan was not of nobility. Arthritic, yes. Cantankerous and stubborn, most certainly. Maybe even senile. But not noble. He brushed leaves from the windshield and climbed in.

He took her to Mama Rosita's, a small Italian restaurant that was messy enough to be quaint, but too clean to be called a dive. They sat at a small corner table, covered with a red and white checkered cloth. A candle flickered from a wicker-covered Chianti bottle and streams of hot wax moved slowly down the glass stem like advancing lava.

After they ordered, Matt poured two glasses of burgundy. "I've seen you in the hall at school once or twice. This is your first year teaching here, isn't it?"

"Yes. Just finished my student teaching last semester. I moved here only two days before classes started, and I was lucky to find an apartment."

Matt cut several slices from the loaf of sourdough and passed it to her on the cutting board. "Where'd you go to school?"

"Boston University. Got my degree in education with a minor in dance. At fifteen I was given a grant to study ballet in Boston. I was good and worked very hard and danced with the Boston Ballet Company as an understudy until I was eighteen, then realized that was it. The problem was that I kept growing, in every way. Too tall, too busty. Ever see a ballerina who was five-eleven with cleavage?"

Matt glanced at her breasts and poured more wine for them, unable to think of anything appropriate to say. Finally he asked, "How did you happen to end all the way up here from Boston?"

The salads came, and after the waitress finished grinding fresh pepper over them, Danielle answered him. "Our family used to spend summers at a cottage in the White Mountains a few miles from here. One of my parents' friends called and told them of an opening, so I applied. There were no jobs in Boston and I wanted to get out of there for a while."

The tone in her voice told him there was more to the story. "Do you have a steady?" Matt asked brazenly.

"Not anymore," she said. "A week before graduation, the guy I had dated for two years landed a job with *The Washington Post* and decided he didn't want to be tied to any commitment. He said it would be good for us to be apart, but I think there were just too many single women and opportunities for him to pass up. So I broke it off. I needed a change of scene."

She looked across at him. "Enough about me," she said. "Tell me about yourself."

"I've been teaching science in Loudonville for eight years, since I graduated from the University of Colorado. . . ." His voice faded and he looked down, staring at his glass.

"Is something wrong?" she asked softly.

He looked up and nodded. "I just learned today that my best friend died of pneumonia."

She reached over and touched his arm. "I'm really sorry." She hesitated for a moment, then continued, "I wish there was something I could say to help you. You sure didn't need to get saddled with me tonight."

"It's okay. I'm enjoying your company and I don't really want to be alone right now. After college, Jeff and I came here to teach. Jeff quit and joined the army. I think he was having some kind of crisis about turning thirty." Matt sighed and put his glass down. "I shouldn't have let him go. It was a stupid idea."

"It was his decision. It's not your fault."

"I should have tried to talk him out of it."

Two plates of Mama Rosita's spaghetti arrived. They ate their dinners and shared a bottle of burgundy. They were just finishing their coffee and were preparing to leave when another waitress walked past.

Matt looked up and caught her arm. "Katie, hello. How are you?" Without waiting for a reply he made introductions. "Danielle, this is Katie Williams, a former student of mine."

Danielle extended her hand. "I'm pleased to meet you, Katie."

Matt continued, "Katie's twin brother, Kelley, was also in my class. He's attending Syracuse University. How is your brother?"

Katie seemed troubled, and she shifted uneasily, as if not sure how to answer. "I thought you knew about Kelley," she said, struggling for composure. "He died three weeks ago. After he went back for fall semester, he called and said he was sick with the flu. When he called, we didn't know how sick he really was. He'd only been sick a couple of days." Her lips quivered. "He died the following day."

Matt sat stunned, not believing what he had heard. The shock caused the words to wedge in his throat. "Katie, I'm sorry."

"I should have called you. But I thought you knew."

Shaken by the news, Matt's heart sank and the blood slid through his veins like cold needles. He felt a stunned detachment. "No. I didn't know. What happened, Katie?"

"The doctors said he died of pneumonia."

"Pneumonia?" he choked. Hot coffee ~spilled as he put the cup down.

With Danielle sitting beside him, it seemed to Matt that the old Nova showed promise of nobility after all. Her alluring profile was softly bathed in the green lights of the dashboard. The Nova seemed to be a shelter against some intangible threat.

The news of Kelley Williams's death had jarred him out of his own small sphere of self-pity and depression and replaced it with a growing sense of uneasiness that something was wrong.

"I can't believe it," he said. "Two people died of pneumonia within a few weeks of each other."

"That's really tragic."

"I think it's more than tragic. Doesn't that strike you as odd? What if there's some connection?" He jiggled the heater switch but only cool air streamed from the vents.

"I think it's just unfortunate circumstances," she said gently. "Your friend was in Colorado, and Katie's brother was in New York. I don't see how there could be a connection."

"Yeah, you're right." But he didn't believe his own words. The irony continued to gnaw at him. The icy feeling that something was wrong wouldn't go away.

It was still early when they returned, and Danielle invited him in for coffee. She flipped on the light in the small kitchen of her apartment, poured fresh-ground coffee into the filter, and plugged in the machine. The smell of percolating coffee soon filled the room.

"Make yourself at home, Matt." When she bent over to take her shoes off, her blouse fell away revealing full breasts restrained by a thin, sheer bra. She opened the door of the refrigerator and stood gracefully on one leg, staring into the interior. One bare foot rested lightly behind the knee of the other leg.

He couldn't tear his eyes away from her. His gaze fell to the curve of her hips, then down the back of her legs. Matt had never seen a more beautiful, sensual woman. When was the last time he'd truly enjoyed himself with a woman?

She pulled something out triumphantly and turned to him. "Split a week-old piece of chocolate cake?" She caught his eyes resting briefly on her breasts when she turned. She looked back at him with a faint, almost-devilish grin forming at the corners of her mouth. His heart reacted immediately to her gaze and he felt the heat of a blush rising in his cheeks.

They stood face to face in the small kitchen, intensely aware of their mutual physical attraction.

She nervously cleared her throat and opened the cupboard, pulled out plates and cups, divided the cake, and poured coffee.

Several cups later, they were still standing at the counter, talking. She took his cup to refill it and kissed him on the cheek, a quick kiss.

He didn't want to go, he wanted to stay and make wild, passionate love to her but reality told him it was time to leave. "I really should go," Matt said, glancing at his watch. "Thank you for a wonderful evening. And for being so kind and understanding."

There was a brief inquisitive look on her face, then she smiled as if she understood. "Why don't you come over tomorrow morning and let me cook you breakfast?" She laughed. "It's okay. I already bought more eggs."

She hadn't asked him to stay. He put his hands around her waist and drew her gently to him and kissed her on the lips. "Good night," he said softly.

He drove home and sat up most of the night in the dark, haunted by the events of the day and unable to sleep. When the first faint orange light came through the window, Matt was lying on the couch, having succumbed to a deep but troubled sleep.

He knocked at the door of her apartment and glanced again at his watch, feeling guilty because he had slept later than he had intended to. From inside he heard, "Door's open, come on in." He opened the door and went in.

Danielle stood at the stove turning bacon. She wore a long, light blue T-shirt with "Boston Ballet" printed in gold script and the silhouette of a dancer. "Hi." She was turning the bacon over in the skillet with a fork. "Do you always sleep this late?"

"Sorry I'm late," he replied. "I was up most of the night. Couldn't get to sleep."

"Coffee's ready. Why don't you pour me some and have a seat while I do the eggs." There was a loud hiss of butter melting in the frying pan, and Danielle started beating the eggs in a bowl.

Matt poured the coffee and dropped wearily into a chair. "Can I help you?" he asked.

"No, everything's about ready. Just a couple of more minutes for the eggs. Do you like scrambled?"

"Sure, love scrambled." He watched her working at the stove and studied her perfectly toned body of a ballerina. Her feet were bare, but thick, blue wool leg warmers extended from her ankles to midthigh and the muscles in her legs were firm and defined.

"I just can't get it out of my head that there might be some kind of connection between Jeff and Kelley, both dying suddenly of pneumonia," he said. "There has to be a connection."

She carried the skillet over to the table and slid the scrambled eggs onto his plate. Matt continued, "Maybe the health department would know if there is some flu epidemic or something."

Danielle carried a hot tin of muffins from the oven and

popped them over, into a basket. She gave him a mock
punch with the hot-pad glove she was wearing, then tossed
it on the counter. "You shouldn't have rushed off so fast
last night."

His face split into a wide grin and he examined the table.
Scrambled eggs, muffins, bacon, sliced tomato, coffee, and
yogurt with strawberries. "Compared to my usual banana
and bagel, this isn't breakfast, it's a feast. You're quite a
cook."

"I don't do this every day—just on weekends." She sat
cross-legged, the T-shirt ridding provocatively up her thighs.

He took a sip from his cup and pushed the eggs about on
the plate while his mind replayed the same nagging thoughts
over again.

As if she sensed what he was thinking, she said, "Look,
if you really think there's something unusual about their
deaths, just call the county health department. Or call your
doctor's office. Maybe they know something."

He nodded and bit into a muffin. He knew he would
pursue it.

7

MATT NERVOUSLY THUMBED through a three-month-old *Mc-Call's* while waiting his turn. He decided that waiting for the doctor was always the worst part of the appointment. Even though this appointment was just to get information, it stirred memories of earlier times, when he was a small boy with skinned knees fearful of some obligatory inoculation.

He glanced around the dim waiting room. Dark, heavy furniture and the yellowing venetian blinds made it look as if nothing had been changed in the office since Dr. Ebner set up practice in the 1940s. An odor of medicine and antiseptic solutions pervaded the place.

Matt glanced anxiously at the clock on the wall for the umpteenth time. There was still a chance he'd get back in time for his one o'clock class, but he would be cutting it close.

The door opened and a nurse stepped into the waiting area. "Mr. Strong? Dr. Ebner will see you now. Please follow me."

He was shown to an examining room, where he was soon joined by Dr. Ebner.

Matt guessed him to be in his late sixties, a stooped man with white, thinning hair and eyes set wide apart on a broad German face. Dr. Ebner was short, barely over five feet, and the lab coat that hung just above his shoes and his rolled-up sleeves gave him the appearance of an old leprechaun. He wore his stethoscope around his neck like a black charm.

"Now, what seems to be the problem?"

Matt wasn't sure how to begin. "I want to inquire about a friend of mine, Jeff Stockwell."

"Let me see now. Jeff Stockwell. I don't recall that name. Are you sure he was a patient of mine?" Dr. Ebner's speech was slow and hesitant, as he thought each question over a moment before answering.

Matt continued, "He died from pneumonia last week. But he had always been in excellent health."

"I'm sorry to hear that. What was it you wanted to know then?" He fingered his stethoscope.

"I'm getting to that," Matt said. "A former student of mine, Kelley Williams, also died recently from pneumonia, about a month ago. He was only eighteen. Do you think there could be a connection, or are you aware of other cases of pneumonia?"

"Other cases? You mean like an epidemic or something? Goodness, no. There hasn't been anything around here like that in decades. I think you are mistaken there. Kelley Williams. I knew the family. Twins, weren't they?"

"Yes." Matt was not getting the answers he had hoped to find, and his voice reflected his frustration. "Can you recall any of your patients who have died unexpectedly in the past month or so?"

"No, can't recall any," Ebner said. Matt had reached a brick wall. There was a long, protracted silence as both men stared at each other.

Ebner tugged on his stethoscope and looked down, searching his memory. "There was one young girl I know of, but she was in Kentucky when she died. Vicki James was twelve. She died from complications of pneumonia."

Matt felt his skin crawl. "Do you know her parents?"

"I've known the James family for many years. Probably would have even delivered Vicki, but her mother gave birth on the way into town. They own the large horse ranch just outside of town on Valley Road."

The paper cover crunched under Matt when he leaned

forward, his hands gripping the edge of the examining table. "But that makes three cases. You said she died of pneumonia?"

"Yes, but the accident killed her. She was thrown from a horse. Pneumonia is a frequent complication of serious trauma. Patients who are in a coma can't swallow or cough. They aspirate on their own secretions, develop pneumonia, and die."

Ebner turned suddenly and was at the door, on his way to see the next appointment. He paused a brief moment and over his shoulder said, "Sorry, but I think you're jumping to the wrong conclusions about your friend's death." And he was gone, already with the next patient as he worked his way through a busy day.

The one o'clock bell rang, halls emptied, classroom doors closed, and silence spread through the building. Matt was late. He took the stairs two and three at a time and thought he was home free until he looked up.

"Matt, you're late." The principal stood at the door, arms folded in a defensive posture, waiting for him. "You're expected to be on time, even for study hall."

Matt adjusted his loosened tie and ran his fingers through his unruly hair. "I'm sorry I'm late, but I was delayed at the doctor's office."

"Nothing serious, I trust?"

"Ah . . . no, I don't think so." Matt knew Thomas Leach had drawn the wrong conclusion about his visit to Dr. Ebner, but a little mistaken sympathy might get him off the hook.

Leach unfolded a piece of paper and handed it to Matt. "Matt, we reluctantly agreed to your request for a live animal lab. But responsibility goes with that. You're expected to see that they get proper care. Check into this and get back to me."

Leach spun on his heels and walked away.

• • •

1:58 P.M. There was a dull thunk as the minute hand of the large wall clock struck off another minute. 1:59.

Afternoon study hall, that wasted no-man's-land of undefined time, a great torturous silence that painfully tested nerves of student and teacher alike. Only the faint sound of paper rattling and turning pages broke the silence.

The room was monotonous, sixty feet long and narrow, with three rows of work tables that stretched back its entire length. Blue fluorescent lights hung down over the tables, utilitarian but cold. One hundred students sat at the tables. Waiting.

Matt paced back and forth behind his desk at the front of the long room, fidgeting with a broken piece of chalk in his hands.

Nothing was going right for him. His disorganized life had become even more chaotic. He hadn't finished grading last week's quizzes over the weekend and didn't have a new lab outline. To add to his problems, the note from Leach indicated that the mice in the biology lab weren't doing well and needed attention. Matt made a mental note to call the supplier and make sure they were getting the right pellets. Maybe they needed some kind of supplements in their diet.

The weekend with Danielle had been an unexpected pleasant surprise. She cooked a late morning Sunday brunch for the two of them, then they spent the morning relaxing with the Sunday *New York Times*. The temperature rose to sixty and a subdued golden autumn sun played magic through the foliage of oak, maple, and dogwood. They went to the park in the afternoon and watched a soccer game, then took a long walk through the leaves. They finished the day with a meal of French onion soup, sourdough bread, and salad at a small café. The closeness he felt for Danielle only made the loss of Jeff seem more cruel. He wanted Jeff to meet her, wanted them to share good times together.

Jeff. Kelley Williams. Maybe Vicki James. There had to be a connection. He couldn't clear his mind of the nagging suspicion that something was happening beyond random chance.

Lost in thought, Matt was gesturing with his hands as he paced back and forth. Suddenly glancing out over the long rows of tables he became painfully aware that the students were staring at him.

He felt the heat rise in his cheeks, and he sat down behind the desk. He didn't know how long he had been pacing back and forth. The room was deathly still.

Just as the silence and stares seemed to become unbearable, the clock mercifully thunked off another minute and the two o'clock bell loudly broke the spell.

Matt stood up and stalked briskly out of the room.

As if he didn't have enough problems to worry about, now he had to baby-sit a bunch of sick mice. He opened the door to the lab at the front of the science room. His appearance sent the hundred or so white mice scurrying madly around. No problem there that he could see. All the mice seemed fine. He shrugged, turned the light off, and closed the door.

He didn't know what all the fuss was about. As far as he was concerned, a mouse that could run was a healthy mouse—for his purposes anyway. He went down the center aisle of the long classroom to the lab at the back. The animal labs were divided into two sections, one at each end of the classroom.

He opened the door to the back lab and flipped on the light.

The sight before him stunned him. At least thirty of the mice were dead, and the rest were obviously very sick, crouched down and shivering, their fur matted. He gently shook the cage, but they ignored the disruption.

What had happened to them? Matt put on rubber gloves, opened the cage, and dropped the dead mice into a plastic trash bag.

He still couldn't believe the difference between the two animal labs. The mice received the same pellet food, and the conditions in the labs were identical. The mice had been delivered in September to the school in a single large wooden crate, then divided between the two labs.

The mice in the back lab had obviously become infected with something and were probably spreading it among themselves. He didn't know what to do for the rest of the sick mice that were still alive. He pulled off the feeder, dumped out the pellets, and washed it thoroughly. He poured in fresh food and put the feeder back on the cage.

He dropped the bag of dead mice into the trash bin outside and headed back to his office. He planned to call the supplier for advice on what to do for the rest that were sick, and maybe see if they knew why thirty of them had died.

And how the hell had Leach found out about the mice? Whoever had gone to Leach should have just come to Matt with the problem.

Damned mice! He was in no mood for this kind of headache now. In the back of his mind was the thought that he might have been exposed to whatever killed the mice. He had to be more careful.

He went to the sink and scrubbed his hands. He scrubbed until they turned beet-red.

Damned mice.

Major Yost read the report from the Armed Forces Institute of Pathology in Washington, D.C. He had sent a copy of all the lab data along with slides to the AFIP for them to review.

The AFIP had reviewed the slides of patient PFC Jeffrey Stockwell, No. 77–8467, and they agreed that the white blood cells looked abnormal. They concluded: "We need more information."

Need more information.

Yeah, don't we though, Yost thought as he focused the microscope on the blood smears for a last look. They'd stumbled onto something, but they'd failed to find any definitive answers.

Yost put the AFIP report in with the rest of Private Stockwell's medical records and closed the file drawer.

8

Albany, New York

MATT THOUGHT HE was emotionally prepared for Jeff's funeral, but he wasn't. Matt was raised Presbyterian and had never attended a Catholic church. The mass was a very dramatic and emotional service, rich with symbolism. Sitting on the front row along with the other pallbearers, Matt became increasingly more uncomfortable as the mass progressed. The air inside crowded Saint Joseph's grew thick and stuffy, and the sweet smell of flowers, burning candles, and incense made him sick, and he fought waves of nausea.

Jennifer Preston, who had just arrived the day before from her home in Colorado, sat in the row behind him, along with several of their mutual friends from college. Matt was to have been Jeff's best man at their wedding, but instead he would be his pallbearer.

After the service he rode in the car with Jennifer and Mr. and Mrs. Chiles to the cemetery. The ceremony at the graveside was brief, the priest saying a last prayer, family and friends placing flowers on the coffin, then everyone left.

On his trip back to New Hampshire, Matt pulled the blue Nova off to the side of the road and stopped beside the low stone wall of the cemetery. Matt got out, staring at the mound of fresh dirt, reluctant to leave. The low afternoon sun found its way through the thinning trees and sent long shadows across the lawn of the cemetery. A brisk wind, growing stronger as the temperature dropped, had already scattered most of the flowers across the lawn along where they lay mixed among the blanket of leaves.

By tomorrow all the flowers would have blown away, leaving only the bare earth, until spring, when grass would grow over to heal the rectangular scar.

But Matt would never forget.

The next week melted into a blur for Matt. He spent more and more time with Danielle while struggling to keep up with his classwork. He tried to put Jeff's funeral behind him but couldn't get it out of his mind.

He had a terrible sense of loneliness without Jeff and found himself being drawn closer to Danielle. He felt different about her than he had about any other woman, looked at her with something deeper than mere masculine interest. But he was determined not to get involved in any serious relationship. He wasn't ready for that, not yet.

The next morning he phoned two other doctors' offices and got the same negative answers that he had received from Dr. Ebner. He called the state health department, and after a dozen pointless questions, he got the same response. No, there had been no fatal cases of pneumonia reported. In fact, the names he mentioned hadn't been reported to them because they were out of state when they became ill and died. The secretary who took the call suggested that he might call the Centers for Disease Control in Atlanta, and gave him the number.

Matt put the phone down and ran his hands through his hair. Obviously his concern about the two cases of pneumonia was unjustified. He sat for a minute, drumming his fingers on the top of the phone book, then picked up the phone and dialed the CDC, was transferred twice, then put on hold. Finally a voice came on. "Evans."

Matt had been on the phone for ten minutes trying to get to the right person, and now he couldn't think of exactly what to say. "Dr. Evans, this is Matt Strong. Three people from our town died from pneumonia within the last few weeks. The state health department here in New Hampshire suggested I call you."

"Yes?" Evans waited for more.

Matt paused a moment, not sure how to phrase his questions, then continued, "They were all healthy people, and each died of pneumonia after only a short illness."

"Did they have the flu? Anything unusual they shared in common?"

Matt was feeling pressure now and his hands were sweating. "I don't know."

"As you know, there could be many explanations for such an occurrence. Sporadic cases such as what you described happen often enough, and many times we never find out the cause. We would need something more specific to go on." Evans cleared his voice. "Send us full duplicate copies of their hospital charts. We'll need all the information you might have, such as convalescent titers, serology, cultures. Doesn't sound like anything to get excited about, but we'll review the charts and get a report back to you."

"I can't do that," Matt said. "I'm not a doctor and I don't have access to that kind of information."

"Any investigation has to be initiated by a licensed physician or state health official before we can act on it. If you are concerned, I'd suggest you call your state health department. Maybe somebody there can help."

Matt added, "I'm a science teacher. Several mice in our high-school lab also died during the same time. I'm concerned about the students. Could the mice have exposed them to something?"

"I can't say, but it's not unusual for laboratory mice to die from some endemic infection. It happens in research labs occasionally. We certainly have no interest in pursuing it."

Click.

The following morning Janet Brown, one of his senior students, came into his office. "Mr. Strong, three of the mice in my science fair project died. Is it too late to get more mice and start over?"

"What?" he blurted out. "Come on. Let's take a look."
He bolted out of the room.

He had forgotten about the mice on the third floor that
were being used for science fair projects. He took the stairs
two at a time and rushed into the room.

She was right behind him. "I'm sorry about this. I don't
know what happened."

He turned and tried to reassure her. "Don't worry about
it. It wasn't your fault. Several mice in the lab downstairs
died. You only lost three."

Flipping through the pages of data on her clipboard that
hung from the cage, Matt quickly reviewed her experiment.
Janet had used five mice for her project. The two mice in the
top cage looked fine, but the three in the bottom were dead.

"Did you touch the mice?"

"Not today. But I picked them up when I cleaned the
cages. Why did they die? They looked fine yesterday."

Matt didn't answer her. He figured it was only a matter of
time before the two mice in the top cage got infected and
died, since they had to be exposed.

"I don't think it is safe for you to be around these mice
anymore. We'll stop the experiment, and I'll put these mice
back in the main lab downstairs. I'm sorry it turned out like
this, but it's not your fault."

Matt quickly checked on twenty other cages being used
for individual projects, but all the other mice looked fine.
He was lucky.

He took Janet's notes describing her project from the
clipboard. He'd review them later. Maybe he could learn
something from them.

Clouds of doubt kept pushing their way into the corners
of his mind, a feeling that he couldn't shake. It was hard to
see any connection between Jeff, Kelley, and the dead mice,
but he couldn't get the suspicion from his head.

He was also worried for the safety of the students, and
debated whether he should stop all the science projects now.

He rubbed his eyes. He was tired.

9

Pine Creek Gorge, Pennsylvania

GAME WARDEN LEONARD Koop wasn't prepared for what he
was about to find.

His gray four-wheel-drive Land Rover clawed its way up
the rocky streambed of the Pine Creek Gorge wildlife refuge
area. Thick globs of mud clung to the tires and splattered
along the side of the vehicle, obliterating the yellow-and-
green federal insignia. Expansive marshlands surrounding
several connecting lakes provided excellent refuge for great
flocks of ducks on their southward trek of fall migration.

Koop was with the U.S. Fish and Wildlife Service in the
central Pennsylvania forests to study the migratory water
fowl. The information he gathered concerning the size of the
migration and mix of species would be used to determine
regulations and quotas for next year's hunting season.

Koop turned off the engine and listened, straining to hear
the low guttural quacking. Luck was on his side today. A
thick morning haze hung in the forest. He knew the ducks
wouldn't fly until the fog cleared. After collecting his
binoculars and a clipboard from the vehicle, he started up
the ravine. Heavy September rains had left the woods damp
and soggy, and his boots squished in the mud. Water oozed
up to fill his tracks.

A solitary canvasback lay dead in the weeds in front of
him. Koop kicked it aside. The death of one bird wasn't
noteworthy. The migration was hard and took its toll on the
weak and the old. Closer to the lake the tart smell of

stagnant water, wet peat, and dead vegetation of the marsh grew stronger. He pushed the reeds apart and stepped to the edge of the lake.

The surface of the water had a strange, clotted texture. A cold feeling—a feeling of death—swept over Koop.

He stepped up onto a fallen tree trunk for a better view and scanned the lake with his binoculars. At first his mind resisted the message feeding double-barreled into his eyes. He tried to comprehend the horror in front of him. Hundreds—thousands—of dead ducks floated on the lake, their carcasses bobbing slightly with the surface ripple on the water.

What the hell? he muttered to himself. Hunters had apparently killed countless scores of birds and left them to rot in the lake. Koop waded forward into the lake, barely noticing the chilled water that filled his boots. Slogging over the mucky bottom he worked his way closer to the carnage that floated in front of him. He picked up the closest duck, an adult male mallard. Its once magnificent plumage of glossy green head and majestic red chest was matted and dulled.

Holding the mallard in his hands brought back a painful memory that had been repressed and locked away.

Koop's father was a hunter and had taught Leonard how to stalk and kill. Leonard's first kill came at the age of ten. It was a cunning ring-necked male pheasant. Leonard had stumbled onto it accidentally at a fence row thick with brush and dead leaves. He almost missed the pheasant and would have walked past it, but it moved, turned its head to look at him—a fatal mistake.

Young Koop swung the heavy double-barreled Remington shotgun to his shoulder, aimed at the pheasant—and fired. The deafening shot shattered the calm and blasted bits of dried weeds and leaves into the air. And it blew the pheasant's head away. The fading echo of the shot was followed by an unnerving silence, and the air thick with the smell of gunpowder and death.

The boy was shaking when he picked up the dead bird, its

blood hot, thick, and sticky. The weeds were splattered with blood and his hands were stained red. He had never killed anything before. The reality of what he had done began to sink in. Leonard threw the pheasant down. With trembling fingers, he opened the breech and the shell casing fell to the ground beside its victim. A blue wisp of smoke filled with the tart, acrid smell of spent gunpowder curled out of the empty chamber.

That moment came back vividly to Koop now as he held the dead mallard. For a moment, standing knee-deep in the lake, Leonard was ten again—and afraid.

Damned hunters! He examined the mallard carefully but was puzzled. There were no birdshot wounds on the mallard. He threw it behind him back into the cattails and moved farther out into the lake to examine more. He checked a dozen more carcasses. But none of them had been shot.

He stood motionless in the lake holding two birds and stared at the slate-gray water, concerned and afraid. Then, what had killed them?

A cold October mist closed in around him and left him alone in a world with no horizon, surrounded by death.

10

Matt winced at the ungraded exams stacked on the kitchen table. His day at school had been hectic and he was too beat to deal with a pile of quizzes waiting to be graded. He went into the living room and sank onto the couch with the evening *Gazette* and his second cup of coffee. While he paged through the newspaper, a familiar name caught his eye.

RICHARD GREY

Mr. Richard T. Grey, aged fifty-eight, died yesterday in Swedish Medical Center, Madison, Wisconsin, after a short illness. Mr. Grey, who owned and operated Grey's Bicycle Shop, died from complications of pneumonia, while visiting family in Madison. He is survived by his wife, Mary. Services will be at two P.M., Saturday in St. Paul Presbyterian Church.

Dick Grey! Matt spilled coffee across the page as he leaned over to stare at the words. He had heard that Dick had died unexpectedly, but nobody had mentioned pneumonia! Matt bought his prized Italian Cinelli at Grey's Bicycle Shop, and Dick did all the maintenance work on it.

Matt looked at the paper again. Since neither Dr. Ebner nor the state health department seemed to be aware of anything unusual, maybe the *Gazette* was the place to start looking for answers. He put on his coat, grabbed his backpack, and left.

• • •

The quiet that permeated the library was interrupted by a chair somewhere sliding across the tile. To Matt, the cold marble pillars and walls of the picturesque building took on the aura of a mausoleum.

The librarian methodically stamped cards and slipped them into the books stacked in front of her. A thin, diminutive woman with silver hair pulled back harshly into a bun, she seemed unaware of his presence. Matt shifted his weight from one foot to the other and cleared his throat.

"I'll be with you in a minute," she said without looking up. He studied the rope-like veins on the back of her bony hands as she went about her work. Her thin, wrinkled skin was blotched with age spots.

She put the last book on the pile and looked up. "Now, may I help you?" she asked. The bags under her eyes hung loose and sagged like that of a desert reptile.

"Yes. I'd like to see back issues of the *Loudonville Gazette*. I want to review the past five months, starting with June."

"That's going to be a large pile of papers. Sunday editions also?"

"Yes."

"I'll have to get them from the stacks downstairs. Have a seat and I'll bring them up."

Matt found an empty table next to a window. Outside, giant oaks, tortured with age, shook and bent in the wind, allowing flashes of light from the streetlight to flicker through branches. The thought of the ungraded exams on his kitchen table kept haunting him. He had never been so far behind in his work, and his life had never seemed more chaotic. He knew his concern with Jeff's death was becoming an obsession with him.

The librarian pulled up a cart piled with newspapers. "This is only June, July, and August," she said wryly. "After you're finished with these, let me know and I'll get the rest."

He thanked her and maneuvered the burgeoning cart beside the table. He stared at the formidable pile of newsprint, then slid the month of June on the table and sat down to the task in front of him, not exactly sure of what to look for.

Matt skipped over the first two sections of each paper and quickly scanned through the obituaries in the last section. It was going to be difficult to spot anything because the cause of death wasn't always given, and when it was, the information was only sketchy.

Swell reading, he thought—endless lists of next of kin, fraternal orders, social clubs, and funeral dates. The pile of papers grew and his eyes stung with fatigue. The names, dates, and causes of death blended and blurred into one meaningless generic obituary. None of the information from the obituaries gave him anything solid to go on. His hunch must have been wrong, so why pursue a hopeless issue? Rapidly becoming discouraged he opened the July twenty-sixth paper.

> ### DEATHS ELSEWHERE
> #### Vicki Loraine James
>
> Vicki James, age twelve, died Sunday morning in Methodist Hospital, Lexington, Kentucky, of injuries sustained after falling from a horse. She was the daughter of Mr. and Mrs. David James of Loudonville. Vicki was an accomplished equestrian, and recently won several tournaments. Visitation will be at the Radnor Funeral Home. The funeral will be one-thirty Thursday afternoon at Saint Mary's Church.

Matt felt a chill in the pit of his stomach. Dr. Ebner was probably right, her pneumonia was a result of her injuries. But—what if there was more to it than that? There was no reason for him to suspect otherwise, still he wanted more information about her death.

Matt thought about it, then went to the pay phone in the lobby, looked up the phone number, and called the Jameses.

He introduced himself, told them his friend recently died of pneumonia, and he wanted to know more about what happened to Vicki. They were with Vicki in Kentucky when she died. She had been sick for two days with a cold before the accident. Nobody else in the family had gotten sick. He thanked them politely and hung up.

Her death was apparently exactly as Dr. Ebner described it. Yet, in the back of his mind, he knew he was missing something. What? He kept grasping for something. There was something else, something he'd missed. How could the three deaths—maybe even four if he included Vicki's—be merely just coincidence?

He jotted down a few notes and looked for a pattern or some clue. How could their deaths possibly be related ? His pencil tapped randomly as he stared out the window.

The words *"Deaths Elsewhere"* leaped out at him from the newspaper.

Everybody had been out of town when they died!

Vicki James, Kelley Williams, and Jeff had all been out of state when they died from pneumonia. So was Dick Grey. Colorado, New York, Kentucky, Wisconsin—every place but Loudonville.

Was it just a coincidence or was there a connection? It explained why neither the doctors in town nor the health department had no record of any of the deaths since none of them were in town when they died.

Matt rapidly flipped back through his notes as another thought occurred to him. There was something else they had in common. Jeff had been in Colorado just three weeks when he died. Kelley Williams had been at Syracuse University less than a month, three weeks and four days to be exact. Vicki had been in Kentucky only four days.

His mind raced over the phone conversation he had just had. Vicki James had been in Kentucky only four days, but she had competed in two other national events and had been traveling for more than three weeks. And her parents had only been gone a day, arriving in time to see the last day of competition.

All the people who died had been out of town three weeks, give or take a few days.

Then what was the connection? And where did the dead mice fit in?

He was confused and excited at the same time, having finally solved at least part of the puzzle. But he still had a mountain of newspapers to plow through.

Matt wondered if his suspicion about Jeff's death had been right, and now maybe he had stumbled onto something that would prove it. Feeling a surge of adrenaline he tore through the June and July papers again, this time looking only for people who had been out of town at the time of their death.

He glanced at his watch. 8:55 P.M. He would have to work fast. While he read, he kept telling himself that he must be crazy, it didn't make sense. But, hell, none of it made sense. Right now it was all he had to go on.

He finished the last issue for August, then looked at his notes. He had made a list of seven people who were out of state when they died, and four even listed pneumonia as cause of death. From the obituaries he knew they had been gone less than a month. Seven more people—all dead!

It had taken him more than an hour to go through three months. The library closed at ten P.M. And he hadn't even gone through September or October. If he hurried, he might have time to review the more current editions. He dumped the papers back onto the cart and returned them to the desk. The librarian went after the other newspapers he had requested.

Matt had just completed the second batch of papers when the lights dimmed. His notes and his face were smudged with black newsprint. After wiping his hands on his jeans, he jammed his notes into his backpack, grabbed his coat, and left.

When he arrived home, he opened a beer, pulled out the

notes he had made at the library, and read through them. Ten names, all out of town when they died. During the last five months there had not been a single reported death in Loudonville from pneumonia.

Was there a link between leaving town and dying? Ridiculous! There was nothing to suggest that any of the deaths he'd found in the paper were even related to each other, other than the fact that they had pneumonia.

There had to be something he was overlooking.

What about the dead mice at school? He went to the desk and took the clipboard with Janet Brown's science project papers and flipped through them again. Maybe there was something in her project that would give him a clue. She had set up a simple experiment, comparing diets to see the effect on weight and development. He flipped back and forth through her notes a couple of times, then threw them back on the desk. Nothing.

With the list of ten names, he was sure he was onto something, but what?

His mind kept going back to Janet Brown's three dead mice.

Matt gulped down the beer, took his notes, and left. Four blocks away he knocked on the door to Danielle's apartment and waited, then knocked again. Loud music drifted through the door. He tried the door and went in. Danielle was sprawled on the couch reading, wearing black dance tights and a faded Boston University sweatshirt. Her stereo blasted out some opera that he didn't recognize.

She looked up and smiled. "Hi, come on in."

Matt walked up to her, bent over, and kissed her hair. She looked sensuous and earthy, almost Amazon-like, with the sweatshirt riding partway up over her stomach. His eyes scanned the length of her long legs.

Matt dropped his notes onto a chair and wandered into the kitchen. "Any coffee?" he called back, but there was no answer as the music built to a fortissimo that vibrated the floor. He found a half-empty pot of cold coffee left in the coffee maker and poured a cup.

He went to the stereo and turned it off. A sudden silence blanketed the room. "The fat lady just sang," he said as a wide smile spread across his face.

Danielle rolled onto her stomach, propped up on her elbows, and looked up at him. "What's that smeared all over your face?"

The sensual curve and firm tone of her buttocks and graceful line of her legs did not escape his gaze. "Newsprint," he said. "I've been at the library going through newspapers, and I think I may have found something, but I'm not sure. I just can't put it all together." He looked at his hands. The cup was covered with smeared fingerprints. Everything he had touched turned black.

She looked at his cup. "What's that, cold coffee? God, I think I'm going to be sick."

"What were you looking for in the papers?" She took the cup from him. "Let me fix you some fresh coffee," and she went back into the kitchen.

Danielle started a fresh pot of coffee, then held up a plate of fudge. "Fresh fudge. Don't you want a piece?"

He grabbed a piece of fudge and took a bite. Warm, soft, rich chocolate with walnuts. "Mmm, very good," he said with his mouth still full. "How can you eat this stuff and still keep that figure?"

She smiled and put the plate down in front of him on the counter. "Why have you been going through the newspapers?"

Matt took another piece of fudge and told her about Dick Grey's obituary, and how he thought the paper might provide some information. Danielle was intrigued and listened while he related the names he had found at the library, about the fact that they were all out of town when they died.

She asked quietly, "So what can you make out of that? You think they could somehow be related to each other?"

"I think so. There must be a connection. I just haven't figured out what it is."

She poured hot coffee. "Let's go into the living room." She put on soft music and they sat on the floor with coffee and fudge. Danielle curled up and put her head in his lap.

They fell silent and listened to the soothing music. Matt ran his fingers through her hair. He stroked her neck and felt the soft hairs on the nape of her neck slide through his fingers. His hand moved over her shoulder, down her arm, then nudged against the side of her breast, paused a moment, then moved on. She stroked the back of his hand with her fingers.

It was after midnight when he glanced at his watch. He put his cup down and stood up to leave. "I didn't mean to stay so late."

She stood up and slowly moved close to him. "Good night," she said softly, her body tall, seductive, now very close to him, her face inches from his face, the aroma of her perfume intoxicating.

His fingers entwined themselves in her hair and he pulled her to him, pressing his lips full, flush onto hers, then kissed her more urgently, pressing her body into his and feeling her breasts against his chest. Her hair was in his face as her mouth opened to meet his and his lips went to her lower lip and sucked and nibbled across its curve. In that moment, piles of newspapers, dead mice, and thoughts of some intangible fear melted away—gone completely from his mind. All he saw and knew at that moment was the primal urge that rose from deep within him.

He bit at her lip and tasted her lipstick, tasted the sweetness of her mouth, felt her hot breath on his face.

"We shouldn't," she whispered in a husky voice as he slipped her sweatshirt off over her head and stared at her breasts. She cupped her hands over her breasts, but he locked his fingers through hers and gently but firmly pulled her arms up full length while he looked at her nakedness. Leaning down he kissed the soft fullness of her breast, and his tongue traced a path over a nipple that grew hard and he nibbled at the skin that felt hot. He could feel her heart beating. Her face was flushed, and her stomach tensed as her breath came fast and shallow.

She pulled him down onto the carpet and he shed his clothes. After pulling off her tights, his hands explored her body, down the smallness of her back, then moving up the white softness of her thigh. She grabbed his wrist but made no move to stop him as his fingers moved higher, touching the soft folds of her flesh, feeling the moisture between them, pushing the tender flesh apart with his fingers, feeling the heat within her. She trembled at his touch and her fingers dug into his back.

There was a primitive scent of raw sensuality that was woman, and it stirred an animal kind of lust from deep within him. He lifted her up against him, her body pressed to his, her long dancer's legs up around him. He had never wanted a woman more than he wanted Danielle now.

Every inch of his body throbbed and he tensed as he pushed against her. She reached down, took him firmly with her hand, and guided him into her. She was wet and he slid into her with one gentle thrust. He inhaled deeply as he penetrated her soft flesh, taking in the taste and smell and feel of her, the heat within her against his flesh. His temples throbbed.

He wanted to be slow, seductive, tender, but a primal urge drove him as he pounded harder, an act of animal aggression, a raw act of possession and conquest.

Their breathing came in gasps with the crescendo of their passion, and with her neck arched back, she moaned a low guttural sound that came from deep within her as she thrusted herself against him in ever-increasing tempo. They met again and again, their rhythm increasing, faster and faster, unable to restrain themselves, sweating bodies slamming until they were consumed by a feverish, spiraling climax.

They made love twice; the first time frantic and rough, on

the floor in front of the stereo, the second time in her bed, this time more tender, slow, and deliberate.

Matt could not sleep. While Danielle drew deep breaths beside him, he stared at the ceiling. Frigid night air poured through a window that had been left open and the room was cold. He fluffed up his pillow and rolled over but couldn't get back to sleep. Lying in the dark and staring at the window, his conclusions seemed absurd. People didn't die because they left town. There had to be more to it than that.

Try as he might, he couldn't get to sleep. He got up and wrapped himself in a blanket, pushed his feet into a pair of Danielle's rubber thongs, and went downstairs to the kitchen. He yawned and rubbed his eyes as he opened the refrigerator and squinted back at the bright light. The first plate held a piece of quiche, but he pushed it aside and looked deeper. Maybe something sweet. He pulled out the sack of fudge and dug inside for a piece. The sack reminded him of the bag filled with dead mice when he'd cleaned out the cages at school.

He looked for milk to wash down the fudge, but Danielle was out of milk. After rummaging through the cupboards, he found where she kept the glasses, pulled one out, and held it under the faucet, testing the water with his finger until it ran cold.

Water. Tap water. *The dead mice had been drinking distilled water.*

That was it!

He stuffed a piece of fudge in his mouth and bolted up the stairs with the thongs flapping wildly under his feet.

11

HE KICKED OFF the thongs and scurried around in his bare feet trying to get dressed in the dark.

"What are you doing?" Danielle asked, tiredly.

"Sorry, but I have to go," he said, pulling on his jeans.

"At two o'clock in the morning?" Danielle sat up, the sheet falling away from her breasts. "You were going to leave without saying good-bye?"

Matt pulled on his sweater, then leaned over and kissed her on the forehead. "Didn't want to wake you up."

"God, I'm freezing. Geez, the window's open. Come back to bed and we'll discuss it in the morning." She pulled the blanket up and fell back onto the pillow.

"I have to get over to the lab at school. I think I know what happened to the mice. The answer was right in front of my nose."

Danielle rubbed her eyes. "What?"

"I think the mice died because of the water."

"And what if they did, so what?" she asked, still trying to understand.

"If I'm right about what happened, then it's damned important we find out as soon as possible." He sat on the edge of the bed to put on his shoes and socks.

She threw back the covers and reached for her jeans. "I'm coming with you."

"Why?"

"You might need help or something. Besides, I don't like

to be abandoned in the middle of the night. I'm going with you.''

''You don't have to do that. Look, there's no reason—''

He could see there was no way he was going to talk her out of going. She had already pulled on a sweater and was pushing her legs into her jeans.

The bank sign flashed twenty-four degrees and the temperamental Nova's cold engine protested with frequent sputters. Their breath fogged the windshield as Matt nursed the Nova down dark streets, lonely and deserted except for streetlights that stood in little pools of light.

''So, tell me what this is all about,'' she asked.

''The three mice that died in Janet Brown's science project had the answer I was looking for. It was so simple and obvious I almost missed it. It's got to be the water.''

''We're out here freezing because three mice died? And what do you mean, it's the water?''

''I mean the mice died because of something in the water. Either something in the distilled water is making them sick, which I don't think is the case,'' he said, wiping clear a spot on the windshield.

''Or . . .''

''Or, if I'm right, it's when they stop drinking the city water that they get sick and die.''

''That's crazy.''

''Sure as hell is, but what if I'm right? And if I am right,'' he continued, ''Jeff and Kelley and at least a half dozen others may also have died from the same thing.''

She cleared her throat as if trying to figure how exactly to pose the next question. ''And . . . you think these people got pneumonia and died because of the *water*?''

''All of them were out of state when they got pneumonia and died. Yet the mice that died were in the same room where others survived. I asked myself why? What did the dead mice share in common with those people? The water.''

''You can't be serious,'' Danielle argued. ''What could the water have to do with it? Nobody in town is sick.''

He pounded the steering wheel. "That's just the point. Now stay with me on this for a moment. It sounds crazy, but just suppose—we're only talking theoretically here—just suppose there was something in the water that the mice needed to survive, and when they stopped getting it, they died."

"Then those people—"

"Those people," he interrupted her, "may have died after they left town simply because they were no longer drinking the same water."

Danielle sat back. "You mean, if we stopped drinking city water we would die? That's the most ridiculous thing I've ever heard."

Matt inwardly agreed; it seemed almost too absurd even for him to believe. "But what if I'm right?" he repeated.

He pulled into the parking lot, turned off the headlights, and drove behind the school. He didn't want to turn on any lights because teachers weren't authorized to use the building after nine P.M. and he wasn't prepared to answer a lot of questions. Not yet. They made their way through the corridors using a flashlight.

The headlights of a car slowly swept past the window. They stopped and listened as the tires of the car crunched slowly over the gravel outside. Matt feared someone had spotted them, but a moment later the car pulled away and continued down the street. He took a key from his pocket and unlocked the laboratory door.

"Can we turn the lights on in here?" Danielle asked, reaching for the switch.

"It's best if we don't," he said. "Follow me."

They went to the cages at the front of the room and Matt shined the beam of light on them. A sea of small red eyes stared back at the light. Except for being aroused out of a sleep, the mice all seemed fine. Matt opened the door and lifted one out by the nape of its neck. The mouse sniffed the air and looked around. "These mice look fine." He put the mouse back and closed the cage.

They closed the door to the front lab and walked to the smaller lab at the back of the room. Matt opened the door to the storage room and snapped on the flashlight. Danielle gasped and Matt stiffened.

It was much worse than he had expected it to be. More than half of the mice were dead, their bodies bloated and the fur matted. The rest were sick and trembling, their sides flaring as they struggled to breathe. The cages smelled of rot and decay.

"Oh, my God, Matt! What happened?"

"I don't know, but that's why we're here. Stay back— don't touch anything. It's my guess that whatever killed these mice also killed Jeff and Kelley and maybe a half-dozen others."

He pulled on a pair of rubber gloves and put the dead mice into a plastic garbage bag and taped it shut. This time instead of throwing the mice out in the dumpster, he would keep them and try to get some answers!

"What's different between these mice and those in the front? Aren't they getting the same water to drink?"

"No," Matt said. "This used to be the old chemistry lab and the only water supply to this room is distilled water from that faucet," and he nodded toward the sink. "So the mice in this room get distilled water to drink."

"So then maybe something in the distilled water killed them."

"No." Matt banged the flashlight as the beam faded. "No . . . that's not it. If I'm right, these mice would be just as healthy as the other mice if they were still drinking the city water. Janet Brown gave three of her mice distilled water as part of her science experiment, and they died."

Matt pulled an empty liter flask from the shelf, rinsed it out, then started filling it with distilled water from the faucet.

Danielle held her hand over her mouth, visibly shaken by what she had just heard and seen. "What are you doing?"

"I'm going to give some of the healthy mice in the front lab distilled water to drink. If I'm right, they'll die."

They took the flask to the front lab, emptied one of the water bottles and filled it back up with distilled. He marked it with a red tag and he was finished.

"Maybe I'm wrong," Matt said as he scrubbed his hands thoroughly at the sink, "but if I'm right, I can prove it very quickly. I intend to do just that with these mice. All we do is wait and see what happens."

"How long before we know anything?"

"I don't know . . ."

He took out a key and locked the door to the mice lab. This was off-limits to the students as of now. Tomorrow he intended to cancel the science projects using mice, and keep everyone away from them.

The feeling he felt was not one of victory for what he'd discovered, but a growing sense of ice-cold terror that he may be right.

12

"You're not going to let me get it tested?"

"Damn straight," the principal shot back. "Why should I? We can't even afford to repair typewriters for the typing class, and you want to have our water tested?"

Matt leaned forward with both hands on Leach's desk and stared down at him. "Mr. Leach, the water is making the mice sick. Something in the water is killing them. It's ruining the science projects. We need to get it tested."

"The mice that died were back in the old chem lab, weren't they? And they were drinking distilled water. There's no reason to test that. Just use tap water. I'll have one of the maintenance men check the distiller in the basement."

Matt wanted to tell Leach that he thought the mice died because of something in the *city water,* not the distilled water, but he knew Leach wouldn't believe him—it seemed too absurd for anyone to believe.

Leach continued, "Change the water every hour if you have to. We can't afford to buy any more mice this year." Leach leaned forward in his chair and opened a folder on the desk. "Your first quarter grades haven't been turned in yet. They were due yesterday. And you were late for class this morning. Anything bothering you at home, anything you'd like to talk about?"

Matt felt the skin on his neck crawl. Last night when they finished at the lab, he dropped Danielle off at her apartment and drove home. When he finally crawled into bed well after four A.M., he'd forgotten to set his alarm clock and overslept.

Without waiting for an answer Leach continued, "Now dammit, that animal lab is your responsibility. Understand?" Leach looked up at the wall clock. "And you're late for your nine o'clock class."

Matt turned and stormed out. The incompetent, stubborn, ignorant bastard.

Matt struggled through his Friday morning classes, but his mind wasn't on biology. During his lunch hour he headed to his office instead of the cafeteria.

There was one more thing he had to check out. He opened the phone book, ran his finger down the page until he found the number, then dialed.

"Culligan Water. May I help you?"

Matt introduced himself and said he was calling to get information for a class project. Could she tell him how many people in Loudonville used Culligan water?

"Just a minute," she said and put him on hold.

If people died when they stopped drinking the water, then switching to bottled water would have the same fatal result. They didn't have to leave town to die! And that should be easy enough to check out.

She came back on the phone. "Here it is. We have 175 customers in the area from this office. Of those . . . 27 are in Loudonville."

Matt thought a moment. He had to narrow down the list. "Can you give me the names of those people who have only started using your service since July?"

"I'm not sure I'm allowed to do that. Why do you need the customers' names?"

"The students only need to ask a few questions for a survey. It's for a school project."

"I'm not sure. Just wait another minute and I'll check," she said.

Matt had missed breakfast because he overslept, and hunger pains made him regret his decision to skip lunch. He hadn't had a square meal in three days. He glanced at his watch. He might be able to grab a quick snack, but he didn't want to be late for his one o'clock class again. He was already in enough trouble with Leach.

After another minute she came back on the line. "I guess it will be okay." She read off five names.

He wrote down the names. "That's all?" Matt asked. "Just five new customers since July?"

"Well, there were actually six. There was one customer who started our service at the end of the summer, but that name won't help you."

"Why not?"

"She was an elderly lady who lived alone. She died over a month ago."

Before he hung up, Matt managed to get her name, Miss Esther Hamilton, an elderly spinster who had lived alone. Matt wondered if she died of old age, or was Miss Hamilton victim number eleven? Had she died because she stopped drinking city water?

He pounded his fist on the desk in anger at Leach. The hell with Leach—Matt knew the answer was with the water, and he intended to get it tested!

13

THE THERMOMETER READ twenty-two degrees, the coldest morning of fall and the first killing frost. The Nova's engine was still cold and Matt nursed the defroster switch, trying to keep the windshield clear. Bright morning sunlight glittered from the ice crystals that clung to the fence and weeds beside the road. Half of the corn in a large field on the right had been harvested, leaving long stubbled rows.

Matt sped north along the winding road to the water plant three miles out of town. He glanced down at the two bottles of water that sloshed on the front seat beside him and wondered what deadly secret lurked there.

The next hill brought two large white water processing tanks into view. In front of them was a white brick building trimmed in navy blue shutters, and a sign over the front door that announced: LOUDONVILLE WATER DIVISION.

Matt turned into the parking lot. He opened the car door, struggled with the two large bottles, and lugged them into the office. He looked around for a place to put them.

A young girl at a small cluttered desk seemed to be doing battle with a typewriter. She finally looked up. "May I help you?"

"Yes. I want to get this water tested."

"Just a minute." After one last assault on the keys she stood up and left. Matt knelt down and slid the heavy bottles to the floor. He looked around the room. One wall was lined with shelves that held hundreds of binders labeled "Water Analysis," with dates written at the bottom.

A short, ruddy-faced, heavyset man came through the door. His protuberant belly hung over his belt, and the tie knotted around his neck seemed like it was about to strangle him. A stubby cigar was wedged into the corner of his mouth. He coughed twice, cleared his throat of phlegm, then asked in a raspy voice, "What can I do for you?"

Matt hated cigars, and that one looked especially disgusting. The soggy butt had been chewed flat and a loose piece of tobacco leaf hung down. Matt said, "I want to get this water tested. I teach science at Loudonville High School, and the mice in our lab are dying. I think it's because of the water they drank. I brought samples of both distilled water and city water to be tested."

The man's thick eyebrows meshed into a frown. "You want to test the city water? Why? You don't think they died from drinking the city water, do you?"

"I'm not sure. That's a remote possibility," Matt answered. He knew it wouldn't be an easy thing to explain.

The man pulled out the cigar, trailing a strand of saliva, coughed again—an act that turned his face a deep purple and made the veins on his forehead bulge—stuck the cigar back in, and said, "When did the mice die?"

"They died this week," Matt said.

"Just a minute." The ruddy-faced man walked over to the shelves and pulled out one of the loose-leaf books. He laid the journal on the desk, flipped through the pages rapidly, then ran his thick finger down a page. "Here is the daily analysis for the past week. Everything's normal. I don't know a darn thing about mice, but this water is safe for humans. Did any of the students at school get sick? Diarrhea, vomiting, anything like that?"

"No, nobody else was sick."

"And you and I didn't get sick, did we? So, either your mice died from the distilled water or from something else. Where do you get it?"

"The school has a distillation unit in the basement. It supplies about twenty gallons a day. It's all we really need for the labs."

"We can run an analysis on it for you, but it's a hundred and seventy-five dollars for a standard test. For that kind of money, I'd just take them off distilled water and forget about it."

Matt nodded as if he understood. "I still want both samples tested," he persisted. "Send the bill to the school at this address, but I'd like a copy of the results sent to my home address. What type of analysis can you do?"

The man pulled the wet, flaky cigar from his mouth and picked up a computer form. "Well, the Class One Systems Analysis is designed to test for safety of human consumption. It's our standard quality test." He ran his finger down the page and read from the book: "Bacterial count, solid particulates as turbidity, metals, free ions, salinity, pH, iron and sulfur for hardness quality. The Class One Systems Analysis also requires microbiological testing. Very thorough."

Matt thought a moment, then asked, "What about toxins, poisons, pesticides—that sort of thing."

"What kind of poison you talking about?"

Matt wasn't sure. "I don't know . . . all of them, I guess."

The cigar was back in his mouth and the words spewed from the corner of his mouth showing stained teeth. "Class B tests for organic chemicals and most petroleum contaminants. Class A tests for radionuclides and radioactive radicals."

"Yeah."

"Yeah, what?"

"I want you to do all the tests you mentioned."

"We can only do the Class One Systems Analysis; we can't do Class A or B analysis here in our lab. The water samples have to be sent to outside labs for that. But you have to identify which specific thing you are checking for, and it's expensive, up to a hundred dollars per test. That can require some very sophisticated testing, like thermal neutron activation analysis and liquid chromatography. If it were me, I'd just give the mice city water to drink and forget about distilled water.''

The man shoved two papers at him that listed all the tests available in Class A and B analysis, with a place to check which ones were to be performed. At the bottom of each page was a place to check if everything listed was to be tested. Matt checked both bottom boxes and quickly shoved them back.

Matt didn't give a damn about the distilled water, but it was obvious that he was going to have to test both city water and the distilled water. ''Do just the standard quality test on the distilled water. On the city water sample, repeat the standard quality test, and I want both Class B and Class A tests done.''

Thick fingers poked the cigar at him. ''You're wasting the school's money. It's already been checked. For the complete Class A and B it'll cost another . . . seventeen hundred and fifty dollars. The total with the two standard tests is twenty-one hundred dollars. You should get the results by the end of next week.'' He started to put the cigar stump back in his mouth, but a coughing fit doubled him over.

Matt left, climbed in the car, and slammed the door. He'd just spent more than twenty-one hundred dollars of the school's money, his department's budget for the semester, and there was always the possibility that it wasn't going to tell him a damned thing!

He just had to make sure he intercepted the bill and somehow buried it among other departmental expenses.

14

The Niwot Project

THE BOLD RED letters served as a warning and not as a greeting:

THE NIWOT PROJECT
U.S. GOVERNMENT PROPERTY
TOP SECURITY CLEARANCE ONLY

"Good morning, Dr. Strassman."

"Morning, Sergeant." Dr. Otto Strassman waited at the security door while the marine sergeant checked his ID badge, then Strassman punched in his access code and went in.

Strassman was a leading candidate for a Nobel prize in physics for his work on hydrogen fusion, but he still had to go through a security check each time he entered. He stepped out onto the metal catwalk sixty feet above the floor and glanced at his watch.

After his escape from Germany during World War II, Strassman made his way to England and after the war came to America. He became a theoretical physicist at Princeton and was the mastermind behind the development of Princeton's "Tokomak" hydrogen fusion reactor. Now he was in charge of the first "Star" fusion reactor.

The view from the catwalk looked down into the center of the giant magnet, surrounded by thick coils of wire that carried the high-voltage current. The superconductive coils produced a magnetic field in the center more than ten tesla in strength, one of the strongest magnets in the world. Gallons of liquid helium bathed the thick electrical coils and cooled them to near absolute zero. Off to the side, two large white tanks that housed the liquid helium "breathed" a white swirling vapor as air came in contact with the frozen metal.

Surrounding the electromagnet were eight enormous Nova lasers, their beams aimed at the zero center of the magnet.

A yellow light flashed and the one-minute warning buzzer sounded. Strassman reluctantly stepped into the control room and closed the door.

One hundred times a day, every fourteen minutes, the powerful lasers surrounding the monstrous superconductive magnet blasted the hydrogen plasma target contained inside. A flashing red light signaled the final ten-second warning. The lasers were armed and hydrogen plasma flowed into the core of the magnetic field. All doors were sealed.

Nobody had ever seen "the event." It had been recorded only by the large array of instruments inside the protected electronics room. Heat and light as intense as the core of the sun would burn the flesh from the eyelids, sear the retina, and blind anyone near it, even with protective lenses.

In one split second, everything in the core of the magnet vaporized. The walls of the control room were six feet thick, made of reinforced concrete and steel and included a sound damper, but at the instant the lasers fired and fusion occurred, the building shook and a muffled but deep, frightening *crack* could still be heard, as if a lightning bolt had just struck on the other side of the wall. He watched the instruments record the burst from the lasers, and he felt the heat even through the protective walls.

At the core of the hundred-ton, eighty-foot magnet—for one ten thousandth of a second—hydrogen fusion occurred at three hundred million degrees, the same event that fueled the center of the sun. All the forces of the universe were brought to life in the center of the magnetic target.

With energies approaching the nuclear binding energy of the atom, everything was in flux; separating, mixing, fusing. Hydrogen fused into helium, then into larger molecules of carbon, oxygen, nitrogen. In the center of the magnet the formation began.

Creation. The beginning of time.

Their early tests confirmed what he had predicted; the "event" had created heavy elements at the end of the periodic table, atoms that existed no place else on the planet. The periodic chart predicted they theoretically should exist, and probably had at one time during the early violent formation of the earth. Now the only thing left was to isolate and study them.

Strassman decided that he wanted to spend the final moment of his life staring into that magnetic ring, and the last image that would be burned into his mind would be the heat of creation—or the fires of hell—he wasn't sure which.

He smiled at the thought and went out to check the data.

After Matt returned home from the water plant, he pulled out his sheet of names and spent the rest of the afternoon calling the five Culligan customers. With each call his excitement grew. Four of the names given to him lived inside the township, but outside the city limits and therefore did not receive either water or sewage services from the city. All had wells as their main water source, and they hadn't even been drinking city water prior to switching to Culligan, so that took them out of the picture.

The fifth person he called lived in the heart of Loudon-ville, but he was a photographer with a studio, and used the bottled Culligan water in developing his film. It seemed that the chlorine used in the treatment of city water caused color distortion on his high-detail film, so the photographer used bottled water in the dark room to eliminate the problem.

That left Esther Hamilton. Matt desperately wanted to get more information regarding the death of the elderly woman. He jumped on his bike and rode to the library, and after scanning through two weeks of the *Gazette,* he found the obituary on Esther Hamilton. She died on Thursday, September seventeenth. She was eighty-four, lived alone, and the only relative mentioned was a nephew who lived in Houston, Texas.

Matt jotted down the information, rode back to his house, and once inside went to the phone. He got the phone number of the nephew and dialed; he was out of town, but his wife was able to provide some information regarding Esther Hamilton. A neighbor found her collapsed on the floor, and the paramedics thought that she had suffered a stroke. She died two days later in the hospital.

He needed more information and sat staring out the window, pondering what to do next. He looked up the phone number of the hospital and stabbed in the number rapidly. When the operator answered, he asked for Medical Records, and nervously tapped his pencil on the table, hoping his ploy would work.

"This is the county court records clerk calling," he said with all the authority in his voice he could muster. "We need to know the cause of death on Miss Esther Hamilton so we can complete her death certificate on our record. She died September seventeenth."

"Just a minute, and I'll check," the secretary said. After a short delay, she returned. "I'm sure the proper forms were mailed in, but here it is. The cause of death was coded out as probable stroke."

Matt persisted. "Since an autopsy was not performed, is there any other information given in the final summary on the medical chart that may help us?"

"It says, stroke with paralysis to the right side of her body. She developed marked shortness of breath and had pneumonia just before she died. That's all that's listed."

"Thank you." Matt put the receiver down, his heart racing as adrenaline surged through him. He was convinced that Esther Hamilton was the eleventh person to die.

He learned that she had been getting Culligan water for

only three weeks before she died. Granted, she was eighty-four and had suffered a stroke, but she was also the only one of all the new customers who had used city water for drinking before switching to Culligan. And she was dead.

Sunday night Matt went back to the school to check on the mice. The mice in the back lab drinking distilled water looked appalling. Their rapid, labored breathing made a wet, raspy sound. Thick mucus ran from nostrils that flared for air as their ribs heaved to suck in air; they were choking to death on their own secretions. Their fur was matted and drenched in sweat, and they were trembling. Matt knew they had pneumonia and showed signs of a high fever; they were going to die just like the other mice. Just like Jeff had died.

He recorded the number of sick mice on a clipboard, and noted the time and date. Then he went up front to check on the other group of mice. The mice that he had switched to distilled water showed no changes, but it had only been three days since he had started them on distilled water. If Janet's lab notes were accurate, the mice died eight to ten days after they were taken off the city water.

In another week he'd know for certain.

Monday morning a secretary from the water division called Matt at school. Was he still certain that he wanted the water tested for all heavy metals and isotopes? Yes. Did he want that done on both the distilled and city water? No, he told her, just do the tests on the city water. He again reminded her to send a copy of the results to his home address.

Matt just had to make sure he intercepted the bill before it got to the front office. He was already in enough trouble, but the hell with the extra cost. He had to find out what was in the water and get the health authorities involved in this.

After his last class at the end of the day, Matt went back to the lab and cleaned the cages and changed the water one more time. Ten more mice back in the old chem lab were dead. He dropped the dead mice into a plastic bag and put it in the lab's freezer with the other dead mice, shoving the bag toward the back where he hoped nobody would bother it. He pulled off the gloves and carefully washed his hands twice. He wondered if he should be wearing a mask.

He wanted somebody to examine the dead mice. He called both the county and the state health departments, stating his concern for the students who were exposed to the mice that died, but they weren't interested, not until any of the students actually came down with something infectious. They had no interest in examining the mice. They did suggest avoiding close contact with the mice until the infection ran its course.

He'd come to a dead end.

He would have the results of the water tests by next week, but he had to figure out a way to get the mice examined. If they died of pneumonia, was it contagious? What had he and the students in the lab already been exposed to?

During the drive home he poured over his options. He went into the kitchen, rummaged through the nearly empty cupboards, and found a can of black olives. He hadn't shopped for groceries for more than a week, and all he had eaten in two days was leftover pizza. He opened the can of olives, dumped them into a bowl, and sat down on the floor, his back resting against the wall, the phone cradled in his lap.

He spit an olive pit toward the bowl on the floor, but it missed and rolled away. Matt tore the note from the bulletin board where he had scribbled the CDC's number, and tapped in the number. He had something definite to go on this time with names and dates from obituaries, the dead mice in the lab, and the death of Esther Hamilton. Maybe there was some way he could convince Evans or someone at the CDC to examine the mice.

Two transfers, another hold, and Evans was on the phone. "Dr. Evans? This is Matt Strong in New Hampshire calling again. I reviewed the obituaries in our paper. Eleven people have died of pneumonia since July."

"Obituaries? You can't be serious."

"Another eighteen mice in the lab at school died, and I'm

convinced it was because of something in the water.'' Matt
told Evans about his simple experiment with the mice, about
the people who died after they left town, about Miss
Hamilton who died when she stopped drinking city water.
''I think we've got a serious problem here that needs
immediate attention. The mice may give us the answer.''

''I don't think you should be concerned about the
mice—''

''It's not about the damned mice!'' Matt shouted back in
anger. ''Eleven people may have died from the same thing
that killed the mice. And it may be because of something in
the water!''

Evans's voice had a sudden icy tone. ''We have no report
from the medical community or health department of any
problem there. I checked after your last call. Nobody has
reported any outbreak of flu and there are no reported deaths
from pneumonia. As for the mice, call Dr. Walter Davis in
Seattle at the Animal Field Division of the CDC. Tell him
your story. Maybe he can help you.'' Evans gave him the
number and hung up.

Matt plopped the receiver back down and let out a deep
sigh. Had he gone mad? Was he imagining a horror that
existed only in his mind? Obviously nobody else believed
him. Matt popped another shiny olive into his mouth and
dialed the number Evans had given him, but the line was
busy.

Danielle came in with a sack of groceries. ''How about
some spaghetti? I also picked up a bottle of burgundy,'' and
she pulled out a bottle triumphantly.

''Hi, beautiful. Got one more call to make.''

Danielle put the groceries on the counter and looked at
him. She picked up the empty can and glanced down at the
pits scattered on the floor. ''Olives? Now there's a balanced
diet. I'm going to fix dinner and we can just spend a nice
quiet night together. You know you haven't had a decent
meal in over a week, and you're starting to look sick.'' She
twisted the opener into the cork and popped it out with a
firm pull.

"I just talked to Dr. Evans at the Centers for Disease Control in Atlanta. I was hoping he might agree to examine the dead mice and see what killed them, but he's not interested." He took a deep breath and let out a sigh. "I've got one more call to make."

Danielle handed him a glass of burgundy and leaned down and kissed him on the cheek.

He ate the last olive and punched in the number again. A receptionist answered and put him through to Davis.

"Dr. Davis, this is Matt Strong calling from New Hampshire. Dr. Evans in Atlanta gave me your number and said you might be able to help me." Matt explained to Davis about the dead mice at school and his concern about the safety to the students. He said that Evans urged him to get assistance from Davis. It wasn't quite the truth and Matt suspected Davis knew that.

Matt debated whether to tell Davis the whole story about the water and the obituaries, or just try to get him to examine the mice. He decided on the latter since it might be his only opportunity to learn anything about the mice, and he didn't want to blow that opportunity. This was his best chance—maybe his only chance—to find out what happened to the mice.

"Evans wants me to examine the mice?"

"Just check to see what killed the mice, because several students working on science projects handled the mice and were exposed to them." Matt wanted to spill out everything—but couldn't risk losing credibility.

Matt continued, "I'm worried that the mice may have exposed the students to something dangerous."

"If there have been several cases of pneumonia in your community, Evans should do an epidemiological investigation. Why even bother with the mice?" Davis asked.

"Well, there hasn't been an outbreak of pneumonia so far. We contacted Dr. Evans just because we were worried about the students. He said to contact you and that you would take care of it."

"Pack the mice in dry ice and have them shipped to me express. I don't want any mice that have been dead for more than twenty-four hours, okay? Our lab will examine them and get back to you."

Matt jotted down the mailing address, thanked him, and hung up. Springing to his feet and taking a long drink of burgundy before setting the glass down on the counter he said, "Good news, I think. Sorry, but I have to go. I'll be back as soon as I can."

Danielle was cutting lettuce and putting a salad together. "Can't it wait until tomorrow? We make love and you jump out of bed and take off in the middle of the night. Now you're leaving before I can even cook the meal."

"I'll hurry right back. I promise." He kissed her and left.

He got a cooler from the garage and drove the Nova to the school, pushing the old car as he raced down the side streets. He ran up the stairs to the third floor and took twenty pounds of dry ice from the chemistry lab freezer, put it in his cooler, then went downstairs to check on the mice again. Three more mice in the back room had died. He grabbed a pair of gloves and dropped the mice in a plastic bag, then put them in the cooler. He took the plastic bag of mice from the refrigerator and put it in the cooler. After scrubbing his hands thoroughly, he loaded the cooler in the trunk of the car and headed home.

Matt knew that the mice and the water were the key to everything, and he was about to get answers to both. For the first time in many days he felt elated. It was dark and cold outside, but hunger pangs reminded him that Danielle and a hot meal were waiting for him.

When he walked into the kitchen, Danielle stood at the sink draining the noodles. "Stir the sauce, would you?"

He walked up behind her and kissed her neck. As he stirred the sauce, he told her that somebody with the CDC was going to examine the mice, and the water tests should be back soon. He was about to get some definite answers!

He promised her he would try to get his life back to normal and pay more attention to her and his classwork.

After dinner, they danced barefoot in the kitchen by candlelight. He held her tightly, felt her softness against his hard body, her warmth, breathed in her fragrance. Every movement she made sent a charge of anticipation and desire through him.

Matt guided her into the bedroom. They fell back onto the bed and he unbuttoned her blouse, caressed and kissed her breasts, then pulled her skirt up around her waist.

Stroking, kissing, touching, he crushed her breasts against his chest and her light perfume rushed into his senses. His lips moved over her flat belly, and he kissed the inside of her thighs as he pushed her skirt higher. His mouth became part of her.

"There—*right there*—oh, God, yes . . ." Her throaty voice was barely above a whisper.

Then she was kneeling over him, the tips of her long auburn hair brushing against the inside of his thighs. She shifted her body on top of him and suddenly, almost by accident, he was inside her. Her thighs tensed as she moved over him, and he ran his fingers deliciously up and down her legs and explored her soft flesh as she moved with greater urgency.

They made love with a furor and abandonment, as if to blot out the world with their ecstasy. After almost an hour, both glistening with sweat, they fell asleep in each other's arms, drained and fulfilled. The early-morning sun bathed their naked bodies as they slept, unaware of the new day.

He was late for school again.

15

*U.S. Centers for Disease Control
Field Research Service
Seattle, Washington*

A COLD RAIN beat against the window and ran down the glass in meandering streams. It was still dark outside and would be for another two hours. The light of dawn came late in the morning to Seattle this time of year. The past ten days had been gloomy from the constant drizzle. Damp, dismal, and dark. "A stationary Pacific low-pressure system," the television weatherman had explained.

The door to the office was open; a sign over the door read:

WALTER R. DAVIS, Ph.D.
Director,
Field Research Service
Centers for Disease Control

Davis's small office was cluttered and cramped for space. Funds for the CDC were limited, and office space was a low priority. His desk sagged under the weight of stacks of reports from completed studies and current projects. Two file cabinets were jammed with journals and abstracts from the world's scientific literature. The department had computer-access to any article published in the world, but personal library space was almost nonexistent.

The smell of brewing coffee and the sound of Tchaikovsky's Symphony No. 6 coming from a small stereo on the bookshelf filled the cramped office and spilled through the open door. It was a sharp contrast to the expansive, sterile laboratory on the other side of the door.

The open, spacious laboratory, while only a fraction the size of the main Centers for Disease Control laboratory headquartered in Atlanta, was well equipped for field research, with an investigative staff consisting of biochemists, research pharmacologists, microbiologists, and immunologists. Any problems that they couldn't handle were supposed to be sent on to Atlanta to the main CDC laboratories, but the field research team didn't let that happen often.

Dr. Walter Davis was a youthful, collegiate-looking man, short at five-seven with thick blond hair and wire-rimmed glasses that framed a friendly face. He was a bright young scientist with credentials a mile long. Harvard undergrad, followed by graduate school at Stanford and research biology at MIT. Davis had been promoted from the CDC headquarters in Atlanta to head the Field Research Section in Seattle. At thirty-seven he was the youngest person ever appointed as a sectional director for the CDC.

Davis had arrived at his office at 5:30 A.M. to examine the mice. He wanted to finish the project and get it out of the way. He had a busy schedule today, too busy in fact to worry about mice. The responsibilities of being director took most of his time away from actual field investigations, and he missed that. But today he had a lot of other important things to do.

He wasn't sure why he had agreed to do this. Maybe it was the desperation in the call, but he wished he hadn't committed himself. He'd been director for only six months and hadn't yet learned when to say no to unnecessary requests. But he wasn't prepared to argue with Evans.

He took the container of dead mice packed in dry ice back to the dissection lab. After snapping on a pair of surgical gloves, he opened a sterile scalpel and slit open the abdomens of the first four mice.

The initial exam was as uneventful as he expected it to be. Generalized sepsis from some pathogen had spread quickly through the small confined lab cages. It happened frequently enough in all labs, even sophisticated research labs with strict safeguards. It couldn't be avoided. He would get gram stains and cultures, and put the matter to rest. He wouldn't even file a report on this one. He didn't know why Evans dumped this on him, but Davis didn't want to raise eyebrows by wasting funds on this kind of exercise. He'd identify the bacteria responsible and get a letter off to the teacher.

The mice were swollen and bloated; their abdominal cavities were filled with foul-smelling fluid. Liver, spleen, and kidneys all had abscesses. This would be easier than he had first thought. Obviously some bacterial contaminant had spread through the lab and killed the school mice. Davis would prove to himself that there was no threat to the students, advise the teacher and Evans of his findings, and be done with it. Nothing more.

Davis attached a three-inch needle to a 10cc syringe, jabbed it through the abdominal wall, and drew thick, yellow fluid into the syringe. After making slide preps, he dipped the glass slides in a series of solutions to get a gram stain, then set the slides aside to dry.

He yanked off the rubber gloves, washed the talc powder from his hands, and finished off his cup of coffee. He wanted to turn his attention to a paper he was giving in Denver on the problem of endemic bubonic plague in small mountain rodents. And his fiancée who was finishing her masters degree at the University of Maryland was going to meet him there for an extended weekend together.

But his mind lingered on the mice another minute. The mice were literally filled with pus. Whatever organism had infected them was damned aggressive and extremely virulent. He scribbled a note for one of the technologists to run serum immunologic profiles, including viral convalescent titers. That was probably an expensive overkill, but something gnawed at the back of his mind. He decided more testing was in order.

He needed blood smears and bone-marrow aspirates. Davis twisted the cutting needle through the hard cortex of bone in the pelvis of each mouse and sucked out bone marrow, then put it aside so the lab tech could decalcify it later and make a smear.

He poured another cup of coffee and added two packets of NutraSweet. After putting on a Mendelssohn concerto tape, he sat down to review the slides. He put a drop of oil on the glass and lowered the high-power lens. The gram stain was loaded with bacteria. But as he scanned back and forth systematically over the slide, something wasn't right. He changed slides and reviewed a blood smear.

He sipped his coffee and stared out at the dark drizzle. Something was definitely wrong.

The slide was loaded with bacteria, but there was a mixture of several strains, not just one type as would be expected. There were gram negative rods mixed with gram positive cocci. The mice couldn't have died because of a contagious bacteria, because there were a hundred different infections going on at the same time. It seemed as if their own lack of immunity had killed them.

He slid his chair back from the microscope and put on another pair of gloves. He picked up the scalpel and dissected out the livers and dropped them in formalin for histology and chemical analysis. As he drank his coffee he began to wonder about the circumstances that could have led to so virulent an infection, identical in character in all the mice.

He wondered briefly whether he should have taken more personal precautions.

He had examined only four of the mice, but they had all looked identical. The abdominal cavity was filled with exudate, and there was fluid in the pleural spaces of the chest. He would have to do more sophisticated tests including serum protein immunoelectrophoresis profiles that separated the immune protein components by application of an electrical field.

He set his coffee aside and picked up the computer printout. All the tests showed the same results. Not only was there no stimulated immune response, the immune complex had completely shut down. The bacteria in their own bodies had overwhelmed the mice and devoured them.

Why? Things weren't going as smoothly as he had hoped. What had started out as a simple exercise was fast becoming a complex problem, leaving him with more questions than answers. He needed more information.

Davis went back to the microscope and put a blood smear under high power.

Something caught his eye. What was different about the white blood cells? He scanned the slide again.

Two staff members arrived and joked to him about being hard at work so early. Davis turned and said, "George, could you schedule me time on the electron microscope? I want to study these white blood cells. Something's wrong with them."

He remembered what the teacher had said on the phone, that something in the water killed the mice. What if the teacher was right? Some important piece of information had to be missing. An alarm went off in the back of his mind, but he dismissed it as implausible. The ramifications of it were too horrible to consider.

Barefoot and unshaven, Matt went out to the mailbox for the Saturday morning paper and mail. He'd just finished off the last of the food from his refrigerator with a cheese omelette, English muffin, and a bowl of peaches. A manila envelope from Richer Laboratories was among the bills.

The results of the water test!

He ran back inside and pulled out the two-page report:

CHEMICAL QUALITY LOUDONVILLE CITY WATER

pH	9.33
Turbidity	0.14
Total dissolved solids	125 PPM
Phenolphthalein alkalinity	8.5
Total alkalinity hardness	80
Calcium	25.8
Magnesium	3.6
Fluoride	0.9
Free Chlorine residual	0.9
Sodium	11.0
Chloride	21.4
Nitrate	1.31
Ortho Phosphate	0.02
Total Phosphate	0.11
Iron	0.0416
Copper	0.0082
Zinc	0.0100
Trihalomethanes	0.057
Arsenic	0.004
Barium	.100
Cadium	.001
Chromium	.020
Lead	.005
Mercury	.0003
Selenium	.004
Nickel	.0019
Silver	.010
Aluminum	.050

SYNTHETIC ORGANIC CHEMICALS	mg/liter
Endrin	.00005
Lindane	.00001
Methoxychlor	.0013
Toxaphene	.001
2,4, D	.01
2,4,5,-Tp	.001

RADIONUCLIDES	PIC/liter
Gross alpha-natural	3 picocuries
Gross Beta-Strontium, Tritium	2.2
*Deuterium	10,000**
see note:	

NOTE: 10,000 picocuries Deuterium exceeds the standard by a factor of over one million.

Matt had no idea what the figures meant. But the special note at the bottom sure as hell implied the level of deuterium wasn't normal. He picked up the phone and dialed the number of the laboratory listed on the letterhead, but nobody answered. He called the Loudonville Water Division. Recognizing the gravelly voice behind the wet cigar, Matt asked him about the deuterium level on the water test.

"Yeah, I got a copy of the test and saw that," the man said. "A mistake in testing, or a misprint. Has to be. Never saw deuterium that high." After a pause he added, "But of course we don't routinely check for isotopes."

"When was the last time you tested for isotopes?"

"Ah . . . let me see." There was a pause while he flipped through several pages. "Eighteen months ago. It's not a test we do frequently because it's expensive and it's not that critical. The rest of the test looks normal, like I told you it would be."

In spite of everything he was hearing, Matt's instincts told him otherwise. He stared at the paper as if something would magically appear and explain everything. What if the deuterium level was not a mistake? Where did it come from, and what did it have to do with all of the deaths?

He pulled out his chemistry textbook and looked up deuterium.

Deuterium: A rare, naturally occurring stable isotope of hydrogen, consisting of two neutrons and one proton, with an atomic mass number two. Deuterium is produced as deuterium oxide, called "heavy water," and is used to act as a stabilizer in atomic reactions.

Deuterium was a rare isotope of hydrogen, so if he wanted to find where there was a source of deuterium, he needed to look for a large source of hydrogen. He picked up the phone book and searched through the yellow pages. He

called several companies in Boston, Concord, and Hartford
that handled nitrogen, helium, hydrogen, and other gases.

Small amounts of the gases were used in glass production, welding, agriculture, and manufacturing, but not in any
significant amounts. A passing comment gave him his
answer. "Of course, the government contract with the
Niwot Project is our largest customer for hydrogen."

The Niwot Project was a large government research
facility thirty miles north of Loudonville, and nobody knew
what kind of research was being done there. Matt looked for
a number in the phone book, then called the operator to
learn that it was an unlisted number.

He pulled out a map and looked at the region. "U.S.
Restricted Area" was all that was listed, and it covered
hundreds of acres near a large marsh. He looked at the water
test results again. If the government used large amounts of
hydrogen at the Niwot Project, it seemed logical that the
plant also could be the source of deuterium in the water.

Glancing at his watch, he studied the map again. It was a
crazy idea, but he was going to do it.

By midmorning, the cloud cover broke up, and scattered
sunlight warmed Seattle. Unaware of the improved weather,
Davis reviewed the paper printout of the immunoelectrophoresis tracings. Davis needed more information. Something was missing. He reached for the paper with the
teacher's phone number in New Hampshire on it and dialed,
but there was no answer.

16

MATT LEANED LOW over the handlebars and pedaled hard against the cold, biting wind that whipped dust and leaves across the road in front of him. His leather biking gloves provided little protection for his numbed fingers. Shifting to a lower gear to maintain his cadence, he started up the long, grueling climb that led out of town. Twenty minutes of hard pedaling made him sweat, and the moisture on the back of his neck felt cool.

He was discouraged and disappointed. For two thousand dollars he hoped he would have gotten more answers about the water. He didn't know if the levels of deuterium in the water had anything to do with the mice dying, but he sure as hell knew that something in the water had caused their deaths when they stopped drinking it. Deuterium was the only thing abnormal on the analysis, and right now it was his only clue. If Davis at the CDC didn't find anything after examining the mice, Matt would be left with nothing.

If he could get a look at the Niwot Project, maybe he could learn something about the source of deuterium. If he had something more to go on, maybe he could get the state health department involved and start an investigation.

At the top of the hill he gained speed as the road leveled, and he quickly covered the remaining two miles to the woods that surrounded the makeshift hangar. He leaned over and loosened the toe straps on the pedals and coasted to a stop in front of a red barn that housed the club's ultralight planes. The long uphill ride winded him, but without stopping to catch his breath, he leaned his bike against the side of the shed and pulled open the large sliding door. The rusty rollers creaked loudly in protest.

He pushed his bike inside and paused while his eyes adjusted to the dim interior. Thick dust and cobwebs coating the windows dimmed the afternoon sunlight that filtered in. The smell of gasoline and oil hung heavily in the old barn. The skeletal cockpit frames and wings of several planes arranged in a long line looked more like resting butterflies with folded wings. The planes had been put in storage for the winter because the weather this time of year was usually too rough for flying.

"Ultralight Aircraft" was the official name of the dacron and aluminum bird-like contraptions. But in simpler terms they were motorized hang gliders, a concoction of airplane, motorcycle, and sailboat. The small 25 h.p. Briggs & Stratton engine with its stubby 3.5-foot propeller could push the 180-pound plane along at 50 miles per hour, top speed. It was a daredevil type of fly-by-the-seat-of-your-pants machine, modern cousin to the old barnstorming biplanes.

Ultralights required only one hundred feet of ground for takeoff, even less for landing. The sparse cockpit consisted of aluminum tubing, a black taped control stick, foot pedals for rudder control, and simple instruments consisting of a floating disc speed indicator and compass. But the best way to judge speed was by the sound of the wind singing through the cables. There were several different models and styles of the strange flying things in the club. Matt's own Hawk-110 model was a fast and maneuverable plane with an overhead engine mounted on the front of the central strut.

He pulled a ten-gallon fuel can from the shelf and wiped spider webs and dust from the spout, inserted a funnel, and poured until gas trickled over the rim. With a full tank he should be able to make the sixty-mile round-trip, but it left him with little margin of safety.

He unzipped the front pannier on the bicycle and pulled

out a pair of binoculars, a pocket camera, heavy lined gloves, and a wool ski cap. These would be necessary as the temperatures dropped through the afternoon. He wore Levi's, a thick wool sweater, down vest, and long underwear.

With the binoculars dangling around his neck, he pushed his plane through the open door at the rear of the building. The club had cut a path through the birch trees and designed a short dirt runway. Now it lay beneath a thick blanket of yellow leaves.

Matt had to hustle. It would be dark in two hours, and his plane had no lights or instruments. He would be cutting it close.

A frayed orange flag that served as a wind indicator snapped and pulled at its grommets in the stiffening wind. The plane wasn't built to fly in these conditions, and under any other circumstances, Matt wouldn't try it. He had no choice now if he wanted to get a look at the Niwot Project. He kept glancing at the flag. The strength of the wind bothered him.

After checking and adjusting the support cables, Matt pulled the choke halfway out and flipped the stubby propeller. The loud whine of the small engine shattered the stillness. He climbed into the cockpit and buckled himself in. He slowly pushed the choke in as the engine warmed, and the exhaust spewed out a pale blue cloud of oil that encompassed the cockpit. A tattered lucky rabbit's foot dangled over the speed indicator, a silent reminder of the real possibility of danger.

Matt pulled back on the throttle, and the Briggs & Stratton roared out in response. Leaves swirled around the cockpit as the fragile plane shot forward, and in a short distance vibration gave way to a sudden smoothness as the fat balloon tires cleared the ground and the propeller clawed through the wind, pulling toward the sky.

A blast of cold air hit him in the face as the Hawk-110 climbed above the protection of the woods. He gripped the stick as he felt the plane fight the wind. The autumn-colored hills spread out below him. Far below him, the red barn hangar seemed like a red hemorrhage among the brilliant yellow birch leaves. A farmer on his tractor gazed skyward, squinting into the sun to catch a glimpse of him.

Ten minutes later Matt pushed the stick forward and dropped down into the ravine already dark in shadow. The Black Fork River began in the mountains of northern New Hampshire and built to a turbulent river that tumbled and wound its way down a deep rocky gorge lined with dense trees. The high western side of the ravine provided a buffer to the strong side wind from the west that had pushed him laterally from the beginning of his flight.

Flying ultralights in strong wind was either dangerous or suicidal, depending on the pilot's experience. Matt sought protection from the lee side of the hill. It took all of his concentration to keep the Hawk trimmed and the wings level.

He felt the same spine-tingling exhilaration every time he flew, but this time it was laced with a growing apprehension from both the wind and the purpose of the trip.

His right hand struggled with the stick while he attempted to hold a map with his left hand. He was mulling over his plan when a large crow, startled by the sudden appearance of his plane, squawked out in protest and flapped wildly in front of him. Matt's arms jerked reflexively and a startled cry died in his throat. The map disappeared in his tail wind. He first cursed at the crow, then laughed at himself.

The sun dropped behind the trees, and the shadows lengthened. He opened the throttle and pushed the engine to its maximum rpm. The wind shrilled through the cables, and below him, leaves floating downstream in the opposite direction gave the illusion that he was flying up the narrow valley at breakneck speed. A glance at the speed indicator showed forty-eight mph, fast enough at treetop height with wind turbulence.

He turned gradually to the left, then sharply to the right

around a steep embankment to follow the tortuous river. Thirty minutes later in near darkness the river valley flattened out to reveal the great marsh that formed one of the tributaries of the Black Fork. The floodlights of the government research complex blinked into view through the trees.

Matt was caught by surprise. It looked like both a prison compound and a military base. But the new research buildings and maze of pipes looked like serious business. He wanted a better look. He banked to the right and followed a chain-link fence that circled the entire perimeter. A paved parking area spread over several acres, with two rows of military jeeps and trucks parked near the entrance.

Four helicopters sat off to one corner. The black Cobras looked menacing, poised and waiting.

Matt trained his binoculars on them. What were they doing at a research facility? Large pods with missile fins were attached to their sides. Air-to-ground missiles. Two machine-gun barrels projected out from the front. A large-caliber cannon underneath completed the flying arsenal.

Fully armed attack helicopters, stuck out here in the middle of a marsh? Matt whistled under his breath. What went on at Niwot to require that kind of security? Seeing the helicopters unnerved him, but there was nobody outside and he wanted a closer look. After glancing around and still seeing no one in sight, he decided to make a pass over the center of the complex.

The buildings in the center were constructed of light brown brick and were arranged in a single long row. A tower at one end with ''272-Z BUILDING'' painted on it in black letters issued a thick plume of steam that was swept horizontally by the stiff wind. A network of large white pipes extended from the tower and continued across the entire complex, disappearing off into the dark woods beyond the fence.

Using binoculars was difficult as he struggled to stabilize the plane in the stiff side wind. He flew above the pipe network back to the tall tower from where they originated.

A sudden gust of wind jerked the Hawk-110 sideways, then into a roll. The primal fear of falling engulfed Matt as the plane was yanked helplessly downward. The tops of the buildings rushed up at him. He began to slip through the seat belt. He grabbed the stick with both hands to regain control. The binoculars swung wildly from his neck and then smashed into his chest as the plane leveled. He had plunged a hundred feet during the roll and was barely clearing the top of the buildings when a man ran out from a small structure near the gate. He was pointing for Matt to leave, then dashed back inside.

They knew he was here and he'd just met the welcoming committee.

Matt glanced at the fuel gauge and flicked it with his finger. It registered just below half a tank. Fighting the head wind had burned more fuel than he had anticipated. He should make it back, but it would be close. He banked back to the left and focused his binoculars for one last look at the pipes before leaving. Two large tanks behind the research building suddenly caught his eye. He saw the bold red letters "LIQUID HELIUM."

The second tank beside it read "DANGER: D_2O."

Deuterium oxide. He'd found it! He snapped off several quick pictures of the tanks. Matt was bursting with excitement and turned again for one more pass over the end building. He chose to ignore the warning gestures of the soldier on the ground for a moment. But just as he turned to fly over the area again, a jeep sped across the open compound toward him. One of the men in the jeep stood up and aimed a rifle at him as Matt flew straight into his sights!

17

Drake Biological Laboratory
University of Washington
Seattle, Washington

A DIM RED light filled the small climate-controlled room. Davis stared at the green monitor, trying to understand what he was looking at on the screen. The Zeiss transmission electron microscope had magnified a white blood cell by a power of fifty thousand. He was focused on the cell wall. The cell wall of the leukocyte was fragmented and torn with large pieces missing, like a snake shedding old scales.

Professor Chonggi Morishima looked at the monitor and adjusted the contrast. "Most unusual. These cells are falling apart. What caused this, Walt?"

"I don't know," Davis answered. "Couldn't this just be cellular decomposition and decay from an animal that has been dead for some time?"

"No, that is not just a decomposing cell, because the cellular organelles are still intact. In the case of old dying or dead cells, the nucleus and mitochondria go first. The cell collapses from the inside, like a deflated basketball." Morishima looked at the monitor, "But this is different. The membrane of the cell wall is just coming apart in sections."

Davis turned to him and asked, "Dr. Morishima, have you seen anything like this before?"

"Infection with some viruses will cause a similar type of response, but the virus particles that are reproducing and devouring the cell would completely fill the inside of the cell. I don't see any evidence of that. There's something else we can do here." Morishima went to the controls and typed in a new set of commands. The monitor went blank as liquid nitrogen was pumped into the electron beam tower.

After five minutes, the pump stopped, and a new image appeared on the screen. "That's hundred thousand times magnification," Morishima said. "At this power we should be able to identify individual virus particles." He focused the electron beam. "But I don't see any."

At hundred thousand magnification Davis stared with fascination at the screen. The membrane around the cell was shredded, and outside of it, whole sections of cell wall were sloughing away or missing. But there were no virus particles, either on the wall or inside the cell.

Davis made arrangements to have five-by-seven Polaroids made at each magnification to be sent back to his office. He thanked Dr. Morishima and told him to call him at the CDC if he had any new ideas about the cells. Davis wished he had been able to contact the teacher who sent the mice. He had to get more information.

It had been a long Saturday, and Davis was hungry. He headed for his favorite pizza joint.

"Son of a bitch!" Matt jerked the stick hard to the left and jammed down on the rudder pedal. The ultralight rolled on its side into a tight turn, with the right wing pointing straight up, the left wing inches from the ground. He straightened out of the turn and aimed at the buildings. Shooting directly between two buildings, the wings just cleared the narrow walls.

He grabbed the throttle and gunned his Briggs & Stratton wide open. He wanted speed, not altitude, and the Hawk skimmed along a few feet above the ground, barely clearing the wire fence that rimmed the compound. Matt aimed for the dark hills that marked the river valley and his route home.

The return trip seemed much longer. A stiff, cold wind buffeted the craft violently, and he fought to keep it on course. Clouds blocked the moon and he flew in darkness;

with poor visibility he couldn't risk flying into the ravine. But without protection from the wind that buffeted the plane violently, he knew his chances of getting back were slim. The engine ran at full throttle to counter the wind and was drinking fuel at an alarming rate.

He held the stick with a steel grip. The increasing force of wind concerned him. Gusts of frigid air blasted into the side of the plane. He felt the frame twist and shudder in protest.

Tears streamed down his face from the stinging cold air. The Hawk struggled on at full throttle against the wind.

Suddenly an entire section of the valley wall in front of him burst to life in blinding light. A powerful search beam skimmed over the trees, then a thunderous noise blasted the night as the dark form of a helicopter shot over the top of the hill to his right and turned directly in front of him, flying low down the valley. The spotlight from the black Cobra panned back and forth over the valley. The flashing blue running light on the tail section disappeared in a few seconds when the plane sped around a bend and vanished.

"What the hell?" he stammered out loud but the words trailed away in the noise and wind. It was one of the helicopters from the Niwot Project. What were they doing out here at night?

The explanation was too obvious. Matt sickened at the thought. They were looking for him. Fortunately, they hadn't spotted him, and he wanted to keep it that way. That overfortified chopper could reduce him to ashes in seconds.

His mind spun. He had violated restricted air space by flying over a military project and now they wanted him.

The bend ahead suddenly lit up again. The Cobra was headed back, aiming straight for him. The blazing searchlight burned directly into his eyes, blinding him for a second. His growing outrage at being chased was replaced by stark fear. Not relishing the thought of being chased down by this mechanical wasp, he jammed the stick back, bringing the nose up, and flew his Hawk over the ridge. He then dropped low over a plowed field as the copter sped past going the other way as it followed the valley.

He skimmed the treetops at the edge of the field, clinging near them for cover. The spotlight panned out over the field. Then the Cobra flew directly over him. He could see the dark form overhead silhouetted against the sky. The sound of its motor was deafening, causing his own plane to vibrate violently under its backwash. His ULA had no running lights, and they hadn't spotted him yet. The helicopter wheeled to the right and settled slowly in the cornfield and killed its engine, the massive propeller lashing the night air with a deafening *swoosh—swoosh—swoosh* as it slowed to a stop.

Matt's heart raced as he began to realize what the other pilot had done. As the sound of the Cobra died, it would only be seconds before his own engine's noise would give him away. They couldn't see him, but now they would be able to *hear* him. He had to land immediately.

He shoved the stick forward, nose down, and flew straight into the tall stalks. The Hawk's propeller tore through the corn, and showered him with bits of dusty stalk and leaves.

He killed the engine even before he came to a stop and took a deep breath. He heard the last staccato swishing of the helicopter's large prop, then it stopped.

Everything was quiet. Had he landed soon enough, or had they heard him?

He sat in his cockpit, listening. He could make out faint voices and the cracking sound of footsteps on brittle stalks. There was an occasional flicker of light as flashlights intermittently penetrated through the stalks.

He waited, listening, ready to make a break for it through the corn if they found him. Muffled voices and feet kicking aside the dried stalks came toward him, then faded.

Without warning, the Cobra sprang to life with the blades beating the air, lifted, and turned back. When it was out of sight he climbed out of his plane and removed a stalk of corn from the wing. His hands trembled, not just from the cold. That was just too damned close!

He had to figure a way out. Looking both directions down the narrow rows of corn, he went back toward the river, pushing his way between the narrow rows to the edge of the field until he came onto a dirt road that ran between the corn and the woods. It was really just a dirt path that the farmer used to get equipment into the field. Matt scuffled his foot back and forth in the packed dirt. He'd found a runway and a way out of there. He ran back through the corn to the plane.

He kicked down stalks to make a path through the corn, and pulled his plane back toward the road. It was slow progress and hard work. He was tired and nearly frozen, but he had to keep going.

Then he heard it. A low grinding sound coming from his right, faint at first, but getting louder. His heart skipped a beat. He stood still and listened. A jeep! He had a bad feeling and knew he wanted to get the hell out of there.

He had just pulled his ULA onto the dirt road when he heard the jeep crashing through the corn. Stalks slapped against its chassis, and the engine grew louder. They were close. The ultralight's engine started with a noise that split the night like a siren. Matt leaped into the cockpit. He knew the jeep would be on him in seconds. The plane had taxied only a few feet when the jeep burst through the stalks and careened onto the road ten yards behind him. Its headlights bounced around him as it rapidly closed the distance between them. Matt had the Hawk's Briggs & Stratton wound out to maximum RPM.

They intended to run him down and were inches from smashing into the tail. Matt yanked back on the stick and prayed. The Hawk struggled into a steep climb just as the jeep shot under him. Circling over the cornfield, he flew back over the ridge and turned again toward home, leaving the jeep behind. Matt didn't want to think about how much fuel he had, but he knew it was dangerously low.

He was just beginning to breathe easier when the Cobra

appeared again out of nowhere, this time its spotlight trained squarely on him. Matt jammed the rudder hard to the right, executing a narrow turn and dropping low over the river. His pursuers hadn't anticipated his maneuver and flew a few hundred yards before turning back. They had lost him again in the night. He had to think fast. The jeep was over in the field to his left, the copter closing on him from behind.

They knew Matt had been following the Black Fork ravine and that's where they were looking for him now, searching through the trees that lined the ravine. He had to leave the ravine. He banked left, and with a tail wind, throttle wide-open, he gained altitude and distance, and slipped off into the black sky alone.

He had given himself a short reprieve.

His hands were clamped vise-like around the control stick, fighting wind and fear. His arms and legs were rigid with tension and his feet shook involuntarily against the rudder pedals. The cold knifed through him. And he had no idea where the hell he was.

It happened sooner than he feared it would. The engine sputtered only once, then died. Out of fuel. With his power gone, the stiff wind immediately blew the plane sideways. Matt gripped the controls as tightly as he could until the blood drained from his knuckles while he fought to keep his plane in a steep but controlled dive. He didn't dare allow the nose of the plane to point into the wind and stall out. The wind screamed past the wings as the Hawk plunged downward.

As he dropped, he frantically searched the black night for a clue as to what terrain lay in front of him. He wouldn't be able to make anything out until it was too late to change course, too late to avoid the trees.

The wind pushed the Hawk straight into a woods and he saw the dark outline of trees rush past him. Branches slapped against the right wing. The plane shuddered as an aluminum wing strut was ripped away with a sickening metallic wrenching sound. Matt braced himself as the black ground rushed up at him.

18

MATT GRIPPED THE stick with all the strength he could muster and struggled to miss the trees, but the branches caught the right wing and drove the nose of the ultralight into the dirt. The impact flipped the plane over onto its back and threw him to the ground with a force that crushed the air from him.

Matt lay on his back dazed, trying to catch his breath, unable to move. When Matt finally tried to stand, a fiery pain shot through his rib cage. After rolling over and staggering to his feet, he quickly examined the plane and even in the dark could tell that the right wing strut would have to be replaced. He remembered trying to dead stick his plane down, using a steep power glide against a strong side wind—a bold maneuver even in broad daylight, but suicidal in the dark. After searching the area, he found his binoculars but the camera was gone.

With an unrelenting stabbing pain in his right side, he made his way back to the road and covered the five miles back to the shed on foot. Dense clouds blocked the moon, and as he took the Cinelli full speed back down the hill into town, he nearly wiped out on a steep curve in the dark as the rear wheel slid out, but he recovered and made it home.

Matt coaxed his stiff, painful body into the hot tub and moaned as he settled back, and was immediately engulfed by a warmth that pulled him into a deep sleep.

He woke up two hours later, long after the water had turned tepid. Shivering and stiff, he climbed out, toweled himself dry, and put on his robe. An ugly purple bruise spread across his chest, and the sharp stabbing pain and crackling sound with each breath told him he had a few cracked ribs. He couldn't fully extend his left arm due to the pain.

Matt glanced out the window. It was still dark outside. He shuffled into the kitchen to make coffee and squinted at his watch—4:22 A.M. His body was racked with fatigue and pain. He touched the large angry-looking area over his ribs and winced. After making himself an extra strong cup of coffee he went into the living room but fell asleep on the sofa before he touched it.

When he woke up again it was almost noon and sunlight was streaming through the window. Matt peeled a brown mushy banana and washed it down with stale coffee. His mouth tasted like cotton. He felt like he'd aged ten years in two days.

The phone rang. Two rings. Three rings. Matt reached for the phone and grimaced as pain brought tears to his eyes. He was surprised to hear Davis's voice.

"You haven't told me everything, have you?" Davis asked. "What happened to the mice?"

"Did you examine the dead mice?" Matt shot back, alarmed by the question. "What did you find out?"

"The mice died of infection, just as you had suspected," Davis said. "But there was no epidemic. It was the bacteria in their own bodies that killed them. The white blood cells of the mice I examined were literally falling apart."

"Why, what would cause that?" Matt asked.

"Don't know exactly, not yet, but we're still running more tests. When you called, you said you were worried about the distilled water. Tell me more about it."

"We had a shipment of three hundred white mice delivered to the school at the end of the summer. They were all kept together in the main lab. Three weeks ago, I moved half the mice to another room, an old chemistry lab. Since the only water supply to that room was distilled water, that's what they got to drink. There was no reason to haul regular tap water back to them since there was already a water supply.''

''So we need to take a look at the distilled water,'' Davis said.

''But it wasn't the distilled water that killed them,'' Matt persisted.

''Oh?'' Davis asked. ''What did then?''

''They died because they stopped drinking city water. I'm certain that there's something in the city water that they need to survive.'' Matt told Davis about the mice in Janet Brown's science project; he told him that he suspected eleven people may have died after leaving town because of the water. And he told him about Esther Hamilton who died shortly after switching to Culligan water. ''If I'm right,'' Matt said, ''our survival is somehow linked to the water. If we stop drinking it, we die.''

Davis was silent and Matt wasn't sure he had heard him. ''Does that make any sense to you? What do you think?'' Matt asked impatiently.

''We're still running more tests. In the meantime, I want you to send me two samples of your city water, one right from your own faucet, and one sample from the source—reservoir, river, whatever—before it has been processed for drinking. Can you do that?''

''I'll get it shipped to you tomorrow. Hey, how much trouble are we really in here?'' Matt's mouth was dry as he waited for Davis's answer.

''I really don't know. Your theory that the survival of the mice is linked to the water is pretty far out. I think you're way off the mark on that one. But''—he paused—''I am curious about the leukocyte breakdown in the mice. Most unusual.''

''Leukocytes?''

''The white blood cells. They are the cells that are the first line of defense in fighting infection,'' Davis explained. ''I just had another thought. Send me a dozen of the healthy mice from your lab that have been drinking city water and we'll follow them and see what happens to them when we give them a different water source.''

Matt picked up the computer printout of the water analysis. "There's something else. I've already had the city water tested and the analysis showed a deuterium level in the city water of more than ten thousand parts per liter. That is more than a million times higher than normal.''

"That sounds like an error. Has to be. Deuterium doesn't occur naturally in that quantity. Besides, deuterium would be of no consequence anyway. It wouldn't do that to the immune complex. Send me a copy of the water analysis and we'll review it.''

Matt hesitated a minute, then asked, "What do you know about the Niwot Project?''

"The Niwot Project? I've never heard of it. Why?''

"Because that's the source of the deuterium. It's a government research complex that nobody seems to know much about.''

"I've got some contacts in Washington that I'll call and see if they know anything about the Niwot Project. But as I said, don't worry about the deuterium. Just send those water samples to me as soon as you can and I'll get back to you. Good-bye.''

Matt stared at the receiver; frustration and fear gnawed at his mind. What was Davis worried about? What *was* wrong with the leukocytes?

The last thing he felt like doing now was driving back up to the reservoir. His chest ached with a constant dull pain.

Finishing off the last bite of banana, he thought about the network of huge pipes that dissected across the Niwot Project and on into the woods. Where did they go? He wanted to get a closer look at them.

Loudonville got its water from a reservoir fed by the Black Fork River. He went to his desk and pulled out a map. He knew the route to the reservoir, but could there be a stream that fed from the Niwot Marsh to the Black Fork

River and into the reservoir? The expansive marsh formed
more than a dozen streams, but none of them flowed into the
Black Fork.

He took out a red pen and traced the Black Fork. The
Niwot Project was identified on the map as "U.S. Government Restricted Area" and he outlined it. But the map
showed no connecting streams between the Niwot Marsh
and the Black Fork.

He pulled out a stack of detailed geological survey maps
that he and Jeff had used for mountain climbing and
thumbed through them. He found the correct quadrant map
and pulled it out. He ran his finger along the Black Fork
again. There it was—a small branch of the Black Fork that
followed a narrow ravine all the way to the Niwot Marsh,
twenty miles farther north of the reservoir. If the Niwot
Project was dumping anything into the marsh, that tributary
would carry it back to the reservoir.

Davis said he needed water directly from the source, and
Matt was going to do better than just take one from the
reservoir. He was going to get water samples as close to the
Niwot Project as possible just in case his hunch was right.

He wanted to follow the pipes and see where they went,
but the terrain around Niwot was rugged. The plane was out
of commission with a broken wing strut, and there could be
more damage once he checked it in daylight. The old Nova
wouldn't make it. He needed a jeep. That meant he would
have to ask Harold Wheeler.

Harold was an overweight history teacher who was
always sweating even on the coldest day. He never quite
found his niche among the other teachers, and they politely
avoided contact with him. Harold had a greasy, unkempt
appearance and a high nasal voice. He smoked dark
cigarettes and the shirt that covered his expansive stomach
was usually covered with flecks of ashes. Every afternoon
Harold would steal into the teachers' lounge and finish off
in quick fashion any stale doughnuts left over from the
morning. Matt pitied him and occasionally chatted with

Harold about the weather, the only thing they shared in common.

But Harold had a jeep. It was a red CJ-5 in mint condition. The red jeep seemed to be the only thing Harold Wheeler truly related to or loved.

Even as the phone was ringing on the other end, Matt wanted to hang up, but he didn't. "Hello, Harold? This is Matt. Matt Strong."

"Matt. Well, hello. How are you?"

"Fine, Harold, thank you. I'm supposed to collect some lichen specimens from the White Mountain range today and my Nova won't start. I need them for class tomorrow. Could you do me a favor and let me borrow your jeep. I wouldn't ask, but I'm really in a bind."

"Well, okay, take the jeep, Matt. I'll be happy to go along for the ride if you need company."

That was the last thing Matt wanted. He explained that he would do better alone, and he wasn't sure what time he would get back. Harold accepted Matt's rather weak excuse.

"I understand. Keep it as long as you need it." Harold was so starved for friends and companionship he would never refuse such a request.

Matt could feel his pain. "Thanks, Harold. I'll be over this afternoon around three if that's okay. See you then."

There was one more thing he had to take care of. He picked up the phone again. "Hi, hon. Sorry, but I can't make it for dinner tonight. I've got something important to take care of and I won't be back until late tonight."

"What are you up to now, Matt?" Danielle asked, with concern in her voice.

"I'm going out to the reservoir to get some water samples. The CDC wants to do some testing on it. I'll call you when I get back."

"You will be careful, won't you? Call me."

Matt found three old Mason jars in the garage and, after rummaging through a box of junk, found lids and rubber seals to fit them. He loaded them into his backpack along with a flashlight, binoculars, and a down jacket, then rode his bike to Harold Wheeler's to pick up the jeep. It was late afternoon by the time he was ready to leave, but he could use the extra protection that darkness would provide. After last night's scene, he wasn't ready to tangle with the military again.

He drove the jeep north along state route 129, a winding road that followed the Black Fork River. At times he could see the Black Fork below through the trees. He knew he was near the section of the valley where the helicopter had chased him last night. He looked for the cornfield where he first landed, but it was on the other side of the ridge, and he couldn't see it from the road.

He arrived at the reservoir that supplied Loudonville's water just before dark, filled one of the bottles with water from the lake, and labeled it. He then continued up 129 for more than twenty miles, turned right onto county road 10, and followed the small stream north toward the Niwot Project and the large Niwot Marsh that bordered it. He passed a newly paved road that was the turnoff to the Niwot Project and could see the glow in the evening sky from its blazing lights. Continuing north for another five minutes, he braked suddenly.

Two overgrown tracks led off into the dense woods, in the direction of Niwot and the marsh. Matt backed up and leaned down to see where the road went, but within a few yards it was swallowed up by the thick brush. He shifted the jeep into four-wheel drive, turned onto the two ruts, and drove into the thicket.

He guessed it was an old logging road that had not been used in years. Weeds scratched at the frame, but the cut through the trees was easy to follow. Low branches slapped at the windshield as all four wheels clawed at the rough ground. Matt was so intent on nursing the jeep along the twisting path that he lost his sense of direction. He wasn't sure if he was still headed in the direction of Niwot.

After twenty minutes the trees thinned and the thick

undergrowth turned to a mucky, water-soaked marsh. Leaves and brush gave way to soft ferns and vines. The jeep lurched when the tires lost their grip and spun in the mud. Matt definitely didn't want to get Harold's baby stuck out here in the middle of nowhere at night. He nursed the pampered CJ-5 down a shallow ravine and spun his way back up the other side.

Off to his left, intense light broke through the trees in thin shafts. He stopped and killed the engine. It was too bright to be the moon—they were the lights from the Niwot Project. He pulled the geological survey map from his pack, spread it over the steering wheel, and turned on his flashlight. He had driven north of Niwot, turned east onto the logging road, and ended up somewhere on the western perimeter of the great marsh. According to the aerial sketch he had made, the pipes he had spotted from the air should be due south of him. He thought the stream that fed into the Black Fork should be nearby.

He climbed out of the jeep, grabbed his pack and flashlight, and headed off on foot toward the light. The ground was spongy from the thick layers of peat moss that had accumulated over millions of years from decaying plants. The damp air carried the smell of musty peat and fungi. Within a few hundred yards he spotted the massive pipes. Using his binoculars, he could see that they passed through the woods like some giant snake, made more mysterious by the vapor that swirled around them.

He stood up and started toward them when a dead branch snapped behind him. He fell flat on his stomach and waited. There was a loud shuffling in the dead leaves, then silence. He held his breath, listening with every fiber of his body; he heard nothing, saw nothing move. Belly pressed to wet, spongy ground, he shifted his position slightly and slowly pulled out his flashlight and snapped it on. Two red eyes glowed back at him, blinked once, then the raccoon turned and ran into hiding.

"Damn!" Matt stood up and breathed a sigh of relief, brushing the damp peat from his pants.

After glancing around the darkness for a final check, he walked up to the large steel tubes that stretched through the darkness. Two of the three huge white pipes were covered with large beads of water that dripped onto the ground. He put his hand on one of them. It was cold. The pipes were sweating profusely as cold moist air condensed into globs of water that bled down the sides and dripped constantly to the ground.

The third pipe was bone dry, and he assumed it was empty and not being used. He put his hand on it.

"*Ouch!*" He pulled his hand back. The pipe was scalding hot. What he wanted to know was where the pipes went and what they carried. Matt turned away from the light coming from the compound and followed the pipes off into the dense underbrush.

He guessed he had gone more than a mile when the trees thinned again, and moonlight broke through the branches and thick shadows blotched the path.

Matt stopped and looked in disbelief. His shoulders sagged and he moaned with disappointment. All three of the huge pipes curved down and disappeared into the ground!

19

M<small>ATT</small> <small>KNELT AND</small> scanned the woods ahead of him with the flashlight, but there was no sign of the pipes.

He swung the flashlight back again. Off to the left he spotted a narrow cut through the trees, a clearing that probably marked where the pipes were buried. He stood up, snapped off his light, and trotted onto a narrow overgrown path that marked the route.

He followed the cut another mile when the woods suddenly stopped and he found himself facing a lake. A sign warned:

U.S. GOVERNMENT PROPERTY

NO TRESPASSING

Moonlight danced on the smooth surface and turned the water a glowing silver-gray. The gravel shoreline sloped steeply into the water. Matt walked down to the edge of the water, pulled out the flashlight, and aimed its beam across to the woods on the other side. To his right, an old planked dock jutted out over the water. He walked along the shore looking, but he could find no evidence that the pipes continued on the other side and no reason to assume that they went any farther than the lake. Matt suspected that they drained directly into the lake, but he wished he could be certain of that.

He walked back to the path, dropped his pack, and spread

the map out on the ground. He guessed he was three miles from the edge of the Niwot Project. The map showed the lake, but listed no name for it. He knew he was inside the restricted area that was outlined on the map. Matt studied the map closer. The lake fed a small ravine and ran twenty miles south to meet the Black Fork River. The lake in front of him would become part of Loudonville's water supply.

But where did the pipes go?

If he was right, the pipes drained directly into the lake. But he had to be certain.

Matt looked out at the lake, removed his shoes and socks, then took off his jeans and sweater. The night was cold and he moved swiftly. He walked out onto the wet gravel at the water's edge, and after turning around to make sure he was aligned with the path, he waded out into the dark lake.

The frigid water cut his breath to short gasps. "Damn!" he cursed under his breath. Probing with his feet along the bottom, he waded out a few steps at a time until he was neck-deep in the lake. The cold was bone-numbing and he paused a moment, trying to decide how much farther to go. He searched with each step for the opening, then his right foot came down on something smooth. It was a metal grate. The turbulent flow of water pushed against his feet as the pipes poured their contents into the lake.

Elated that he had proven to himself that the pipes ended in the lake, he was at the same time scared of what the pipes might be carrying. There was a warning sign, but he had ignored it. What if the pipes were spilling acid or some other corrosive sludge? Or radioactive material. He was being careless and might be exposing himself to a very serious danger.

He turned around and waded back to the shore, filled the jars, then carefully labeled and sealed them.

He shook uncontrollably and his teeth chattered. He pulled on his jeans and sweater, then sat down and put on his shoes and socks.

He looked at the two bottles and wondered what secret they held. He put everything back into the pack and pulled out his thick down jacket.

At first he dismissed it, but a distant noise grew and tripped an alarm in his head. He froze and listened. The distinctive baying of dogs on a scent, and human voices, headed toward him from the direction he had come. From the Niwot Project.

Matt knew he was on restricted property. He sure as hell didn't want to get caught. He scooped up his pack and turned and started running along the gravel bank. The barking behind him grew louder; they were close to the clearing. He wouldn't be able to circle the lake to the other side and slip into the woods before they spotted him.

He sprinted at top speed, pumping his legs hard and breathing through clenched teeth, ignoring the burning pain of broken ribs. The voices were louder and the barking seemed deafening. Time had run out, he wasn't going to make it. He hesitated a moment, then ran out onto the dock and slid quietly into the frigid water. He found his footing on the bottom of the lake and moved under the dock. The water came to his chin and he had to arch his neck to breathe. The black rotted planks of the dock were inches from his face and thin slits of moonlight streamed between them.

He was still trying to catch his breath when men and dogs burst into the clearing and ran to the water's edge. Matt tried not to move because any ripples on the water would give him away. He stood staring straight up at the planks, and tried to shut out the penetrating cold.

His lungs ached. The muscles in his rib cage spasmed from the cold and his breathing was shallow and strained.

The loud barking muffled the conversation, and he couldn't make out what they were saying. Gravel crunched under boots as a man ran by. Suddenly the man stopped, turned around, and walked back to the dock. Matt was trapped. Had they seen him dive into the lake? The heavy boots thundered onto the dock and Matt saw a dark silhouette directly overhead. Wet sand and mud from the boots dropped into Matt's face; he blinked and fought back a cough. The old planks groaned under the weight. Matt was afraid they would give under the strain and dump the man on top of him, but after a few agonizing seconds, the man turned and left.

The dogs were at the end of the dock and barking frantically. Voices and flashlights were everywhere. After what seemed an endless agonizing wait, the commotion turned away and slowly faded to an unsettling quiet. Matt didn't know how far they had gone, or if they were hiding nearby, waiting for him.

But that didn't matter now. The cold numbed his legs; painful cramps knotted his feet. He had to get out of the frigid water, or his frozen legs would become useless, and he would sink slowly away into a black tomb. He tried to move, but his legs buckled. He grabbed the edge of the dock with his right hand. His left hand was nearly useless, and when he moved, the pain in his ribs was excruciating. With a great deal of effort he pulled himself painfully out of the water, holding on to the dock for support.

He shivered uncontrollably. He had to dry off and get warm soon or he was going to die of exposure. His stiff limbs and fingers were almost useless, and it took him several tries to remove his backpack. He unzipped the down vest and dropped it to the ground, then got out of his soaking jeans and sweater. His pale, wet skin was the blue pallor of death in the moonlight, like a cadaver.

After wringing as much water as he could out of his clothes, he slipped them back on. The jeans were freezing, but the thick wool sweater provided much needed warmth to his chest and arms. The soaked down vest though was useless without its fluff. He pulled nylon Windbreaker out of the pack and put it on. He wrapped the down jacket around the two bottles of water, stuffed them in the pack and started back along the path.

Walking proved to be difficult and slow going at first, and he had to stop once to rub away a painful cramp in his calf. He told himself to keep moving, he had to get warmth back into his limbs.

He wondered who had followed him to the lake. Were they just a bunch of raccoon hunters with their beagles, or had the same people as last night come after him? He wished he had gotten a better look at them.

His mind searched for answers as he trotted back along the pipes. He slowed to a walk; why had they followed him to the lake—unless they had found the jeep. If they had, they would be waiting for him. He didn't savor running into a trap; Davis *had* to get the water samples.

He stopped, knelt down, and pulled out the soggy map. Maybe he could find a different way back. The wet paper came apart in his hands as he tried to read it in the moonlight. Frustrated, he tossed the crumpled map off into the brush and followed the pipes back toward the marsh.

When he was near to where he had parked the CJ-5, he slumped down to the ground and listened. The woods were silent. Too silent he thought. Matt didn't like it. He made his way as stealthily as possible on the peat until he spotted the dark outline of the jeep ahead. Squatting a moment he waited and listened, then ran crouched down toward the jeep, threw his pack onto the front seat, and leaped in. After listening for a second, he started the engine, jammed it into gear, and spun around for a quick exit.

He didn't want to turn the headlights on, but he wouldn't find his way through the trees without them. He kept glancing back in the rearview mirror, but it reflected only the black empty night. The jeep passed the small ravine that marked the edge of the marsh and was once again on firm ground, matted with thick underbrush. The engine roared as he tramped down on the accelerator and the jeep bounced wildly up the other side. The tires flung globs of thick mud that thunked loudly against the underbody. He glanced into the mirror again.

"What the . . . ?" he yelled above the engine. Headlights were closing in on him from behind. The trees were so thick he couldn't turn off the road even if he wanted to. He kicked in the clutch and jammed it into third gear. The jeep careened through the woods at speeds that threatened disaster as he fought the wheel from side to side and tires tore around turns. Deep ruts and rocks battered the tires and fighting to control the steering wheel required great effort.

The jeep bounced over a boulder, launching him up out of his seat and dropping him onto the steering wheel.

"Ahh!" he cried out in pain as the wheel slammed into his cracked ribs, sending hot, searing pain through his lungs. His eyes smarted and he fought to get his breath. Too fast. He shifted down to second gear but kept the accelerator to the floorboard, all four wheels clawing at the ground. He shot a glance into the mirror. They weren't gaining, but he certainly wasn't losing them.

Remembering a sharp turn ahead, he decided on a plan. He tensed, ready to make his move at the approaching curve in the path. Trees in front of his headlights marked the sharp turn, and as Matt spun the steering wheel, he snapped off his headlights and careened around the bend in darkness. Large branches beat against the windshield and he knew he had gone too far left. He jerked the wheel back the other way to stay on the road, feeling his way through the narrow clearing in the dark. If his plan had a chance at all, he had to act now.

He took a deep breath, braced himself, then spun the wheel hard to the right and veered off the path, straight into the dense woods. He didn't know if he would hit a tree dead center or with luck slip between them. The jeep jerked violently to the right with a sickening crunch of wood as he tore off a huge branch, nearly flipping the jeep over onto its side.

He hit the brake hard, and turned off the ignition.

Looking back at the roar of engines, he saw the headlights from four jeeps speeding by. After twisting the key in the ignition, he shifted into reverse and spun back out onto the road, threw it into first gear, and with tires spinning dirt out behind him, he sped after them. It went against every fiber of his instinct to follow his pursuers, when his own common sense told him to get as far away as possible. But their own loud engines would mask his, and their headlights would lead him through the trees. He stayed back and followed patiently.

The trees thinned and the moon tinted the ground silver. He was at the edge of the woods, near the logging road he had come in on. Matt knew he'd never find the overgrown road in the dark. He slowed and let the other jeeps pull ahead, then he turned sharply to the left and bounced into the dense brush. He kept his headlights off because the brush was too thick for them to be of any use anyway. If he was right, this direction would take them back to the ravine road. A ditch camouflaged by brush flung the jeep violently upward and nearly separated his head from his body. He slowed down and rubbed his neck.

After fighting through the brush for more than ten minutes, he was beginning to wonder if he had made a mistake, when the brush gave way to grass, and he saw the paved road ahead. He moaned again. A split rail fence blocked his path.

Too tired and cold to be stopped by some half-rotted planks of cedar, he shifted into first gear, aimed straight at the center of the rails, and burst through them with a sharp, splintering crack.

Turning south toward town, he shifted into high gear and sped away with mud slapping into the fenders. He kept his lights off, and drove down the center of the road that the bright moon turned into a silver ribbon. A piece of broken fence vibrated off the hood and fell to the ground.

Harold was going to croak when he saw his jeep.

Washington, D.C.

The phone rang again and jolted Lee Higgins from a deep sleep. Higgins fumbled in the dark, dropped the receiver, then pulled it up by the cord. But the phone kept ringing.

"Oh, hell." Higgins rolled out of bed and groped for the other phone in the cabinet. He grabbed the receiver on the agency's secured line and rubbed his eyes, fighting sleep. "Hello."

A woman's voice was on the other end. "Mr. Higgins, I have Mr. Reintraub on the line for you."

Reintraub? Why in blazes was the deputy secretary of defense calling him in the middle of the night?

"Lee? Jim Reintraub here. It's about TOPAZ. The Old Man just received a situation report of TOPAZ penetration. The SIT-REP suggested terrorist action."

Higgins was fully awake and alert. The deputy secretary of defense in his usual terse manner was on the phone in the middle of the night with bad news. The President had just gotten a situation report of attempted entry to TOPAZ, code name for the top-secret Niwot Project in the mountains of New Hampshire.

"When?" Higgins asked.

"Tonight. The Old Man is furious, wants answers fast. Heads are going to roll if he doesn't get them. TOPAZ security has been upgraded from controlled to critical."

After a long empty pause Higgins asked, "What do you want me to do?"

"Your unit is being assigned to a special operations interagency group. Your Special Intelligence access code is SI: NP 07224. I want to see you first thing tomorrow morning. Eight o'clock sharp."

Click.

"Good night," Higgins said to a dead phone. He put the phone back in the cabinet, flipped on the light, and glanced at the clock. 2:30 A.M. The middle of the night. What was he supposed to do about it now? Reintraub had just ruined a perfectly good night's sleep. Higgins pulled on his bathrobe.

Lee Higgins was sixty and section chief of the FBI's Foreign Counter-Intelligence Division. His thinning white hair and short height gave no hint of the stature of the man, a gritty, determined administrator. His pipe and unique eyes were his trademark; penetrating eyes, light steel-gray with the faintest blue rim that could twinkle with humor and in the next blink could bore through someone in anger, eyes that some believed could see into the very soul of a man. He walked slightly stooped and gave the appearance of a defeated man. Higgins was often tired from a demanding job, but he was never defeated. His reputation in the intelligence community was that of a feared adversary, or a trusted and devoted friend, depending on how one saw him.

He might as well salvage what remained of the night. Higgins could brief himself and make a few notes for tomorrow. He knew little about TOPAZ, and didn't want to face Reintraub already two steps behind. He turned on the computer, accessed the secured line with the modem using his seven-digit key, then typed in his personal access code, and he was on line:

SECURED LINE, 2:33 A.M.

SUBCODE RESPOND:

Higgins typed in his name: HIGGINS

ENTER CODE:

He typed in the special code Reintraub gave him: NP07224

Higgins pushed tobacco into his pipe and lit it while he watched the monitor and wondered how much information the SI code would allow him access to within the highly secretive and classified DARPA files.

DEPARTMENT OF DEFENSE, RESEARCH AND DEVELOPMENT

ADVANCED RESEARCH PROJECTS AGENCY

THE NIWOT PROJECT

CODE NAME: TOPAZ

DARPA FILE
TOKOMAK, HYDROGEN FUSION REACTOR
CLASSIFIED: TOP SECRET

Higgins stared at the screen and bit on his pipe. He was staring at the biggest undertaking since the Manhattan Project, an undertaking that could change the world forever— just as the A-bomb had done.

He turned on the printer, then took out a bottle of Glenfiddich and poured the Scotch over a fistful of ice while the printer tapped out sixty pages of classified information about the top-secret Niwot Project.

The printer stopped and Higgins tore off the scroll of pages. He sat down on his favorite reading chair, Scotch in hand, to review the information.

Damn, this was going to be a long night.

20

THE DOCTOR WALKED in, shoved an x-ray onto the viewbox, and flipped the switch. The light flickered on and he pointed at the film. "Broke three ribs. Lucky you didn't puncture a lung and end up with a pneumothorax."

He pulled the dressing gown away from Matt's chest and pushed his finger against his pectoralis, causing him to wince in pain. "Got a real nasty hematoma here, though. I'd normally wrap your chest with tape, but I don't want to put tape directly on that," he said, pushing softly on the large bruised area. He took Matt's wrist and raised his arm, and he cringed with pain. "Real nasty bruise," the doctor said again. "We'll see what we can do," and he left.

Matt had crawled out of bed at the crack of dawn and gone to the school, taken a dozen mice from the front lab and packed them into a box, then took the box and the sealed water samples to the parcel depot. He shipped them same-day-express to Davis in Seattle.

The pain in his ribs stabbed through him like a knife every time he twisted or turned, and the bruise over his chest, an ugly purple-stained swelling, had grown dramatically. The jeep's steering wheel had slammed into ribs and muscle already battered by the crash landing. The pain had become almost unbearable, so he'd gone to the hospital ER to be examined.

The doctor returned with a large gauze pad, held it against the bruised chest wall, and taped it firmly in place. He scribbled out an illegible prescription, tore it off and handed it to Matt. "Get this filled and take two every six hours for pain. That's the best I can do for a dressing, so you're going to have to be careful and protect this. It's going to hurt like hell for a few days, but these should help."

Matt drove home, then called the school to tell them that he was sick and would be absent for a day. After grading his homework papers, filling out the grade sheet, and bringing his assignment book up-to-date, he took two capsules and fell into a deep sleep.

He was awakened when his front door opened and closed. "Who's there?"

Danielle walked into his bedroom carrying a sack. "Heard you were sick, so I brought you some soup and hot tea. How are you feeling?"

"I'm not sick. Just had a bad weekend."

She leaned over and kissed him and saw the bandage and gauze on his chest. "What happened?"

"Minor accident. Broke a few ribs. I'll be good as new in a few days." He climbed out of bed, grimacing with pain as stiff muscles resisted his movement. He slipped on his robe and they went out to the kitchen. "I'm fine, just a little sore," he said, trying to reassure her. But the look of concern on her face told him he hadn't succeeded.

Low, gray clouds had blown over the Potomac basin during the morning. Now a drizzling rain soaked into the gloom of the dark afternoon. The streetlights along Independence Boulevard reflected from the wet pavement. As he walked past the government offices, Lee Higgins shoved *The Washington Post* under his arm to keep it dry.

He never hurried home anymore. The house was empty and lifeless since the death of his wife ten months ago. His position as section chief, Foreign Counter-Intelligence Division of the Federal Bureau of Investigation, consumed all of his time now. It helped to fill the void her death had created. The phone call last night gave a surge of excitement to his otherwise routine existence.

The situation report on the Niwot Project had caused more concern in Washington than any other security matter he could remember, including the security assignment during the visit of the Pope. Phone calls, meetings, and poring over classified material had consumed his day. He had to admit that all the commotion was energizing.

Higgins wasn't sure what role his section would play in the investigation since there were three other intelligence agencies involved. That would be spelled out tonight at the first SOIG meeting.

He turned onto Seventh Street and entered Piete's, a small cozy restaurant that featured fresh seafood. After a dinner of filet of sole with a dry white German wine, he glanced through the *Post* while sipping coffee.

When he came to an article on the OPEC cartel, he read it with more interest. According to the article, OPEC ministers had managed to agree to a cut in production quotas, an obvious threat to the rest of the world. It would drive the price of crude sky-high, cause a return to long gas lines, and strike a powerful blow to an already weakened U.S. economy.

Internationally, both Russia and Germany, with all the new political changes that were occurring there, would suffer the dangerous destabilization of their newly formed governments.

Higgins began to realize the growing importance of the Niwot Project, and of the threat to it.

At 7:15, Higgins gathered up the paper and left. He headed down C Street and turned up his collar for protection against the cold rain. His breath sent gray puffs into the freezing mist.

21

The Pentagon

TWO MILITARY POLICE closed the doors and stood guard outside. Inside, the large room grew silent. Higgins pressed aromatic-blended tobacco into his pipe, struck a match, and drew several long deep puffs while glancing over the men seated around him.

Deputy Secretary of Defense James Reintraub sat at the front of the table and leafed through a document that had just been handed to him. To Reintraub's immediate right sat Samuel Peterson, director of Special Operations in the CIA, then Daniel Berger of the National Security Agency, and finally the head of the DIA, Thomas Strunk, Division for Intelligence of Special Activities. Across the table from them sat Air Force General Hugh Zachery, director of Special Military Operations, Higgins next to him, and finally Army General Bryan Morgan, the commander in charge of the military operations at Niwot.

Major Robert Smith, aide-de-camp to Deputy Secretary Reintraub, sat at the end of the table, next to Reintraub. Major Smith had just placed folders marked "SPECIAL OPERATIONS INTERAGENCY GROUP" in front of each of them.

Higgins knew he wasn't there for his political savvy, but because of his ability and skill in intelligence operations. In physical stature Higgins was the smallest man in the room, but he was also the most experienced and was highly respected. Still, he wasn't sure what role he and the Bureau were to play in this SOIG. He and his division were the smallest fish in the pond here. When the pipe was lit to his satisfaction, Higgins blew a thick cloud of smoke and opened his folder.

Reintraub leaned forward on the desk and spoke. "During the past five years, the prime target of East European and Soviet espionage activity has been the stealing of high technology and defense systems from the U.S. They have been successful. Our own Minuteman nuclear missiles and the Soviet's SS-13 missiles are identical. The materials used in nose cones of Soviet missiles were developed at MIT. And the Soviet-built SA-7 antiaircraft missile contains the same technologic features as the U.S. Redeye missile system."

Reintraub's eyes darted from man to man, demanding their attention. "This stolen technology has saved the Soviets hundreds of millions of dollars and years of research time. We estimate that there are over one thousand KGB, GRU, and East Bloc spies operating in the U.S. The confiscated material is usually shipped to the Soviet Union, or to Czechoslovakia and Romania and other East Bloc countries by way of Germany.

"That brings us to the Niwot Project. Until recently, obscurity and a low profile provided protection for it. The military security deployed there has been kept intentionally out of sight and to a minimum so as not to draw attention. The Niwot Project has monumental global significance and total secrecy is absolutely essential, especially so with the OPEC conference next month. This DARPA project is the most damned important undertaking this country's ever done. Major Smith, if you would please."

Higgins struck another match and drew the flame deeply into his pipe. Reintraub glared at the smoke swirling up from the pipe, but Higgins ignored him.

Major Smith walked to the front wall and tacked up a large detailed map. The map covered six square miles, with the four thousand acres of the Niwot Project in the center highly detailed and outlined in red. He handed Reintraub a long wooden pointer, then sat down.

Reintraub stood up and continued, "In the past forty-eight hours there were two attempts to gain access to the complex. One from the air, one from the wooded swamp area to the north. Here," he said and outlined the swamp with the pointer.

"The plane was a small recreational ultralight craft with no markings. A Jeep drove into the swamp area here, but it managed to escape. Footprints were found leading to the perimeter. We're not even sure if the two events are related, but our butts are on the line because of this. Nobody was supposed to get that close to Niwot. I want to know who in the hell was in the plane, who was in the Jeep, and what they were after.

"I met with Higgins and Peterson today. As of now, we have no knowledge of any foreign government's interest in or knowledge of TOPAZ. Two Libyan agents carrying detailed information about the Mercury underground testing site were apprehended in New York last week. And a KGB agent trying to ship a microchip computer system to Bulgaria was arrested in Boston yesterday. But neither event seems even remotely related to the Niwot Project.

"Obviously the biggest risk up to now was considered to be espionage activity, stolen technology. But because of events during the past forty-eight hours, we have to consider the threat of terrorists and radical groups. I've been informed that any damage to that magnet could set the project back ten years. A small plane or a truck loaded with explosives could destroy the Niwot Project. The White House wants to know how it was possible for a small plane and a Jeep to get that close to Niwot and still get away. I didn't have the guts to tell them that it wasn't even a plane for God's sake—just a small powered glider.

"We can't figure out why the sudden outside interest in the Niwot Project unless there has been a serious security leak. This SOIG was formed because of the complexity of the problem. First, internal security has to guarantee that there is no technical information being smuggled out. Higgins, that's where your section takes over. We want a complete rundown on the entire staff at Niwot. Family background, medical history, any heavy debts, mistresses. Everything. Give us a computer profile scan when you get the data.''

Reintraub turned to Peterson, head of the Internal Security Division of the CIA. Peterson was a quiet, white-haired man of medium build. His pale skin and fragile appearance made him look much older than his fifty-eight years. ''The CIA will try to find out what terrorist group or foreign government is interested in Niwot. This could be a monumental task. As you might well imagine, any OPEC nation would have every reason to try and cripple the Niwot Project to protect their own self-interests.''

Reintraub paced in front of the group while Higgins relit his dying pipe, and continued, ''Second, Niwot has to be totally impenetrable from the outside and safe from acts of terrorists by air or land. Zach, we want immediate deployment of surface-to-air missiles in this wooded area here,'' and Reintraub pointed to the map again. ''There will be electronic surveillance twenty-four hours a day. Sonar and infrared scanning. There is to be nothing visible to the casual observer, but Niwot has to be made absolutely impenetrable. I want this to make Fort Knox look like an open-air flea market by comparison. I don't want a muskrat moving through the woods that we don't know about.''

General Zachery stood up and went to the map. He walked with a slight limp from an injury he sustained during a nighttime glider landing on Normandy. ''Four Cobras have already been placed at the Niwot Project. The Air Force is supplying eight Lockheed X-47 Interceptor helicopters. These are fast rigid-blade turbo-powered planes, with tremendous firepower. Each craft carries a 40mm grenade launcher on each side of the fuselage, firing four hundred rounds per minute, and four 30mm rapid-fire guns mounted on the nose turret, with all radar scan-lock firing devices. Mounted under the belly are six 2.75-inch rockets.''

Zachery leaned forward with his hands resting on the long table. ''These choppers are capable of stopping a small air strike and could quickly annihilate any ground assault, including armored vehicles. The Interceptors deployed at Niwot will have no special markings and will be kept out of the way, near these large storage tanks.''

General Zachery pointed to the northern wooded area. ''As an additional precaution, eight SAM Falcon missiles will be placed here and here as requested. Twelve assault jeeps with 14mm guns mounted on them are being moved to Niwot. A new radar mobile station will be moved into place by the end of the week. No plane, parachutist, or vehicle could possibly penetrate the area.''

Reintraub put his pointer on the table. ''For everyone here, this is your first priority as of now. We want immediate action from each section. Zach, I want to know the moment the defense system is completed. Peterson and Dodd, send everything you get over to my office. Higgins, same for your section.

''One other thing,'' Reintraub continued. ''There is to be no hint of anything unusual. No other officers are to be informed. There is to be total and absolute secrecy. The military personnel at Niwot know nothing of the research that is being done, and they are to be kept separate from the scientists there. Dodd, I want the guards at the gates doubled immediately. Nobody is to enter or leave the facility except for those we have already designated. Only people with Q-clearances will be allowed into the main building. All delivery and service vehicles must be stopped at the gates and the military personnel will complete the delivery into the area.''

Reintraub stood. ''We will hold regular briefing sessions to keep everyone informed. The Old Man wants this locked up. Top priority. The timing on this is extremely sensitive. Any questions? Good. Gentlemen, that is all for now.''

22

THE BELL RANG and Matt shouted Wednesday's assignment above the clamor as the students scrambled from their seats. He gathered up his own papers and turned to leave when the principal's secretary came to the door.

"Mr. Leach would like you to go to his office as soon as possible." She turned and was gone before he could respond.

Matt suspected this was the fallout for his absence from school yesterday.

This morning he hadn't had the chance to turn in his work at the main office and had planned to do so during his lunch period. He went to his room and picked up the grade sheet and assignment book, then went down the hall to Leach's office, braced himself, and knocked.

Leach opened the door, his stern eyes were narrowed and the muscles in his jaw twitched. "Sit down, Matt," he ordered.

Matt knew Leach was mad about something; there was probably more to it than just a late quarter grade sheet. Matt took a chair in the corner.

When the door was closed he saw Perry Chapman, superintendent of schools, sitting across the room. Chapman was a heavyset man, hair cropped short, thick neck bulging above a starched white collar, dressed in a bland brown suit that showed no wrinkles. He was a strict disciplinarian who wanted everything done by the book. Chapman was an overweight, uptight prick as far as Matt was concerned, more interested in rules than the students or their education.

Matt stood and leaned over to shake Chapman's hand, then sat back down and turned his attention to Leach. Matt wasn't sure what the meeting was all about, but he had a bad feeling about it.

Leach opened a folder. "Yesterday, Perry tells me he got a call from the state health department asking if we knew anything about an epidemic in our school that involved mice, and inquiring if any of the students were ill. Then, Culligan Water called my office and said it would be best if you didn't use the list of customers' names they gave you because they hadn't gotten permission from the customers."

Leach then took a paper from an envelope and opened it. He stared at it a moment, then shoved it at Matt. "That is a bill from the Water Division for more than two thousand dollars. Would you care to explain to us what this is all about?"

Matt had checked the mail every single day so he could intercept the bill before it got to the front office, and on the very day he was home in bed, it had landed in Leach's lap. Matt scanned the bill while his mind raced for something to say.

Matt started to speak but Leach cut him off. "And they told me that you locked the labs and canceled all the science projects with the mice. Just what in the hell is going on here?"

Matt leaned forward, staring straight at Leach. "The mice died from infection. The Centers for Disease Control lab in Atlanta said there's something wrong with their leukocytes—the white blood cells."

"The CDC? How did they get involved in this?"

"My concern was that the students not be exposed or infected with anything from the mice, so I contacted them."

"So, that's why you closed the labs and canceled all the science projects with the mice?"

"Yes," Matt answered.

"Well—that seems reasonable. That was probably the safe thing to do," Leach conceded. "But why in the hell did you waste the school's money getting the water tested?"

"I'm convinced that the mice died because of something in the water, so I had it tested."

"And what did the tests show?" Leach asked, staring at the forms in front of him.

"Well—nothing except for high levels of deuterium."

Leach let out a sigh and dropped the forms on his desk. "Your department will be charged one thousand dollars against its budget, and the remaining eleven hundred will come out of your salary over the next six months. I guess we should probably have the rest of the mice destroyed and the labs scrubbed down."

"No, not yet," Matt argued.

"Why not? I thought you were worried about the students being exposed to something."

"I've closed the labs to the students, so their safety is not an issue. The CDC and I are doing a small experiment with the mice that may tell us why they are dying. The mice may provide some important answers."

"This time, keep me informed about what you're doing. And don't spend any more of the school's money without written permission." He looked up. "That's all, Matt. You can go."

23

Adirondacks National Forest, New York

BILL HARRIS PULLED his Chevy pickup camper deep into the forest and found a clearing to set up camp. It was a gorgeous afternoon, and he still had five days left before he had to go home. After putting the last of his beef stew on the stove for dinner, he downed a quick cup of coffee, loaded five .270-caliber rounds into his Browning rifle, and set out for wild turkey.

He felt a ripple of chills and the flush of fever. An icy sweat soaked into the back of his flannel shirt. Just a passing chill from a cold, he thought—but he ignored colds. Harris never let a cold stop him from doing whatever it was he was doing, and right now that was bagging a big gobbler. He pulled the canvas hunting coat around his neck and hunched down against another wave of chills. He started out through the brush with the Browning over his shoulder. The big tom turkeys would be in full display, like the fall foliage they were hiding in.

He loved autumn with the smell of wood smoke and apples rotting on the ground, the sound of dry leaves rattling in the trees and crunching underfoot, and the colors, earth tones blended and splattered like excess paint on some artist's palate. He liked the shafts of sunlight that broke through the shedding trees, illuminating the veils of spider webs that hung between thistle.

It was on the eighteenth day after leaving his home in Loudonville, New Hampshire, that the immune cells of Bill

Harris's body began to break down and fragment. He had three days to live. It would not be a quick death, nor would it be a prolonged illness. Just three days—and the bacteria would devour his body like maggots on garbage.

His head was throbbing and he felt weak. He wouldn't push himself too hard today, just a short trip out to kick through the leaves and maybe get a shot at something before dinner.

Harris decided that if he still felt sick by Saturday he would just stay in the camper and watch the fighting Irish of Notre Dame beat the living daylights out of Michigan State. It wasn't a hard alternative, since he loved football almost as much as he did hunting.

But on Saturday as Notre Dame beat Michigan State in the last forty-three seconds with a desperate fifty-yard field goal into the wind, Bill Harris lay dead in his camper, the victory as meaningless now as the autumn leaves that scattered in the wind.

24

MATT FELT LOUSY. The tape bound tightly across his chest did little to relieve the constant pain. His body ached, he had chills, and his head was stuffed up. Probably just a cold. He always got a cold this time of year. He kept telling himself he wasn't dying, but at night when he was alone, his fears told him otherwise. What was Davis in Seattle doing with the mice that was taking so long? Why hadn't he heard from him?

Matt opened the bottle of pills and poured a glass of water. He tried to remember how often he drank water. He didn't want to deviate from whatever he drank normally. He was very conscious of it now and every drink was anything but routine. Matt held the water in his mouth before swallowing and tried to taste it.

Water—just plain old water taste.

But it wasn't just plain water. What was the water doing to his body right now each day, with each drink? He knew there was a reason to fear the water. After swallowing two of the pain pills that had been prescribed, he tossed his robe on a chair and climbed into bed, hoping sleep would come.

The phone rang at 1:15 A.M. and tore Matt from a deep, badly needed sleep. "Sorry," Davis apologized when he realized he had gotten Matt out of bed. "I always forget about the three-hour time difference. It's still more than an hour before the late evening news comes on out here."

"That's okay," Matt lied, feeling like he'd just been

awakened out of a coma. He tried to clear his mind of the fog caused by the medication. "Did you get the water? Have you tested it yet?"

"Yes, we're testing it now. I've got some more information concerning the Niwot Project. It is one of the Department of Defense's secret DARPA projects."

"What kind of project?"

"DARPA. Defense Advanced Research Projects Agency. The Niwot Project is a new hydrogen fusion reactor of some kind. It's all very hush-hush and hard to find any real information about it. It's supposed to be the first on-line functioning fusion reactor. It has enormous political and economic ramifications. If they are right, it will crush OPEC and the oil cartel. Your senator from New Hampshire, Senator Midgley, is on the committee that oversees the Department of Defense funding of special projects. That's why the Niwot Project is in your state. Maybe his staff would be willing to look into the situation. Sorry about waking you up in the middle of the night, but I think you've stumbled onto something big."

"Have you found anything new about the mice I sent?"

"We're still doing tests. We should know something soon. Next time I'll try to remember to call earlier."

Matt thanked him and went back to bed.

Dr. Walter Davis checked the mice in his lab. He had switched the water supply on half the mice that Strong had sent him, substituting Seattle's tap water for the water they had been getting. The teacher was right—the mice were dying! Davis had ordered nasal cultures for virus and blood cultures on all the mice, but he knew the results would be negative. The water tests confirmed high levels of deuterium, but he knew something else was killing the mice.

He wasn't convinced that the town was in any real danger, but there was just enough lingering doubt that he couldn't take a chance. There were still a few more tests he could run, but it was time to call Atlanta and get help on this one. Evans had to get an investigative team to New Hampshire immediately and look into the situation. And Evans should get in contact with the Defense Department in Washington for more information about the Niwot Project that might shed some light on the problem.

Davis still didn't know exactly what was going on, but he was growing more uneasy about it by the minute.

Matt threw the *Gazette* down in anger after reading a story that was all too familiar. Bill Harris, a pharmacist in town, had been found dead in his camper two days ago. He had been hunting wild turkey in the Adirondacks of New York. According to the article, authorities initially thought Harris had died from a heart attack or from carbon monoxide poisoning in the camper. But an autopsy showed that he died of neither one.

Bill Harris had died of pneumonia.

Matt wasn't going to sit around any longer and wait for outside help. It was time for action. If word got out to people about the danger of leaving town because of the water, every death from here on could be prevented.

And people like Bill Harris would still be alive.

He called Davis but he was gone for the day. Matt had another plan. He was going to play out a hunch. He called long-distance information and got the number he wanted, then dialed. Matt wasn't sure if he would be able to reach him on a late Friday afternoon, but it was worth a shot.

"Senator Midgley's office."

"Hello, I'm a reporter with *The Boston Globe*," Matt said, "and I need to speak to Senator Midgley regarding an article we are going to run in the paper."

After waiting a full three minutes, another voice came on. "I'm Doreen Nickles, Senator Midgley's press aide. Can I help you?"

"I'm a reporter with *The Boston Globe*," Matt repeated. "I need to speak with the Senator regarding an urgent matter."

"I'm sorry, but Senator Midgley will be tied up in meetings for the rest of the day. Perhaps I can help you," she said.

"Give the senator this message," Matt said sternly. "We are going to print a story on the Niwot Project. There have been problems there, and I wanted the senator's side of the story before we print it."

"I'll give him the message, but it may be some time next week before I can discuss this matter with him. May I have your phone number in case we need to get back to you on this?"

"If I were you, I'd make sure the senator gets the message very soon. We're going to do the article, and I'm sure he would like to have some input on what we are going to publish. I'll be in New Hampshire for another day or so while I finish research for the article. While I'm here, you can reach me at this number," and Matt gave her his home phone number and hung up.

Matt went to the kitchen and was rummaging through his refrigerator for a Coors when the phone rang.

It was Midgley's receptionist who put him through directly to Senator Midgley.

"Senator Midgley," Matt began, "I'm a reporter with *The Boston Globe*. We have learned that the Niwot Project has been dumping deuterium into a lake that supplies drinking water for a nearby town. And there have been several cases of fatal pneumonia in that town that are believed to be related. We also understand that the Centers for Disease Control is investigating this."

"The Niwot Project? Pneumonia? What the heck are you talking about?"

"Our paper wants to know what the government is going to do about checking the water and the material that the Niwot Project has been dumping. As the senator representing the people of New Hampshire and the one responsible for bringing the Niwot Project to their state, we want to know what steps you are taking to protect them."

"To be honest with you, my office has not heard of anything unusual regarding the Niwot Project. Did you say the CDC was investigating it?" There was a pause and Matt heard a deep sigh, then Senator Midgley continued, "As you know, this is a very sensitive and classified item. Could I speak to your managing editor?"

"He's out of town until next week, and I'm in New Hampshire finishing the last research for the article, but I'll have him call you and answer any questions you have about the story we are going to run. In the meantime, when we run this story, can we say that you are looking into the situation and will be starting a full investigation?"

"When are you running the story? This is top-secret classified stuff, and we should talk it over before you run it. Your paper knows the rules on this."

"For your information, *The Boston Globe* doesn't think that the disclosure of several deaths or the disregard for the safety of a town is considered classified stuff, and I don't think the people of New Hampshire will either."

Then Matt slammed the phone down to dramatically end the matter right there.

He sat back and let out a slow, deep breath. That should stir things up enough to make Midgley do something. No politician liked bad press.

The speed with which Midgley called him back on a late Friday convinced Matt that he had indeed stumbled onto something big, a story so important that Senator Midgley, chairman of the Defense Systems Appropriation Committee, would make time to call him back in less than five minutes.

Matt had an idea that might keep the heat turned up on the senator. If Midgley thought there were two different papers breathing down his neck, he would be forced to take it seriously and take some kind of action. And that's just what Matt wanted him to do.

He picked up the phone and called Danielle.

. . .

"Coffee, please," Matt said to the waitress. "Danielle, listen . . ."

"Do either of you care for cream?"

"No, just black," Matt said.

The young waitress at the diner persisted. "How about a piece of fresh pie to go with it?"

Danielle opened the plastic menu. "What kind do you have today?"

The waitress turned to the side and looked at the round glass case. "The Dutch apple is fresh and very good."

Danielle shrugged her shoulders and nodded. Matt said, "Sure, bring us two pieces of Dutch apple."

When the waitress finally left, Danielle put her elbows on the table and leaned across, chin resting on her hands. "How's your chest?" she asked.

"Hurts, but that's to be expected for a few days."

"You're sweaty."

"Got a small cold. It's nothing," he said.

Her brows furrowed as she looked at him. "You look sick."

Matt leaned across the table and spoke. "I want you to call your friend at *The Washington Post*. I want to see if he's interested in investigating this story."

"You want me to call Dick Cahill?" She stirred in a packet of sugar.

"This would make a great story for an investigative reporter," Matt said. "Davis at the CDC is convinced there is something going on here, and Senator Midgley is going to look into the matter."

Danielle looked at him over the top of her cup. She swallowed and put the cup down slowly. "Senator Midgley? How do you know that?"

The waitress returned with two pieces of apple pie and a refill of coffee.

"I called his office in Washington and talked to him personally. Midgley was the one who helped get the Niwot

Project into New Hampshire. He sure as hell doesn't want to see anything go wrong because it would be political suicide.'' Matt dug into the pie and washed it down with a long drink of coffee.

"I'll call Dick and tell him what's going on," Danielle said. "If he's interested in pursuing it, I'll have him contact you. But I can't promise anything."

Matt slid a note across the table to her. "Have him call Senator Midgley and tell him he's with *The Washington Post*, and ask Midgley if there have been any recent problems reported at the Niwot Project. Nothing else, just have him ask that. There, I wrote it down for you to read to him." Matt looked at her.

Matt drummed his fingers nervously on the table. He would have to find a way to convince Dick Cahill to pursue it. Matt wondered what would happen when she talked to Dick again. Had she really gotten over her old boyfriend? Matt was worried, and felt twinges of jealousy and self-doubt. It was a gamble—but one he had to take.

He pushed away from the table and picked up the bill. "Let's get out of here."

25

J. Edgar Hoover Building
Federal Bureau of Investigation
Washington, D.C.

HIGGINS WAS AT his desk reviewing all the personnel files from the Niwot Project with Q-clearance when his phone rang.

"Higgins, Jim Reintraub here. There's a SOIG briefing tomorrow night. I know it's sooner than you expected, but I need your report then."

"Tomorrow night? You can't be serious. We've got over fifteen hundred files on scientists, technicians, electricians. That'll take two weeks, ten days tops."

"We don't have ten days. I've just learned that the Centers for Disease Control in Atlanta has made inquiries about the Niwot Project. And this morning Senator Midgley called to see if we knew of anything unusual that had happened at Niwot. He'd just gotten off the phone with some damned reporter from *The Washington Post*. And last Friday a reporter from *The Boston Globe* called him and said they were going to print a story on the Niwot Project. Now how in the hell did the papers get involved in this? Goddammit, at this rate we'll have a profile of the whole project showing up on the evening news!"

"Why is the CDC interested in Niwot?" Higgins asked.

"Never mind why, it doesn't matter. We just told them to bug the hell out!" Reintraub screamed back. "The only important thing that should concern you is maintaining security of the project. The DIA is taking care of Midgley to get him off our backs. I don't want any leaks. I want this project sealed up tighter than a fly's ass, not spread all over the TV. I've scheduled a SOIG meeting tomorrow night, and I want an update on everything at that time.''

"I can't possibly put together a complete report, but we'll do what we can.''

"One more thing," Reintraub added. "We don't have much time on this one, and there's only one way this can be sealed up. This has to be a completely sterile operation. The TOPAZ SOIG has been authorized to take executive action from this point on. No exceptions.''

Executive Action! A sanitized euphemism for assassination. "Sterile operation" meant the termination of all sources involved with breaking the security of TOPAZ.

The sound of the words sent a chill through Higgins. He knew the rationale for taking executive action. The government couldn't arrest those involved with top-secret, classified information and risk having the details come out in court or the press. In this nasty business executive action was the preferred way—the only way—of closing a case. It wasn't meant to mete out justice, but simply to eradicate a problem.

Mistakes were rare, but they happened. Innocent people were occasionally the victims of executive action. How many people would accidently be "eliminated" this time? Higgins felt ill.

Higgins should have guessed this assignment would call for wet work. He knew he was getting too old for this; he didn't have the stomach for it the way he did when he was younger. He didn't like it.

"Who made the decision?''

"The order came from the top. There wasn't time to let your section know sooner," Reintraub answered.

Higgins knew that was a lie. Who at the top? The President? The secretary of defense, advisers, who?

"It shouldn't involve your section anyway," Reintraub inserted.

Higgins hung up and sat back. Why was the CDC interested in Niwot?

Davis finished taping up the last of the cartons and labeled them for shipment to Atlanta. His request for assistance from the Atlanta section of the CDC hadn't gotten the response he'd expected. Instead of giving him the help he'd asked for, they had unexpectedly demanded that he stop any investigation regarding Niwot immediately. It was too sensitive for his section they said, and they would handle it in Washington. Evans had given Davis specific instructions to send all his records and test results to the Atlanta office immediately. The material would be reviewed, then sent on to the Department of Defense in Washington, D.C.

Davis told himself it probably didn't matter anyway. Admittedly the white blood cell walls looked bizarre, but he knew there was no infectious agent. The students who had handled the mice hadn't been exposed to anything, the town seemed to be in no real danger. He was comforted by the fact that the Atlanta section of the CDC and the DoD in Washington would both be looking into it.

There was no reason for him to worry about it. The matter was out of his hands now. He had done what Evans had asked him to do, and Atlanta would complete the investigation along with the Department of Defense.

Then why did he still feel uneasy about the situation? He had to let Matt Strong in New Hampshire know what was going on.

He picked up the phone and dialed: "Matt, this is Walter Davis. The Niwot Project is classified and my section isn't authorized to go any further with the investigation. I've shipped all my reports and test results to Atlanta and after they are reviewed, they will be sent on to the Department of Defense in Washington."

"Who in Washington is going to be in charge? Who can I contact?"

"I really don't know. Atlanta is better equipped to pursue

it than we are." After a pause Davis said, "I'll monitor their investigation as much as I can and keep you filled in on what is happening. But you can at least take comfort in the fact that the Atlanta office and the DoD are pursuing this."

Matt walked into the school gym and spotted Danielle. She was dressed in black dance tights, working on the exercise bar. She stretched over to touch her toes with the smooth graceful flow that only dancers had. She smiled when she spotted him.

He kissed her on the neck. "Good morning," he said. "Don't you ever sleep?"

She looked at him and saw his bloodshot eyes from lack of sleep and his tired face lined with concern. "Yeah, but it looks like you haven't in a long time. Matt, you look terrible."

"Have you called your friend at *The Washington Post* yet? Is he going to look into this?"

She took a towel from her duffel bag and they sat on the floor together. "Dick called Senator Midgley's office the same day you gave me the note. He didn't learn anything, but he did say Midgley sounded very upset. What have you heard from the CDC?"

"Davis called from Seattle last night. They've decided to handle the investigation of the mice and the water from the Atlanta office. All the material he had regarding the mice has been sent there. He's been told not to interfere in any way with the investigation from here on. Some agency in Washington is going to handle it."

"Doesn't that make you feel encouraged that authorities in Washington are finally going to start checking into this?"

Matt sighed. "I suppose I should be, but I'm not convinced that anyone really knows yet just what the hell is going on here." He kissed her. "Meet me for lunch? I'll buy. Today's menu is toasted cheese sandwich and chili."

"You got a date," she said. "Toasted cheese."

26

WALTER DAVIS, STILL upset about being pushed out of the Niwot investigation, almost failed to make the connection to the most important problem he would ever face.

The door to his office opened. "Walt, the toxicology screen chromatography is almost finished. Are there any other tests you want to do on all these ducks?"

"What?" Davis asked, irritated at the interruption. "Ducks? What ducks?"

Dr. Peter Trent, a biochemist on the staff, stepped into Davis's office and handed him a manila envelope. "The U.S. Fish and Wildlife Service sent twenty ducks for us to test. The ducks were found dead in Pennsylvania. Thousands of them died during their fall migration, and they can't seem to find out what killed them."

Davis took the report out of the envelope and glanced at the pages. Ducks in Pennsylvania? As if he didn't have enough to worry about already. Peter Trent continued, "The Fish and Wildlife people are really concerned. Their lab and Penn State University's lab have already cultured for bacteria, viruses, rickettsia—the works. No luck. They hoped maybe we could help them out."

The scenario triggered an alarm of recognition, and Davis took the folder and flipped through the tests that Penn State University had done. All their cultures were negative.

"A game warden found them at a lake on the Pine Creek Gorge wildlife area in Pennsylvania," Trent continued.

"They tested the water in the lake and came up with nothing. It's all there in the report."

Migration!

Davis put the folders on his desk, a feeling of alarm and dismay gripping him. "Do blood smears and stain them. Also, call Morishima at the university. I need to use the electron microscope again." Davis hit the intercom button on his desk. "Jackie, get the U.S. Fish and Wildlife Service in Pennsylvania on the phone for me. I want to talk to the game warden who found these ducks!"

Davis pulled down a wall map of the Northeast and scanned it. "Peter, you're an avid 'birder.' Where were these ducks migrating from?"

"From the northeast, New England and Canada. They'll travel thousands of miles to winter in either Florida or Mexico."

Davis traced a line north with a finger and came to rest over the center of New Hampshire.

When Davis turned toward him, Peter Trent saw a look of fear on his face.

Higgins read the notes in front of him. His section had found nothing on any of the Q-clearances that would trigger suspicion. Reintraub wanted all the information on the situation at the Niwot Project "contained." On the surface it seemed routine, but Higgins had a nose for trouble and something didn't fit right. Something was wrong with Reintraub's conclusions. There were too many parts of the puzzle that were missing. It smelled of a cover-up.

Reintraub was hiding something.

Higgins had pulled out the personnel records of the men who were the brains behind the Niwot Project. At the moment he wasn't interested in the technicians, electricians, and maintenance staff. He had assigned that task to one of his assistants. Higgins was looking for something else.

With the DIA and CIA also involved, Higgins knew the Bureau would never be fully informed of what was going

on. Each of the intelligence sections would be keeping
something from each other. He wanted to know the whole
truth, not just fragments and pieces of the truth. The truth was
never a top priority in Washington these days. He needed help
on this and had sent for Special Agent Frank Parker.

There was a knock at the door.

Higgins went to the door and opened it. "Frank, thanks
for getting here so quicikly. Have a seat."

Parker was a quiet, gentle-appearing man in his late forties,
showing gray through his temples. He was a trim, well-dressed
man, and the best agent Higgins had working for him.

For the next half hour Higgins brought Parker up-to-date
on the situation at the Niwot Project. He then explained to
Parker what he wanted to do next. "Frank, I want you to
contact the Centers for Disease Control in Atlanta and find
out what their interest is in the Niwot Project. I want names
and copies of any reports, memos, or studies they have
regarding the Niwot Project."

Parker had been taking notes, but put his pen down.
"Who do I contact at the CDC?"

"I don't know. That's one of the things you'll have to find
out. But remember when you talk to the CDC that we want to
keep a low profile on this one. The Niwot Project is classified
and the Department of Defense wants to keep it that way."

He pulled out a folder he had tagged from the pile and
opened it. "Dr. Otto Strassman, physicist at Princeton
University, and the brains behind the Niwot Project. As a
young scientist, he was the leading pioneer in Germany's
atomic research during the Second World War."

Higgins handed Strassman's folder to Parker. "This is
your second assignment. Talk to Strassman and see what he
knows about the CDC interest in the Niwot Project and find
out if they have contacted him. Maybe he knows what the
hell is going on. You should also look into his background,
although I doubt if he is any security risk."

Parker opened the folder and paged through it.

"One other thing, Frank. There are three other intelligence sections mudding up the water on this thing, and that's not good. Don't talk to anyone about what you're doing or what you find. I want to keep it simple and quiet.''

Higgins walked to the window. ''We have an order for executive action jammed up our ass because of a top-secret project that isn't secret anymore, and everybody but *People* magazine seems to have some interest in Niwot. Innocent people are going to get hurt.''

He turned and faced Parker. ''People are going to be killed unless we can close this thing up.''

Davis put a dead female mallard on the dissection table, pulled on a pair of surgical gloves, and slit open its abdomen with a single long incision. He watched as purulent, thick yellow fluid oozed out behind the path of the scalpel. It was the same picture as with the mice he had dissected.

Davis pushed a needle into the heart, pulled back on the plunger, and filled the syringe with blood, then separated it into three tubes and diluted it with phosphate-buffered saline. It was the first step for the most definitive test he could run, the ELISA. Enzyme linked immunosorbent assay. It was very specific, and when combined with the electrophoresis would leave no doubt.

The horror of what might be happening to the town slowly sank into his conscience. He hoped he was wrong—it seemed too unbelievable. But the thought that he might be right made him nauseated.

He put a slide with a blood smear under the microscope. As he focused on the leukocytes, his hand began to tremble.

He wanted Dr. Morishima to see this.

Davis focused the electron microscope and stared at the white blood cells from the ducks. The wall of the leukocyte was fragmented and torn, with large pieces missing.

''No doubt about it. These leukocytes look exactly like those of the mice,'' Morishima said. ''The cells are falling apart. That beats anything I've ever seen.''

"We separated the basement membrane from the cell wall and ran a spectroscopic analysis on it," Davis said. "It's just protein. Our DNA analysis drew a blank."

"You mean you can't match it?"

Davis answered in a low voice laced with fear. "No, I mean there is no DNA."

"Do you know what you're implying?" Morishima asked.

"Yes—there's no genetic material. Just pieces of living protein," Davis answered.

"*Prions?* Are you suggesting that the mice and ducks died because of prions?"

"That's exactly what killed them!" Davis said as he stared at the green monitor in front of him.

Prions: an alien life-form spawned at the beginning of time on earth. Just chemicals, having no genetic code: a life without purpose. It had finally happened, and he and the rest of the CDC would have to move fast to save the town.

He reached for the phone.

The time for investigating was over. The time had come to do something—and soon! Evans could throw his weight around and cut through all the bureaucratic tape and get the DoD involved.

Davis now had proof of what had happened. He was going to call and demand help. He was going to insist that the CDC launch a Class One priority field investigation immediately! He called the CDC in Atlanta and asked to speak to Dr. Evans, but Evans was gone. No one knew when he would be back. His position with the CDC often required trips around the country, but neither his wife nor his secretary knew of any scheduled trip.

Davis finally spoke to a vice-director, told him what had happened, and demanded immediate help. The vice-director said he would look into it and get back to him.

Matt was heating a can of chili on the stove when the phone rang.

Davis's voice had an icy tone, but the words were even

more chilling. "We think we know what killed the mice." There was a pause. "You're lucky to be alive. The whole damn town is lucky to be alive."

Fear gripped Matt when he heard Davis. He thought of Jeff, Kelley, Vicki James, and the others who weren't so lucky. "What did you find?"

"Prions," Davis said. "The water from the Niwot Project is loaded with prions."

"What is that? Some kind of toxin?"

"More like an infection. We come across one or two cases of infection every year that we suspect are due to prions, but it's almost impossible to prove because the quantity is so small. This time it's different."

"What are they?" Matt asked, feeling a knot form in the pit of his stomach.

"Prions are living chemicals, a primitive life-form left over from the beginning of creation, different from all other life on this planet. They have no cell wall or structure, no genetic code, no reproduction. It's a life-form that doesn't belong in our time."

"How did they get into the water?"

"Prions are formed by heat, incredible searing heat. Prions came from the blazing chemical soup fueled by the sun, volcanoes, and a constant barrage of lightning during the cataclysmic formation of the earth. The Niwot Project is experimenting with hydrogen fusion that produces temperatures that equal that of the sun. And it's my guess that they are creating life, making millions of prions in the process."

Matt's mind was reeling at the thought that some kind of prehistoric chemicals were living in his body. "But what will we do? We'll die if we stop drinking the water!"

"Since it behaves like an infection, there must be a way to treat it. God help us if we can't find out what it is."

Higgins leaned back in his chair and bit on his pipe as he opened the report that Parker had just delivered. "What did you find out about the Niwot Project?"

"Professor Strassman was anything but friendly. He was surprised to see me. Apparently Strassman and the rest of the staff know nothing about the SOIG or outside interest in the Niwot Project."

Higgins put the report down and turned his full attention to Parker.

Parker continued, "Strassman came from the Princeton Plasma Lab where he worked on the Russian-designed Tokomak fusion reactor. Reintraub recruited him from Princeton, and Strassman has a very prestigious staff under him from Brookhaven, Yale, and MIT. There are two main types of reactors, one using massive lasers to blast the hydrogen and the other—like the Tokomak—uses huge magnetics to squeeze the hydrogen together. When they fuse two hydrogen atoms together it forms helium and in the process produces a tiny thermonuclear explosion, reaching temperatures of more than a hundred million degrees, the same temperature as the center of the sun."

"What's so special about Niwot that has generated all the attention?" Higgins asked.

"The Niwot Project—code name TOPAZ—is a new concept and uses a combination of factors to achieve fusion and, according to Strassman, is designed to be the first operational commercial plant. Until now, nobody was able to contain and put to practical use the incredible temperatures that they generate. But Strassman and his staff have figured out a way to do it. They can use seawater to get an inexhaustible supply of energy. Strassman insists that fusion is safe, produces no waste or isotopes. And he has absolutely no knowledge of the CDC's interest in Niwot."

"Do you believe him?"

"There's no reason not to," Parker said.

"If Strassman doesn't know about the CDC's interest in the project, who would? What's Reintraub's involvement in it, anyway?" Higgins asked. "This project should be the baby of the Department of Energy."

"A lot," Parker answered. "The project is funded

entirely through DARPA, not through the DoE as you would expect it to be, and that leaves everyone else on Capitol Hill out in the cold with no say in anything that happens at Niwot. Congress has its thumb on the DoE. The DoE has to account for every dime it spends, but the secretly funded DARPA section answers to no one. This project was too big and too important to go through financial channels in Congress. Nobody knows exactly how much money gets funneled into Niwot, but I heard an estimate of fifty billion dollars.''

Higgins whistled softly at the amount. ''So Reintraub puts this project through DARPA, controls it himself with no outside interference, and is accountable to no one about the amount of money spent.''

''There's one more catch to it,'' Parker said. ''The geopolitical ramifications of fusion are enormous. OPEC would be stopped dead in its tracks and left with little bargaining power.''

Higgins nodded. ''And Reintraub stands to reap all the political benefits. Good work, Frank. This report answers a lot of questions. Now we have to find out why the CDC is interested in TOPAZ.''

Walter Davis had called the CDC in Atlanta several times trying to reach Evans, but he still hadn't returned. Davis gave a detailed report of what he had discovered about the prions to Evans's assistant. He had also sent a full report to the Department of Defense to inform them. He hoped that with the DoD and the CDC working together on the situation at Niwot, they could find some answers.

Davis telexed the report, carefully detailing his findings, to both the Atlanta office of the CDC and to the DoD, demanding an immediate investigation to avoid a potential disaster. Davis figured that would get fast results.

Higgins answered the phone. It was Parker. ''Sorry I couldn't get back to you sooner on this, but there were problems. Only one man at the CDC knew specifically about the inquiry into the Niwot Project. Dr. Evans, the head of the Epidemiology Section, but he has been missing for three days. His wife hasn't heard from him, and nobody at his office has a clue as to where he may have gone. The Atlanta police have officially listed him as a missing person.''

Higgins didn't want to think about the obvious conclusion. Evans may have been "coded"—a euphemism used to describe the victims of "executive action." But why? What had Evans done that was enough of a security risk to get coded?

"Evans's assistant said that the Field Research Service of the CDC in Seattle, Washington, was the lab that had been investigating Niwot.''

"What investigation? Why were they interested in Niwot?'' Higgins asked.

"I don't know,'' Parker said. "The director, Dr. Walter Davis, has been in charge of the initial investigation. I tried to reach him, but he wasn't there. It seems that the Department of Defense called off the CDC's investigation into Niwot because the project was classified top secret. All of Davis's reports and papers were sent to the Department of Defense.''

"Can you get me a copy of those CDC reports?'' Higgins asked. "They might give us some answers to this mess.'' He hoped he could find a reason to cancel the executive action order.

"I went through the DARPA files in the Architect's Building in Rosslyn,'' Parker said, "and couldn't find any papers from the CDC. I called a friend inside the Defense Intelligence Agency, same story. Nothing.''

"They're not with the DIA or DARPA? Reintraub. That son of a bitch has the CDC reports. That's the only explanation. See what you can find out about it.''

Higgins hung up. What kind of cover-up was Reintraub involved in? Higgins grew more enraged by the minute. Reintraub had positioned himself politically to make a big move, but something must have happened to jeopardize his plans. And he had dragged all the intelligence groups into the Special Operations Interagency Group to do his dirty work for him. Then he—or someone—had decided to take executive action to guarantee that no information regarding TOPAZ would ever leak out.

Higgins didn't know how far the cover-up extended, and whether or not it went as far as the White House.

He would have to move more carefully on this one.

27

DAVIS PULLED HIS raincoat over his head and ran around to the rear of his apartment building. The rain was heavy and steady, and as usual, the front entrance was flooded. When he opened the back door to his town house he knew immediately something was wrong. Dusty, his two-year-old female retriever, was not there to greet him. She was always there, anxious for a quick trip to the yard and eager to play. He closed the door and listened but heard only his own heartbeat above the eerie silence. He ran his hand along the wall in the dark until he found the switch, then turned on the kitchen light.

Shock and fear flooded over him, making his legs tremble and his heart beat wildly in his chest. Every drawer and closet had been emptied and scattered on the floor. He walked through the rubble into the hall, the living room, and into his bedroom. Every room in his town house had been torn apart.

He saw something dark on the bathroom floor. Dusty. He couldn't go in. He knew she was dead.

Why would anyone want to kill Dusty?

Davis's first impulse was to call the police. But an inner voice told him he hadn't been robbed. Somebody had come after information, and maybe they had come to get him.

Then an icy fear gripped him when he realized he didn't know if he was alone.

Davis ran out the back door and down the alley and

melted into the shadows. He watched his car from a distance for more than an hour before deciding it was safe. He crouched down and unlocked the door, then slipped in and drove off.

He didn't spot anyone, and there was no car in the mirror behind him.

Still uneasy, he drove around the block twice by his apartment, but spotted nothing unusual. Davis drove back to his office at the CDC lab. What was going on? Who had ransacked his apartment? Why would they kill Dusty?

He turned the headlights off while still a block away and pulled into the dark corner of the parking lot, away from the safety light. He walked in the rain back to the lab, hanging in the shadows, and slipped into the rear of the building. He made his way to his office without turning on any lights. He unlocked the door and started to go in but stopped.

Even with the faint light coming through the window from the yard light outside he could see what had happened. It looked the same as his apartment. Every drawer and file had been emptied and dumped on the floor. In the short time it had taken him to drive home and back someone had ransacked his office.

Who are they? What did they want? *What the hell was going on?*

Davis tore out of the building, ran to his car, and sped off. He drove around a quiet residential section until he was convinced he wasn't being followed, then left Seattle and headed north toward Bellingham on Interstate 5. He could stay with a friend there.

He glanced in the mirror again and saw nothing.

The phone rang seven times before Matt could manage to get himself out of bed to answer it. The clock read 4:30 A.M. "Hello."

Davis was on the other end. "Somebody just ransacked both my apartment and my office at the lab. I think they were there to get me."

Matt rubbed his eyes and sat up. Fear swept fatigue aside. "Who is after you? What did they want?"

"I don't know yet—but I think we've stumbled onto something big, something we weren't supposed to know about. I was only able to make a quick check of the office, but all the information about the prions was missing. They've taken everything. All I have left are some photos that I sent to Stanford. Something strange is going on. I don't know what the hell we've gotten ourselves into, but I don't like it. Watch yourself. I'm going to a friend's house. I'll call you in a couple of days."

"What have you heard from Atlanta or Washington? Somebody has to do something to help the town so we don't die!"

"You don't get it, do you?" Davis snarled. "They don't intend to help us. There's been some kind of mistake, and they don't want anyone to know about it. I called Atlanta and sent a telexed report to Washington, but nobody called me back. There's no word from Evans. He just disappeared, and they've listed him as a missing person. Because the Niwot Project is classified top secret, they insisted that all of the material I had regarding the mice and the water you shipped be sent to Washington for a review. Two days ago I phoned all ten hospitals requesting copies of the medical records using the list of names you gave me. I called the army hospital at Fort Carson. I called the student health clinic at Syracuse. Every single record was gone. Someone has the names from your list of obituaries! Now there are no records left."

"Why did they want the medical records?"

"They don't want anyone to see them. It's part of a cover-up, and we're right in the middle of it. You'd better be damn careful," Davis said. "I'm scared. We need help, but I don't know who to ask. Our lives may be in danger."

Click.

Matt replaced the receiver and sat up, staring into the black night and wondering what would be next.

· · ·

Matt never went back to bed and called the school office and told them he was sick and wouldn't be in today. The secretary put him on hold a moment, then informed him that he had no sick time left. Matt hung up. His mind was still reeling from last night's phone call. He had called Davis's office in Seattle twice, but Davis hadn't reported for work.

Evans had disappeared and Davis had gone into hiding. At the moment Matt was left with nothing except the fear that maybe he was in danger not only from the water, but because he already knew too much about the people who had already died.

Matt wondered why the Department of Defense had taken all the medical charts? What information did they have that could be damaging to them? What were they trying to cover up? He was furious with himself that he had inadvertently supplied them with names when he had sent the list to Davis.

His heart suddenly leaped in his chest. If all they had to go on was his list, they didn't have all the charts yet! There was still one chart they didn't have. He hadn't included one name on the list because it was an oversight on his part. It didn't seem important then.

Matt tried one more time to reach Davis, then he dialed the airport in Boston.

28

FLIGHT 492 FROM Boston to Lexington took just over an hour, time for Matt to have a cold glass of wine and a chicken and rice dinner with its plastic-wrapped salad, then catch a quick nap.

The plane was on its final landing approach, and the Boeing 727 lurched as the wing flaps were extended and the landing gear dropped. Matt tried to plan what he was going to do once he got to the hospital. He worried about details like whether the office doors in the hospital would be locked. Vicki James had died more than two and a half months ago. Where would her chart be? What happened to the charts after a patient died?

Ripping off a hospital chart in the middle of the night didn't seem as dangerous as robbing a bank, but it definitely posed its own peculiar problems. He had purchased a cheap stethoscope in Boston and hoped it would enable him to get around the hospital.

A twenty-minute cab ride from the airport brought him to Methodist Hospital. He glanced at his watch. 10:05 P.M. He decided against the front entrance, since he hadn't seen any visitors coming out. If he used the front door at this time of night, he might be stopped since visiting hours were over.

He walked around to the back and hung around the emergency-room entrance in the dark. He waited ten minutes. During that time a rescue squad arrived in silence, bright blue and red lights flashing, and delivered their passenger with a flurry of activity. A few minutes later a silver Porsche 911 squealed into the parking lot and a well-groomed man jumped out. Matt presumed he was a doctor and followed him in.

Staying right on the heels of the man, Matt found himself inside a busy ER and trauma center with a maze of halls and cubicles, nurses, patients, doctors, and equipment everywhere he looked. He yanked out the stethoscope, hung it around his neck, and followed the doctor in front of him through the emergency-room maze.

The doctor turned left. Matt followed. The crowded emergency room, as with all large metropolitan hospitals, served as a night clinic for indigent patients with no means for a family doctor, as well as for major trauma and medical emergencies. Patients on carts and wheelchairs cluttered the halls. The noise of phones, beepers, moans, babies, and voices drowned out normal conversation. Matt wasn't prepared for this. He stayed on the heels of the doctor who walked past the chaos, seemingly ignorant of the suffering around him.

He led Matt down the hall and into an already crowded trauma room. Other doctors and nurses swarmed around the patient who had been brought in by the emergency squad. Matt got a glimpse of the man on the gurney and heard someone say something about "damned motorcycles." A jagged piece of femur protruded through a gaping laceration of his leg. Nurses were packing gauze into the hole and applying pressure to try to stanch the flow of blood that gushed from the wound. Blood soaked the front of the man, and a dark pool spread under the leg. A forest of IV poles, bottles, and tangled plastic tubing surrounded the patient. The air was thick with the antiseptic smell of alcohol and the coppery odor of blood.

Matt spun around and left as he fought off both shock and nausea. He went down the hall, opened the door at the end, and walked straight into a linen closet. He was losing confidence fast. He couldn't even find his way through the emergency room—how could he even hope to find and steal a medical chart. The thought of leaving crossed his mind, but he knew he couldn't.

He found a door marked "Exit" that opened to a stairwell. He went up a flight and quietly opened the door to the second floor. The dim corridor was deserted. A sign read "Department of Radiology." He glanced inside a few rooms and could make out the large shadowy forms of x-ray machines that filled the rooms, like something from an old black and white horror movie. He moved on down the hall.

The next room was marked "Film Reading Room." He looked in. Empty. After slipping in quickly and closing the door, he found himself facing walls that were lined with banks of glass viewing boxes and a tangle of Dictaphones. Stacks of x-rays were piled on a shelf. Several long white coats hung on a rack by the wall. He found a hospital phone book and looked up Medical Records. It was on the third floor, just one flight up.

Matt decided it was time to improve his disguise. He found a white coat that fit him, put the stethoscope around his neck, and pulled an x-ray from the stack.

He started off to find Vicki's chart. Deciding against using the elevators, he went back to the stairwell and took the stairs three at a time. He caught his breath, opened the door to the third floor, and started down the hall to find the records room.

The door marked "Medical Records" was open, lights were on, and for all the activity inside, it could have been the middle of the day. Typists in small cubicles were taking dictation from headsets, and others were sorting, filing, and shuffling papers. Matt stepped up to the desk.

"Are you here to sign your charts, Doctor?"

Matt looked up and shook his head. "No, I'll catch up on them tomorrow. I need the chart on Vicki James."

After several minutes she returned with a pink sheet of paper. "I'm sorry. That chart has been signed out for conference tomorrow."

Matt stammered in disbelief. "I have to have it tonight!" She seemed startled by his demand, but he continued; "I'm presenting the case at conference. That's why I have to review it now."

She looked at the paper in her hand. "It was checked out to Dr. Eller, Neurology." Just when Matt resigned himself to defeat and was turning to leave, she spoke up. "It's probably on his desk on Four-North."

"Yeah, probably. I'll check with him. Thank you," he said and left.

Matt went up another flight of stairs to the fourth floor. A nurse was delivering medications, pushing a drug cart in front of her. The rest of the nursing staff was busy filling in charts at the large desk area that separated the north and south sections.

Matt walked on down the hall, but he had no idea where to look. All he saw in front of him was a long row of doors to patients' rooms. He went back to the nurses station. "Excuse me. Do you know where Dr. Eller's desk is? He has a chart that I need to review."

Several nurses looked up. One pointed to a small room behind them. "Back there, Doctor."

"Thank you." He walked past them and over to the small office at the back of the nurses station. The sign on the open door read "Neurology." Vicki's chart was on top of a mountainous stack of other charts. It was a thin, neat chart, unlike the bulky charts of clinic patients piled under it. According to the face sheet in the front of the chart, she had been in the hospital less than twenty-four hours before she died, not long enough to accumulate the large volume of information that was customary with chronically ill patients.

Matt grabbed the chart and turned to leave. The next folder on the pile beneath it caught his eye.

AUTOPSY REPORT
Vicki Loraine James
No: 89–7008

He had almost missed it. The autopsy report was exactly what Davis wanted. Matt quickly went through the rest of the stack to make sure he wasn't missing something else, but they were charts on other patients and a few journals.

A phone rang at the nurses station. Matt turned the light out and left.

A nurse looked up. "That was Dr. Eller calling. He's on his way up to see a patient, and you could talk to him about that chart when he gets here."

Matt kept moving toward the stairs. "I'll see him at conference tomorrow."

"He'll be here any second."

In his haste to get away, Matt had gone down the south wing, into another patient ward—and straight toward the elevators. Cold sweat poured down his back.

A nurse came out of room 411 and reached toward him. "Doctor, I need help in here. I can't get this IV to drip and I think it's infiltrated."

The elevator doors opened and a hulk of a man with thinning blond hair approached them. Matt snapped back, "I'm on my way to surgery. You handle it." He moved into the empty elevator and watched the doors close safely in front of him.

Higgins opened the folder of material that Parker had obtained from the CDC in Atlanta that contained photocopied data from the field lab in Seattle. He bit on his pipe and sat reading for twenty minutes without saying anything while he downed its contents. During that time Parker filled his coffee cup twice and watched from across the room.

Finally Higgins closed the thick folder of material and looked up. "Damn, can you believe that mumbo-jumbo about living chemicals? That's the most incredible thing I've ever read."

"After I reviewed the material, I called the Biological Sciences Lab at Stanford University and spoke to Dr. Miga in the microbiological research section. He confirmed what was in the report. They've known about these things called prions for the past two years, but it was always a very rare occurrence and occurred in such small amounts that they were hard to test for until now.''

"Has anyone at the CDC heard from Evans yet?" Higgins asked.

"No, sir, no word."

Higgins knew there never would be. He looked out the latticed office window and clenched the stem of his pipe firmly in his teeth, a growing cloud of cherry blend enveloping him. "At least we know what the cover-up is all about. Now we just have to find out who is involved. Have you spoken to the director at the Field Research Service in Seattle that did this work? Maybe he can add something to this that will help us out."

"Dr. Walter Davis. He's been missing for two days."

Higgins turned to Parker. "Dammit, have they killed everybody?"

29

THE FLIGHT BACK to Boston had been delayed three hours because of fog, and the Nova didn't pull into the driveway until 6:40 the following morning. Matt had less than an hour to get to school, but he called in sick again. He figured he couldn't make his position with Leach any worse than it already was. He tried to call Danielle, but there was no answer.

He alternated between chills and drenching sweats, and even though he thought he was fighting off a cold, Matt was scared, and for the first time truly afraid that he might die. He took two pain capsules, fell across the bed exhausted, and in seconds was in a deep sleep, ignoring the pain of broken ribs.

The phone awakened Matt from the first sleep he had gotten in more than thirty-six hours. It was Davis calling from Bellingham.

"I think we've found something." There was an excitement to Davis's voice that carried a promise of hope. "We may have found the way the prions are interacting with the leukocytes. If we're right, we may be able to figure out a way to reverse the process."

"Where are you?" Matt asked.

"I'm calling from a friend's apartment in Bellingham. Here's my number in case you have to get in touch with me." Davis read the phone number off to him.

Matt jotted it down. "I've got some news of my own. I

have Vicki James's medical records including her autopsy. I flew to Lexington, Kentucky, last night and took it from the hospital.''

"Nice work," Davis said, "but I don't know what good it will do us now, since I won't get a chance to review it for a while.''

"There's a reporter from *The Washington Post* who might be willing to look into this and help us. Maybe he can find out why the Department of Defense wants all the medical charts.''

"Maybe. Call me after you've talked to the reporter and tell me what happened," Davis said. "I've got a new idea I'm working on at the lab, but I can't go near the place. There have been federal agents asking about me. My assistant is running the tests for me, then he calls from a phone booth so they can't trace the calls and fills me in on the results. We're really walking a tightrope on this. Be careful.''

Davis's warning hung in the air like an evil presence. Matt opened Vicki's medical chart and flipped through the pages of lab tests and progress notes. There must be something important buried among the pages, something nobody was supposed to see.

But what?

Higgins was reviewing classified microfilm of recent expenditures by the Department of Energy when his phone rang.

It was Reintraub and he was furious. "Higgins, I must insist that you stick to your own assignment. If everybody does his job, the situation at Niwot can be adequately contained. This is a complex operation and we can't waste time duplicating someone else's assignment, or going off on some tangent.''

"What are you implying, Mr. Reintraub?" Higgins asked, even though he knew perfectly what had set Reintraub off.

"I'm talking about contacting Strassman at Niwot and your calls to the CDC. That has nothing to do with security. Stick to your assignment and see if you can manage to do it properly."

Higgins knew he was getting close to something sensitive. But as he hung up, something troubled him. How did Reintraub know what he had been doing?

Higgins wondered how far up the cover-up went. Did it go all the way to the White House? Would the White House really be so callous as to attempt a completely "sterile" cover-up?

He didn't think so, but how could he be certain?

30

Matt called Danielle. "Have you heard from Dick?"

"Yes, Dick thinks it would be better if you flew to Washington and told him everything you know so far. He said that if there is any validity to what you claim, this could be a really big story."

"I have something to show him that may help convince him. How soon can he meet with me?"

"I suppose anytime."

"Call him back and tell him I'm leaving for Washington tomorrow morning."

"Tomorrow? You just got back from a trip. Wait a day or two. You need to get some rest."

"There isn't time."

"I'll bring in your mail," Danielle said. "Be careful, and call me when you get there." There was a pause on the phone, then she spoke in a voice filled with concern. "I'm scared, Matt."

"I know." He wanted to tell her that there was more than just the water to worry about, that he was caught in the tangled web of some government cover-up operation that could prove more deadly than leaving town and the water source that was his lifeline, but he couldn't.

Early the next morning he threw some clothes into an overnight bag, then filled two thermos bottles with tap water and packed them carefully among his clothes. He didn't intend to be gone more than a day—two at the most—but he didn't want to take any unnecessary chances. The water supply would give him some leeway if he had to stay longer.

Just as he was leaving, the phone rang. Danielle said that everything was arranged, and Dick Cahill was anxious to talk to him. She gave Matt the address in Georgetown where he was to meet Cahill, then told him to be careful and to let her know how things were going.

He drove to the bank and withdrew the last of his meager savings in cash, then turned the tired Nova toward Boston and Logan International Airport.

In less than two hours he was aboard Flight 138 to Washington, D.C.

At the moment Flight 138 from Boston touched down at Washington National Airport, Harold Wheeler's body was discovered hanging from the stairwell at his home in Loudonville.

Dr. Ebner had been called to the house by a frightened neighbor, Mrs. Willis. Ebner felt an unsettling eeriness as he walked down the hallway, not sure of what he would find. A still, breathless chill greeted him.

Mrs. Willis followed him through the house. Mess and squalor were everywhere, not out of character for Harold Wheeler. A rancid odor came from the end of the hall.

Ebner knew instantly that Wheeler had been dead at least two days. The rope dug deeply into the neck from the weight of his heavy body. Ebner reached up and felt the neck for a carotid pulse, an act that made the body sway slightly on the rope.

"Is he dead?"

"Yes, he's dead."

"Aren't you going to cut him down? Don't seem right to leave him hanging like that."

"It's a coroner's case," Ebner said. "Can't touch the body until the authorities have examined it." But something about it didn't seem right to Ebner. He wasn't the coroner and didn't have to make a ruling, but he had seen two other hangings, and something was different here. Thick phlegm hung between Wheeler's blue lips.

But the glazed eyes that stared out at nothing were sunken into their sockets, not bulging out. The face was drawn and pale, not bloated and purple as it should have been from strangulation.

Ebner looked closer at the heavy body sagging below the rope. There were no rope burns on the neck. In most suicides by hanging, the rope is too short, and as the victim starts to choke, the primitive will to live overtakes the need to die. A desperate struggle ensues as they try to rescue themselves, which they could never do, and they die an agonizingly slow death by strangulation.

Ebner moved up closer and looked at the face. With strangulation, the increased pressure inside the head is tremendous, causing hemorrhage into the brain and delicate membranes behind the eyes, but Harold Wheeler's body showed none of these.

"Something's wrong here," Ebner said in a low voice, talking to himself.

"Yeah, he hung himself. That's pretty obvious, ain't it?" Mrs. Willis looked at him, her eyes wide.

He ignored her crude mannerism. Something was wrong. Harold Wheeler had met a violent death. And it wasn't suicide.

31

After getting a room at the Hotel Lombardy, Matt took a taxi to the coffee shop in Georgetown to meet Dick Cahill. He glanced around and spotted a man sitting in a booth by the window, and as he approached, the man stood.

"Hello. I'm Dick Cahill. Here, have a seat." Cahill was similar in build to Matt.

Matt shook his hand. "Matt Strong. Thanks for finding time to talk to me about this." He glanced around the place as he slid across the vinyl seat.

"Danielle filled me in on the problem you're having at the school with the mice. Maybe something to do with the water? What's this all about?" Cahill asked as he waved for a waitress.

Matt told him about the mice dying in the lab, the people who died of pneumonia when they were out of town, and of his trip to the Niwot Project to get water samples. "I sent mice and water samples to Dr. Davis in Seattle."

"When I mentioned the Niwot Project to Senator Midgley on the phone, it sent him into a tailspin," Cahill said. "What is the Niwot Project?"

"It's a big top-secret project, some kind of new thermo-nuclear reactor that uses hydrogen fusion. And that's why our inquiry about the water has stirred up a lot of activity," Matt said.

Cahill took out a pad and started writing. "What's the name of the man at the CDC who you contacted?"

"Dr. Walter Davis, who's with the Field Research Service, an extension for the CDC in Seattle. But you can't reach him there."

"Why not?"

"He called two days ago and said that someone had ransacked his apartment and his office at the CDC. And all of his records have been sent to Atlanta. He said he had figured out what happened, and that's why they are after him."

"Who?"

"Maybe the Department of Defense, maybe the FBI or CIA. I don't know."

"Why would they want him?" Cahill asked, intensity creeping into his voice.

"Because somebody in Washington doesn't want anyone finding out what's happening in Loudonville. Maybe there's been a mistake, and now there is a cover-up. I sent Dr. Davis a list of ten names of people who had died after leaving town, and now all their charts are missing, confiscated by the government."

"Why? What's in the medical charts?"

"I don't know," Matt said, "but they didn't get all the charts. Here is one I told you about. Maybe you can find something in here that would give us a clue." He pulled out Vicki James's medical records and autopsy report and pushed them across the table to Cahill.

A man in his early twenties wearing white trousers and carrying a black medical bag walked in and slid into the booth beside Dick Cahill. "Sorry I'm late, but I had a new admission to the floor."

Cahill made introductions. "Matt, this is my friend, Dr. Tom Grant. Tom is a resident in internal medicine at George-town University, and I've asked him here to hear your story." Matt leaned across the table and shook hands, then Cahill turned to Grant. "Tom, look at these records and see if you can make anything out of them, anything unusual."

Cahill tried to bring Grant up-to-date on as much as he knew of the situation thus far.

Grant opened the folder and started through Vicki's medical record. "What exactly am I looking for?"

"I don't know," Matt said. "Dr. Davis from the CDC can explain it. He said he had figured out what happened, and that's why they're after him."

Grant shot glances at them, then turned his attention to the chart. When he had finished reviewing it, he opened the autopsy folder. The waitress returned with refills of coffee. Matt drank water from the thermos he'd brought with him. They both looked at him but said nothing. Grant made a few notes and flipped again through the lab reports, then closed the folder.

"Vicki James died of pneumonia, probably staphylococcal. The injuries from being thrown from the horse were incidental. She was already septic when she arrived at the ER. There were a few notes in the progress sheet about their confusion with the case, but no conclusions were drawn. There was nothing in the lab or pathology reports out of the ordinary."

"Was there any mention about the leukocytes? Dr. Davis at the CDC said he'd found something abnormal with the leukocytes of the mice that died."

Grant opened the folder again, read through the pathology reports again, and shook his head. "Sorry, no mention of anything here." He looked at his watch. "Look, I have to run. I wish I could have been more help to you. Good luck." He shook Matt's hand, grabbed his bag, and left.

Matt looked at Cahill. "What do we do next?"

Cahill leaned forward on the table. "Look, this is all very interesting, but I need facts. Specific dates, names, lab reports. And I want to talk to the guy from the CDC."

Matt nodded and sighed. "Well, can you arrange for us to meet with Senator Midgley?"

"Can't do that either—he's out of town."

Matt looked up, surprised to learn that Midgley had left Washington. "When is he due back?"

"Tomorrow."

Matt took the medical records and his thermos and stood

up. "Thanks," he said and turned to leave. "The moment I hear from Davis, I'll have him call you."

"Tell me, how is Danielle?" Cahill asked. "I haven't seen her since I left Boston."

Matt should have been prepared for the question, but the words sent a chill through him. "She's doing fine. Small-town life seems to suit her, and she loves teaching."

Cahill nodded. "Call me when you get something. I've got a few things I can check in the meantime. Where are you staying?"

"At the Hotel Lombardy, room 842."

"How are things going at the lab?" Davis asked.

"Federal agents have been back in twice asking about you." Peter Trent had called Davis from a phone booth so there would be no chance of anyone tracing the call. "They're questioning everyone. I've tried to keep my distance from them."

"I have a new idea I want you to start work on immediately," Davis said and outlined to his assistant exactly what he wanted him to do next. "Keep a close eye on the mice that were shipped to us from New Hampshire," Davis instructed him. "Monitor their blood count and temperatures daily. When they show the first signs of infection, sacrifice them."

"Okay. What tests do you want me to do on them?"

"I need complete immunological profiles, globulin levels, CBC, sed rates, and I want Dr. Morishima to do electron microscopy on the leukocytes. I've called him and he is expecting you.

"Peter," Davis continued, "this is critical if we are going to figure out how to treat this thing. Be careful, and don't talk to anyone about this."

Concord Air Field
Concord, New Hampshire

The fuel truck drove along the tarmac and pulled alongside the twin jet engine Cessna Citation. The driver climbed down and pulled the fuel hose over to the wing tanks and screwed on the nozzle. The truck's tank was marked "GASOLINE" in large red letters, but he pulled the lever and gas started flowing into the jet tanks. As the tanks filled, he glanced around nervously.

The driver took in the graceful lines of the silver Citation with forest-green trim and rich brown leather interior. A beautiful plane, three, maybe four million, he guessed. Too bad he had to trash it.

There were still a few gallons of jet fuel left in each wing tank. That, along with the fuel already in the lines and pumps, would allow enough jet fuel for the power needed during takeoff. But when the two Pratt & Whitney 5-A jet engines called for maximum thrust during the critical part of climb, they would stall and that would be that.

A waste of a perfectly good airplane, he thought. And it would be a "dirty" action, because it would involve a few innocent people. But that couldn't always be avoided.

Matt went back to his room at the Hotel Lombardy. Suddenly, everything seemed bleak. He had struck out. The medical records he had stolen were of no help. He wondered why the government had even bothered with them if there was nothing important in them. And Midgley was out of town. It had been a wasted trip that accomplished nothing.

He picked up the phone and called Danielle.

"Hi, Matt. How are things going? Did you talk to Dick?"

"Yes, he's going to see what he can come up with that may help. But he's not ready to print anything until he gets something more definite to go on."

"When are you coming back?" Danielle asked. "I may have some news for you."

"I'm going to stay over another day and try to talk to Senator Midgley. News about what?"

"It'll keep until I see you. I'm going to cook us a fabulous Thanksgiving meal, so don't make any other plans. Be careful."

The coroner wasn't as observant as Ebner had been, and the limited autopsy on Wheeler that was mandatory in such cases turned up nothing unusual. The heart was normal, the brain showed early lysis and fragmentation of the neurons, and the blood toxicology tests were negative.

The coroner missed the fractured sixth cervical vertebral body of the neck, a full four inches below the rope mark. His report did not detail how Wheeler's head had been viciously wrenched around backward, fracturing the spine. The splintered shards of bone had ripped through the spinal cord, causing immediate death. His murdered body had been strung up by the neck where it would eventually be found and called a suicide. Tidy, clean, quick job.

Harold's jeep had been dismantled, and nothing was found. But before he died, Harold had given them a name, the name of the friend who had brought back his jeep covered with weeds and mud.

"'Alpha' code has been arranged."

"Good." That took Senator Midgley out of the picture. "Just make sure you get the CDC report Midgley had with him. That's classified material. Nobody is to read it."

"We got the name of the man who we think is the primary operative; he is Matt Strong, a high-school teacher. We've got a tap on his phone."

"Code him," Reintraub said.

"He's in Washington," the agent answered.

"What? Find out where he is and who he talked to, then code him. The situation at Niwot has to be contained!" Reintraub's face was contorted in anger as he slammed the receiver down.

The security of the Niwot Project was of paramount importance for the U.S.'s negotiations with the OPEC cartel, as well as his own political future.

Nothing was going to get in the way of either.

32

MATT WAS LEANING over the sink shaving and listening to the news when something on the radio suddenly made his skin prickle. His hands were weak as he turned off the faucet to hear better.

The radio continued, "Senator Donald Midgley of New Hampshire and three of his staff were on their way back to the capital last night when their small plane went down. Senator Midgley was chairman of the powerful Defense Systems Appropriations Committee. He is survived by his wife and . . ."

Matt's razor froze in midstroke as his mind raced. He turned the radio off and sat down on the bed. Midgley was dead and Matt was fast running out of options and ideas.

What if Midgley's death wasn't accidental? Davis had warned Matt that they had stumbled onto something big. How big? How much danger was he in?

He pondered the situation for a minute and tried to think what his next move would be. The trip had been a failure; Cahill wasn't interested in printing the story yet without more details and Midgley was dead. Evans was missing and Davis was in hiding. Having decided that there was nothing else he could do in Washington, Matt checked out of the hotel and took a cab to the airport.

Washington National Airport swarmed with the crush of Thanksgiving holiday travelers. Taxis were lined three abreast and backed up for two blocks, waiting to deliver their fares at the terminals. Inside the airport, airline counters were jammed with people buying tickets. Banks of monitors overhead showed arriving and departing flights, which occurred more than once every minute. The noise inside the crowded airport was deafening, the activity frantic.

Matt purchased a ticket and checked in at the gate. He had more than an hour before his flight back to Boston. After going through the security checkpoint, he headed for a phone booth.

He was glad to hear Danielle's voice again, but what she said was disturbing.

"Listen, Matt, I've got some bad news. Harold Wheeler committed suicide."

"What? How?"

"He hanged himself. They found his body yesterday."

"Why?"

"Why does anybody commit suicide? There's more. Two men showed up at school today asking questions about you."

"Who were they?"

"I don't know. After they left, Mr. Leach called me into his office to find out where you were and to see if I knew anything about what's going on. What *is* going on, Matt?"

"I'm caught in the middle of something big, something that could be dangerous. I'll call as soon as I get home. Be careful, Danielle."

Matt waited in an empty corner of the airport, away from passenger traffic. He slumped back in his seat and wrapped his coat around himself, trying to keep warm. His body was drenched in cold sweat, but he was shaking with chills. His cold was getting worse. He had to get some rest.

Matt closed his eyes. Exhaustion had seeped into the marrow of his bones and drained him of will and resolve. He shifted slightly to east the pain in his side. Broken ribs and bruised muscles ached painfully with each breath. He was cold and shivered uncontrollably. He wanted to go home.

The speakers in the concourse crackled to life: "United Airways Flight 482 to Boston has been delayed indefinitely due to fog. Passengers ticketed on Flight 482 should report to the ticket counter."

But Matt didn't hear the announcement for his flight. His weary, battered body had slipped into a deep overdue sleep. He lay curled under his coat in a dark corner, getting his first real sleep in more than a week, unnoticed by the swarm of travelers.

Four DIA special agents scrutinized the passengers of Flight 482 as they came into the gate area. But the person they were looking for didn't appear. The agents had delayed the flight, but so far, their efforts were wasted.

After two hours of waiting, one of them went to a phone and dialed. "This is Kaufman. We're at Washington National. We delayed the flight and checked all of the passengers, but he's not here."

"What have you found?" Reintraub asked.

"Nothing, sir. But there are agents at all the gates covering flights back to Boston. We'll get him."

Matt woke up, stretched his cramped legs, and went to the ticket counter to cash in his ticket. He headed for the exit. He wasn't going to fly back to Boston yet. There was something important he had to do first. Something was bothering him. Why had Midgley flown to New Hampshire? Who had he met with? Why couldn't his business have been handled by phone? Unless he was delivering something!

Matt left the terminal and walked out into the wet snow, searching among the chaos for an empty taxi.

Reintraub picked up the phone. "Yes, what is it?"

"He was at the airport. He purchased a ticket on United

Airways to Boston, but he never boarded. We're checking everything—both airports, bus stations, car rentals.''

"How did he get through your men?"

The agent detected the anger in Reintraub's voice. "We're not sure. But he must know we're onto him. We'll get him in New Hampshire as soon as he shows up.''

"Don't bother. He's still in Washington. Stay with the phone taps. Wait long enough and he'll tell us where he is, then we'll get him." Reintraub was furious that his agents had let him slip through their fingers so easily. "No more fuckups. Got it?''

"Yes, sir.''

"Find out who Strong has been in contact with in Washington. Check with both *The Washington Post* and also Midgley's appointment book. Let me know the minute he's been coded.''

Deputy Secretary Reintraub slammed the phone down. He wasn't going to let some dumb-ass nosy teacher set the project back. Things were on schedule now and he wanted to keep it that way.

33

MATT TOOK A taxi to the downtown Capitol Hill section and checked into the posh Hyatt Regency. It was expensive, but it was worth the extra cost because of its convenience. Time was a more valuable commodity to him now.

Matt called *The Washington Post* and left a message for Cahill that he would be at the Hyatt Regency for a few days if he needed to get in touch with him. Then he unpacked, took a quick shower, and left. It was 4:10 P.M. and he would have to hurry to get everything done. He stopped first at a "one-hour photos" shop and had two passport-sized shots taken. He paid the five-dollar fee and left.

His next stop was a print shop that displayed fake IDs in the window. He had a card printed up with the name: Michael Woods, U.S. State Department, Special Agent, Intelligence. Matt explained that it was a gag gift, and the woman helping him smiled. He had a duplicate made, glued on his photos, and then laminated them both in plastic.

He had just fifteen minutes before the stores closed and he hurried into a fine men's clothing store on Constitution Avenue. He bought a navy-blue blazer, gray dress slacks, and a maroon tie. His uniform was complete.

Matt went back to his room at the Hyatt Regency and changed into his new clothes, attached one ID to the lapel of his coat, and slipped the second one into the ID case he had purchased, with his photo and name showing through the plastic window.

Just before leaving, he tried to call Danielle but she wasn't home. He left a message on her answering machine with his new phone number at the Hyatt Regency and asked her to call him when she got back. Where had Danielle gone? He wondered what she wanted to tell him. He was afraid it might have to do with her and Dick Cahill.

Matt just wanted to finish what he had to do and get back home.

He set out on foot for the Senate Building just two blocks away. It was past seven P.M. and most of the offices would be closed, but he guessed the staff in Midgley's office would still be there to take care of all the problems that the senator's sudden death must have created. Matt was counting on some degree of turmoil and confusion for his plan to succeed.

Matt went into the Senate Office Building across the street from the U.S. Capitol, looked up Senator Midgley's number on the directory, and went upstairs to the second floor. Inside Midgley's office there was shock and confusion; office personnel were stacking boxes, answering questions for reporters, all the while wondering what would happen next. The death of the chairman of the powerful Defense Appropriations Committee would cause temporary chaos as Washington braced for new power moves.

Matt moved past everyone and approached a woman at the desk. "I'm Special Agent Woods, State Department. I need to speak to Senator Midgley's private secretary immediately." He opened his passport case and flashed his ID at her.

"Mr. Woods," she said as she glanced at his photo, "this is not a good time for us right now. As you can see, we are swamped with phone calls and dozens of unexpected problems, to say nothing of the personal loss the staff is experiencing right now. The earliest we can talk to you will be the first part of next week."

He leaned over the desk and looked her directly in the eye. "That was not a request but an order. This is an urgent state matter and cannot wait. I need to see her now!"

Matt was led past the clutter of boxes, files, reporters, and cameras into a smaller inner office. "Mrs. Steines, this is Special Agent Woods from the State Department to see you on an urgent matter."

Matt stepped forward and tried to sound authoritative. "I'm sorry to bother you now. I know this is an awkward time for all of you, but we have a critical situation on our hands."

She glared at him. "What can I do for you?"

"According to the State Department's information, Senator Midgley flew to New Hampshire to meet with someone at the Niwot Project. What we need to know is who did he meet with, and what was the purpose for his trip?"

She looked at Matt somewhat more suspiciously. "Senator Midgley flew to New Hampshire to meet with Dr. Strassman."

"Dr. Strassman?"

"Dr. Otto Strassman, the director of research at the Niwot Project."

"Do you know why he flew there to meet with him? What was so important that it couldn't be handled by phone?"

She avoided a direct answer. "Why don't you ask Dr. Strassman. I'm sure he could tell you what you need to know."

"What the State Department wants to know is whether the senator took any important papers with him regarding the Niwot Project. We searched the wreckage but no papers were found. This is a matter of some urgency."

"What he was doing was classified and I cannot tell you more than that. As I said, you could ask Dr. Strassman or contact someone at the Centers for Disease Control. Maybe they could help you."

Midgley had been in contact with the CDC!

Matt's mind was spinning with the possibilities and what they meant. Maybe Midgley's death wasn't an accident after all. Maybe he had stumbled onto something and it cost him his life.

"Thank you for your help, Mrs. Steines. I'm sorry to have imposed on you at such a difficult time. Please extend our sympathy to the senator's family." As he turned to leave, he stopped. "One more thing before I go. Could you look up Strassman's phone number for me? That will save me valuable time."

She pulled out a book from her desk and read off the number to him.

"Thank you," he said and left.

Higgins took a decanter from his cabinet and poured himself a Scotch. He offered a drink to Parker, but he declined. Higgins took a drink and walked to the window.

Parker watched and waited in silence. It seemed to him that his old friend was drinking a lot more these days. The current situation was taking its toll on him; the strain showed in his eyes.

Higgins turned toward him. "Reintraub may have inadvertently given us a lead. Somebody from the *Post* contacted Midgley. Find the name of that reporter. Maybe he can shed some light on this mess."

"That isn't going to be as easy as it sounds. It may take me a day or two to find out who the reporter was," Parker said.

Higgins finished his drink and put his glass down. "Frank, we don't have time on our side now. Find him."

Parker hesitated a moment, as if to say something, then nodded and left.

Higgins lit his pipe and stared up at the swirling smoke. He knew there was a cover-up. Who were they protecting? What were they hiding?

Back at his room, Matt pulled out the note with Strassman's number and hesitated. Was Strassman involved in the cover-up or was he, like Midgley, merely an innocent person caught in the ever-increasing tangled web? If Strassman was part of the cover-up, Matt would be playing right into their hands.

But he had to take the gamble. He sat on the edge of the

bed and dialed the number. A deep voice with a thick German accent answered.

"Dr. Strassman, this is Matt Strong from Loudonville, New Hampshire. I know that Senator Midgley met with you before he died. Did he tell you what happened to Loudonville's water?"

"Yes, I did meet with the senator, but what we talked about is quite confidential. Who are you, what do you want? And how did you get this number? It's unlisted."

"Wait!" Matt said when he sensed that Strassman was about to hang up. "Midgley talked to somebody at the CDC and he knew what happened in Loudonville. That's why he came to see you, wasn't it? Dr. Strassman, we need your help. If you told the newspapers or authorities what you knew, they would listen to you. Dr. Evans talked to you about the problem, and now nobody knows where he is. He just disappeared."

"I've already talked to the FBI. But I can't talk to you or anyone else about our work here because it is strictly classified."

Matt was stunned and caught off-guard. Why would the FBI question Strassman? Matt's mind raced over what he had heard. Strassman wasn't part of the cover-up, but how much did he know, and would he help?

Matt knew he was taking a big gamble but felt he had no other choice. "I had an appointment with Senator Midgley for tomorrow. Look, Dr. Strassman, Senator Midgley knew what happened in Loudonville and knew of the government's attempt to cover up the mistake. He was going to expose it when he got back, but he never made it. Whatever Midgley gave you may have cost him his life."

Strassman's next words were unexpected. "The CDC reports have been classified top secret."

"Then you've seen them?"

"Midgley wanted me to look at them to see what I thought, to see if there was any validity to their claim."

"What did you find?" Matt asked excitedly.

"I only glanced at the material, but couldn't make anything out of it. We're physicists, not microbiologists. It's just not our area of expertise. I told the senator to discuss it with the people at the CDC, and he said that was out of the question."

"Why? Why didn't he go to the CDC?"

"I don't know," Strassman said softly.

"Yes you do. It's because somebody in the government wants to keep a lid on this thing. That's why Midgley couldn't go to the CDC. Dr. Strassman, we need those papers. We need your help. The lives of an entire town are at stake."

"I told you. I can't."

Matt screamed into the receiver. "You know what happened to the town. Midgley must have told you."

Strassman mumbled a feeble "Sorry," and hung up.

Matt slammed the receiver down in disgust. He sat back and rubbed his eyes. He was tired and hungry. The last thing he had eaten was a cold plate on the plane. He took a hot shower, then called room service and ordered a medium-rare prime rib, a baked potato, and a bottle of burgundy. After the meal, he stretched out on the bed and fell asleep.

Davis read through the lab results that Trent had sent him. The biological half-life was alarming. The lab animals died in ten days, but the irreversible changes to the leukocytes occurred in half that amount of time. Fear gripped him as he tried to think of how to reverse or slow the lethal clock once set into motion. The town was fast running out of time.

Davis took out the note with Matt's hotel phone number in Washington and dialed.

Matt was curled up on the bed in a sound sleep when the phone rang.

"Matt, this is Walter Davis. I'm afraid I've got some bad news."

Matt didn't think he could take more bad news. He had reached his limit. "What is it?" he asked resignedly.

"We know exactly how the prions kill. Prions bond with proteins in the walls of leukocytes. Prions become absolutely vital to the immune system. But their life-form is very primitive and short-lived. At some point, for whatever reason, they revert to just lifeless chemicals and the cell wall of the leukocyte disintegrates unless there is a constant new supply of prions to form new bonds with the cell walls. Without leukocytes, the victim is left with no immune system, and infection overwhelms the victim before the body's immune system can rebuild itself."

Davis continued, "What we still don't know yet is how to treat it, but we have an idea. And if I'm right, I'll know the answer to that in a few days."

Matt was encouraged. "I'm going to call the reporter from the *Post* and tell him we're getting closer to an answer on this thing."

"As soon as I get the results of the tests, I'll fly to Washington and we can both talk to the reporter. Once this thing comes out in the press, we'll get action on it. And once this mess hits the news, we can breathe a lot easier. There's nothing they can do to us then."

"How soon can you get here?" Matt asked.

"This is the bad news. Listen to me, Matt. You can't stay longer than two more days, do you understand? The actual half-life for humans appears to be less than two weeks, but there are irreversible changes in the leukocytes that occur even sooner. You've got to get back."

When Matt hung up, he walked to the window and ran his fingers through his hair as he looked out over the city. If he stayed in Washington too long, he would die. And if he flew home, there were federal agents looking for him. He was trapped and running out of time. Every move had to be carefully thought out and well executed.

Some Thanksgiving. He wanted to be home with Danielle, eating turkey. Not really much he could think of to be thankful of at the moment.

• • •

The phone rang and Higgins answered it. It was Parker.

"I have the name of the reporter who contacted Midgley. He's Dick Cahill, a reporter for *The Washington Post*."

"Let's go see him. Meet me there in twenty minutes." Higgins hung up and arranged for a car out front, but without a driver. He didn't want anyone else involved at this point. He grabbed his coat and left.

Higgins wove the car expertly through Washington's crowded evening traffic as he raced toward the *Post* building. Why had the reporter called Midgley? What did he know about this whole damned affair?

Higgins and Parker showed their IDs to the guards in the lobby of *The Washington Post* and then took the wide marble stairs to the second floor. They spoke briefly to someone on the floor and were directed to Cahill's desk.

The newsroom was a gigantic room filled with rows of desks, word processors, fax machines, phones, mail carts, and general chaos as another day of news in the nation's capital went to press. They walked down a cluttered aisle to a desk where a young man sat studying a computer screen.

"Dick Cahill?"

"Yes," he said, turning around. "Can I help you?"

"FBI," Higgins said, flashing his ID. "Could we speak with you in private?"

Cahill took them into a small conference room cluttered with a coffee machine, stacks of foam cups, and boxes of sugar packets. "Now, what can I do for you?" he asked them, nervously shifting in his chair.

"We understand you made a phone call to Senator Midgley's office, inquiring about the Niwot Project. Is that correct?"

Cahill was clearly stunned and caught off guard by their question. He stammered for a moment, then said, "Yes, that's correct."

"What was your interest in the Niwot Project? How did you learn of the project?" Higgins asked.

"I'm not required to divulge the sources who provide information to us."

Higgins closed the door to the small conference room, then moved close to him, put his hand firmly on his shoulder, and said, "Listen, this is not an ordinary story we're talking about here. We're trying to stop a lot of innocent people from being hurt, and you may be able to help us. Now, just what the *hell* do you know about the Niwot Project?"

34

MATT OPENED HIS second thermos and poured the last of his water into a glass and held it up to the light. It was clear. He drank it and tasted only water. Nothing else. But he knew that with the last swallow, his own life was draining away. That was the last of the water that had been both his salvation and his death warrant. He put the empty glass down and felt a chill slide through his body.

He hadn't planned on staying in Washington more than an overnight. Davis's warning stayed in the room like an intruder, constantly facing him, not letting him forget the danger. An invisible doomsday ticking clock inside his body had been set into motion with his last drink of the life-sustaining water. Matt knew he had to get back to Loudonville soon; without water, he would be dead in less than three weeks.

Matt punched his fist in anger. He had to convince Strassman to help him. He picked up the phone and dialed.

"Dr. Strassman, this is Matt Strong. I just talked to Dr. Davis from the CDC. He's working as fast as he can to figure out exactly what happened to the town and how to prevent any more deaths, but somebody in Washington is trying to stop him. We need your help. Would you at least talk to a reporter from *The Washington Post*—off the record—and tell him what you know?"

"You know I can't do that. The project is strictly

classified and is too important to jeopardize. Besides, they're watching every move I make."

Matt shouted into the phone. "Dr. Evans and Senator Midgley were probably both killed because of a cover-up of some mistake that happened. Dr. Davis's life is in danger, and an entire town is doomed to die! Is your damned project important enough to kill an entire town?"

After a long, silent pause Strassman spoke.

"There might be a way we could do something," Strassman said. "I could authorize to have the tests repeated at the CDC labs and see what they say."

"There isn't time! To duplicate all the work that Davis has done would take weeks and cost more lives."

Strassman spoke in a soft voice, almost a whisper, and the words sent a shiver up Matt's spine. "You should know one thing: they want you. You're the last thing in their way. But I might be able to help you. After this, though, you're on your own. I can't do anything else. Give me your phone number."

Strassman called five minutes later from a phone booth. He had papers that confirmed that Deputy Secretary Reintraub and the Department of Defense knew about the situation in Loudonville, documents that proved there had been a cover-up. "It's not possible for us to meet," Strassman said. "Security here's been turned up, and they're watching me constantly. Do you know where the old All Saints Church is?"

"The old stone church at the top of the mountain outside of Loudonville?" Matt said.

"Yes. I'll leave the papers there," Strassman said. "Listen carefully." He proceeded to give Matt specific instructions.

Matt hung up and sat for a moment while he tried to formulate a plan. Strassman said that Deputy Secretary of Defense James Reintraub was in charge of the Niwot Project, and knew of the situation in Loudonville. He was a part of the cover-up. Matt called Davis and told him what had happened.

"Great! Good work, Matt. You stay where you are," Davis said. "It'll be safer for you. I'll fly to Boston, rent a car, and drive to the old church and get the papers. Then I'll fly to Washington and we'll talk to the reporter. Our problem now isn't prions, it's with the Department of Defense. We'll get this whole damn thing out in the open and finally get somebody to do something."

Matt gave him Danielle's phone number in case he needed help while he was there. Then he called Danielle and filled her in on everything, telling her every detail of the plan, and instructed her to wait by the phone. If Davis had problems or didn't make it, she would have to get the papers.

"Matt," Danielle said, her voice pleading. "We shouldn't be doing this. It's too dangerous. Call the police or some-body."

"There's nobody to help us now. Until we get the story to the papers and go public with it, we're on our own."

"Matt, I love you." She was sobbing.

"I love you, too, Danielle. Don't worry, everything's going to work out fine."

But he wasn't sure. He stared at the empty thermoses and hoped Davis and his assistant would find an answer soon. He went to the window and looked out over the city. On the street below he caught sight of Dick Cahill walking toward the hotel with two other men.

Who were they? Matt paced the floor while he tried to decide what to do. What was going on? Why hadn't Cahill called first to tell him what was happening? He went to the window again, but they had already entered the hotel. He decided he couldn't risk waiting around to find out.

He stuffed his clothes and toiletries into his suitcase, looked around the room one more time, then turned out the lights. He opened the door, checked to see that the hallway was empty, then left. He decided against using the elevators since someone might be waiting for him in the lobby. He ran to the end of the hall, opened the door marked "Exit," and started down the stairs.

The steel fireproof door slammed shut behind him with a metallic explosion that rolled off the cavernous cement hollow of the stairwell and echoed back in waves. He stopped for a minute until it was quiet to listen. When he was sure he was alone, he ran down the ten flights of stairs, opened the service door at the bottom, and found himself outside the back of the hotel. He went down the dark alley and melted into the night.

35

EARLY THE NEXT morning with only the first faint hue of orange on the horizon, Strassman drove out the security gate at the Niwot Project and turned south on state route 129. He passed a Christmas tree lot, with newly cut pine trees still stacked in bundles.

As he maneuvered the car through the hills of New Hampshire, he thought about how politics always seemed to be changing the course of his life. His mind flashed back to Germany.

As a young, brilliant scientist caught up in a war he didn't understand, Strassman had grown tired of stale Nazi propaganda and wearied of the war that threatened to destroy Germany. He became a bitter, disillusioned man, and when the Gestapo came during the night and took away Rachel Juditz, a young Jewish assistant with whom he had fallen in love, Strassman knew he had to escape. While avoiding the security police, he boarded a train for Bonn, then fled over the mountains to Belgium, taking with him his notes on hydrogen.

Now, more than forty-five years later, he found himself again caught in a web of political deceit; he always seemed to be in conflict with evil people, driven by greed.

But this morning he was about to do something about it.

He had made the fifty-mile trip to the old church every month for the past year since his wife died. He had chosen the place for a reason. He visited the grave often to be alone with his thoughts, so it seemed the most logical and safest place for him to go now without arousing suspicion. But this time he brought more than flowers. An unmarked sealed folder lay on the seat beside him.

Ten minutes after leaving the compound, he pulled into a gravel driveway and waited. After making sure that no one had followed him, he pulled back onto the highway and continued south.

A one-hour drive through the winding hills brought him to the old graveyard where his beloved Gretta was buried. There were a few hundred graves, but less than a dozen were recent.

All Saints Church and cemetery had been built on the bluff more than a century ago overlooking the New Hampshire community of Loudonville. A larger cathedral had been built in town years ago to accommodate the growing parish. Now the ornate old stone church was deserted. Only the cemetery was still used occasionally.

After delivering flowers to her grave, he took the folder and slipped quietly into the church. He finished his task in the dark abandoned building where life and death were now entwined by a bizarre twist of fate.

The sky grew dark and the temperature dropped as a wicked-looking storm raced out of the north. By the time Strassman arrived back at the entrance gate at the Niwot Project the sky opened up and a torrential rain beat the ground.

After parking outside his apartment, he climbed out of his car and stood for a moment, looking up into the cold rain as it beat against his face. It felt good. A cleansing of the soul.

It was well after midnight when Matt checked into a cheap, run-down hotel built beside an all-night convenience store. He decided it would be too risky to use one of his credit cards to pay for a room, so he paid cash for two nights, which left him with only a few dollars.

The place was dark and dingy, the carpet worn and

frayed, but at least he had a place to sleep. Matt cracked the window for some fresh air and lay across the bed for a night of troubled sleep, alone in the city with his water supply gone, and temporarily out of contact with everyone, since they only had his phone number back at the Hyatt Regency. Cahill couldn't have mucked things up at a more critical time.

Matt realized he had left his pain capsules back in the other room, and cursed the damned reporter under his breath as he sought to get relief from the constant throbbing of broken ribs.

The following morning, his mood soured after a miserable night, he called Cahill at the *Post*. "What was going on last night? Who were those people you brought to the hotel? Why didn't you call first?"

"Where the hell were you?" Cahill shot back. "They were FBI."

"FBI? Are you crazy? Did you decide to turn me in just to get a good story?"

"Mr. Higgins is the director of the Counter-Intelligence Division of the Bureau and he wants to talk to you. Your life may be in danger, and he says they may be the only people who can help you. Where are you now?"

"Never mind where I am," Matt said. He already knew his life was in danger; both Davis and Strassman had told him that. At the moment Matt didn't trust Cahill any further than he could throw him. But he still needed Cahill's help to get the story to the press. "Listen, I've got something for you. We're about to break this thing wide open. Davis from the CDC is flying here to talk to you, and he's bringing documents that prove there was a cover-up operation by the government. You'll have enough to print the story."

"Don't be stupid!" Cahill screamed into the phone. "You can't do this by yourself. There's more to it than you realize. You'll get yourself killed and accomplish nothing."

Matt froze a moment. What else was going on that Cahill was involved in? "I'll call you as soon as Davis gets here,"

Matt said. "Maybe then you can arrange some kind of meeting with Higgins, but not until Davis gets here."

"Look," Cahill said, "if you change your mind, at least give Higgins a call and talk to him. There's no risk in that." Cahill gave him the number and hung up.

Matt next called Danielle to give her his new phone number so she could call if anything came up. He decided not to tell her why he changed hotels, choosing instead to tell her it was more convenient for his purposes.

"When are you coming home?" she asked with growing desperation in her voice.

"Two days, three at the most," Matt said. He knew that was all the time he had anyway. If he didn't finish this mess and get back by then it would be too late anyway. "Just wait by the phone today in case Davis calls and needs your help."

"Mr. Leach called me into his office yesterday. You've been suspended without pay until you can meet with the school board to discuss all the unexcused absences. I tried to tell him that something very important had come up, but he wouldn't listen. He said federal agents were investigating you. Until he knows what you're involved in, you're suspended."

"Well, that's something I'll have to deal with later. I'll call you when Davis gets here."

He'd spent the last of his savings, he was out of a job, and he was fighting an uphill battle for his life against some kind of prehistoric life form. And now the FBI wanted him. Why?

He had to get some answers.

Matt took off his watch and set the stopwatch. Then he dialed the number Cahill had given him and was put through to Higgins immediately. "This is Matt Strong. What I want to know is why the hell you bother to send agents around investigating me? I haven't done anything wrong."

"You should turn yourself in before you get hurt,"

Higgins said. "There's been too much hurt and killing already. I can help you."

"Why waste your time on me? I haven't done anything. What about the town? You assholes, you're killing the whole damn town!"

"Listen to me, son," Higgins said with a tone to his voice that turned Matt's blood cold. "Those agents looking for you weren't FBI. They were DIA—Defense Intelligence Agency—and they intend to kill you."

Matt slammed the receiver down. Thirty-five seconds. Not enough time to trace his call. The words *"they intend to kill you"* stuck in his head.

That, along with something about his conversation with Strassman, haunted him. His mind replayed the conversation over again and again. What was it he had heard?

Then it hit him, he stopped in his tracks and his knees went weak. There had been a faint extra click on the phone after Strassman hung up. And he'd heard the same sound the last two times he'd called Danielle.

What if their phones were tapped? He didn't think so, but he couldn't take a chance. Matt's heart leaped into his throat when he thought of the consequences.

That meant somebody else knew details of the plan for Davis to get the incriminating documents from Strassman. Davis could be walking into a trap! Danielle would have to drive up and warn him. Matt reached for the phone.

Her line was busy. He hung up and dialed again to make sure he had the right number. Still busy. Matt called the operator and asked that they cut in and put his call through since it was a life and death emergency.

After a series of clicks as the operator tried to cut in, a busy tone sounded. "Just a minute," the operator said in a soft voice. She tried again and got another busy signal. "Sir, that number is out of service."

"What? It can't be. I just spoke to someone at this number."

"The line has been disconnected. I'll call repair and see if they have a report of any service interruption."

Matt hung up. Danielle was in danger and there was nothing he could do to warn her. And he had sent Davis into a trap and didn't know how to stop him.

Matt went to the sink and splashed cold water onto his face. He was fatigued, his chest throbbed, and his eyes stung. He looked into the mirror and staring back at him was a haggard man with a stubbly beard, the face aged and the eyes dark. It was the look of a defeated man. Matt didn't know if he was dying or just worn out. The problem was too big for him. They had won.

He'd already decided what his next move would be. He hoped it wouldn't be his last.

36

New Hampshire

A DRIVING RAIN fell with a vengeance and hammered the windshield. The windshield wipers batted ineffectively at the streaming sheet of water, and visibility was poor as gusts of wind whipped the rain across the road in dense sheets. Walter Davis fought both the storm and his mounting anxiety. The radio mentioned showers but had not predicted the deluge he found himself in now.

The old dirt road that led from town to the top of the bluff had become a murky stream that twisted upward through a dense woods. All signs of autumn were gone now and only the gray void that preceded winter remained. The torrential storm blotted out the fading afternoon light, and barren trees turned black by rain were dark skeletons towering beside the road.

Leaning over the dashboard Davis stared intently at the muddy road and wiped again at the condensation that stubbornly re-formed on the glass. The rented Ford suddenly lurched and slid sideways on the steep incline as the wheels spun in the mud. His sweaty hands gripped the steering wheel tighter.

"Goddam pain-in-the-ass car!" His mood was sour. Thanksgiving weekend, and he was spending it alone in some godforsaken place, risking his life. His life had been turned upside down and it seemed very probable that somebody was trying to kill him.

Davis struggled up the treacherous route that finally

leveled off on a broad stretch of winding road. Another
quarter of a mile it turned abruptly up into a clearing at the
top of the hill. Out of the mist a tall, dark apparition slowly
materialized in the distance as the car crept forward.

He drove within a hundred feet and stopped. He killed the
engine and peered through the rain-streaked window at the
eighteenth-century stone church. He felt a shudder of
apprehension.

Davis cracked the window a few inches to listen, straining his ears to hear something—anything—beyond the
storm. Only an occasional rumble of thunder and the
staccato drumming of rain on the car roof filled the fading
afternoon. The place appeared deserted. Rain blew through
the window and soaked him. His eyes stung and he wiped at
them as he tried to peer through the downpour to assure
himself that he was alone.

Davis struggled to quell his uneasiness. He was irritated
at his own timidity. No one would think to look in this
unlikely setting. A shiver rippled through his shoulders. He
was cold and scared. Something didn't feel right.

His eyes searched the gloom. Dark vertical forms protruded from the cemetery, all but obscured by the dismal
mist of rain splattering off the tombstones. A deserted
rectory sat directly behind the chapel. The front door of the
rectory gaped open, probably blown by the wind, he
thought.

The remoteness of this place was unsettling and he could
see why Strassman had chosen it.

The dark stone church seemed to loom more menacingly
as the storm intensified and darkness grew deeper. Its
silhouette stood out boldly with the next blinding flash of
lightning. The tall steeple cut into the black clouds.

He had to get the documents.

The lightning intensified. Brilliant terrifying bolts came
in quick succession. Double, triple loud cracks, each flash
showing the low angry clouds and trees blowing violently in
the wind. Davis looked around again, pulled up the collar of

his coat, and ducked into the storm. He ran toward the church and leaped up the three steps into the protective arch over the double oak doors. Water poured off the tile roof and drenched him.

He grabbed the cold bronze latch and shoved. The door opened with a reluctant groan and he entered. Rain pelted against the slate roof and stained-glass windows. The sound wasn't loud but came from every direction, muffled and echoing through the empty structure. Damp musty air hung thick inside the church. Davis thought it was an awful place to be in a storm; a mildewed monument to the past and the dead. He stood silently and waited.

When his eyes adapted to the darkness he stepped from the vestibule into the sanctuary and surveyed the dusky interior of the old building. Graceful nave arches rose above the pews and massive truss beams spanned the cavernous ceiling. An altar sat on the platform across the front. Mute carved statues seemed to hover in the shadows at the sides of the altar and a large crucifix floated in front. Figures cut in stained glass burst to life surrealistically during a flash of lightning.

His footsteps resonated crisply on the cold marble floor. He turned again toward the vestibule and noted a choir loft upstairs. He wiped his dripping hair back from his forehead and stepped back into the entry. A narrow, wooden stand held a thick book containing the burial records of the community for nearly a century. The green cloth binding showed its age with water stains and worn, frayed corners. A tarnished brass chain secured it to the wall.

The book that chronicled death ironically now also held the last hope of life for the small town, because the documents were hidden within its covers.

The book was heavy. He opened the cover and thumbed carefully through the brittle pages. It was empty—there was no envelope! He nervously thumbed through it again. It had to be there! He held it upside down and shook the pages apart. The overwhelming musty odor of mildew poured from the pages.

His fingers froze. Above the sound of the storm he thought he heard something. A shuffle, a footstep maybe; he wasn't sure. His breathing stopped a moment as he directed his senses toward the source of the noise. A chilling knot formed in the pit of his stomach. What had he heard? Merely a piece of tile giving away? He listened but heard only the pebbling of the rain on the roof. He breathed deeply and returned to the book.

Several pages were stuck together with the back cover into a thick, unbending mat. He tried to pry the stuck pages apart, but they were fused solid. He examined the water-soaked papers carefully. On closer inspection a telltale drop of dried glue oozed along the edge. The smell of glue was fresh.

The back pages had been cut out and glued together to hold the papers. Strassman was a clever and cautious man. On casual inspection no one would notice. Davis opened his pocket knife and started to cut along the back cover.

There! He heard it again. It wasn't his mind playing tricks on him this time. It came from the balcony overhead.

He wasn't alone!

Impulsively he grabbed the thick book, braced a foot against the wall, and yanked. Plaster exploded across the vestibule as he lurched backward with the book, its chain still attached and dangling with a piece of wall. He shoved it under his coat and lunged for the door.

Davis threw open the door, then froze in disbelief.

There was one last desperate thing Matt could do to try and save Danielle and Davis. He was going to turn himself in to Higgins and the FBI. But it would be on his terms.

Matt reached for the phone. He needed Cahill's help. Matt had no choice but to trust him. "Dick, I'm going to turn myself in to the FBI. I want you to arrange it, and I want you to be there to record everything that happens."

''Why the sudden change of heart?'' Cahill asked.

''I think Danielle and Davis are in serious danger and this may be our only chance to help them. Davis may be walking into a trap. They'll kill him to get those documents back. But I have a plan.''

''I'll arrange it,'' Cahill said. ''So what's your plan?''

A flash of lightning revealed a black sedan parked by the cemetery gate. They were waiting for him. He had been followed! Davis ran back down the aisle through the sanctuary, stumbled on the altar steps in the dark, and careened into a votive light stand. Glass splintered across the marble floor with a high-pitched tinkling sound. Footsteps hammered down the stairs from the balcony and echoed through the darkness.

Davis ran to the wall behind the altar, frantically searching for another exit. Nothing. Why hadn't he gone out the front door when he had the chance?

He ran to the side of the sanctuary and ducked behind the first pew. He sprawled beneath it and crawled as quietly as possible on the cold floor under the benches toward the rear of the church. The silhouetted dark form of a man rushed past him down the center aisle.

Silence. Prey and hunter listened.

Davis slowly raised his head, but from his crouched position he couldn't see over the wooden benches. As he worked his way under the next pew, the kneeler dropped onto his right shoe. He reached back and pulled his foot out, but the shoe was caught. He knew he couldn't make it back to the front door this way. He was trapped and defenseless.

He sucked in a deep breath and scrambled silently to the end of the bench. As quiet as a shadow, he faded into the dark recess of one of the two arched confessionals that lined the wall. His heart raced and his pulse pounded in his temples. He crouched on his heels, tensed and ready to spring as he peered out from the opening of his small protective grotto. Who was it? Who could possibly have known?

The sight of his apartment and of Dusty lying dead flashed in his mind. An icy fear gripped him.

Stagnant, musty air caught in his throat. He gulped in deep breaths, but the feeling that he was being smothered wouldn't go away. His skin was cold and clammy. He gripped the thick journal against his chest, and the chain made a faint rattle.

A flashlight snapped on; its shaft of light swept over the altar. The beam shortened as its arc moved slowly toward the confessionals. With the next bolt of lightning Davis caught sight of the man just as he was turning toward him. For just a split second during the flash, the man looked directly at him. Davis stiffened and braced his hands on the walls in order to lunge for escape. He froze as the light swept over him and moved on.

He hadn't been spotted.

The light disappeared for a second and reappeared on the other wall. Gilded icons flickered to life as the light slid over them. Then the beam lit something far more interesting: a door behind one of the supporting columns. An escape route. The flashlight receded back to the vestibule. Davis felt a sudden cold draft and knew that the front door had opened, then closed with a dull thud. Had the man left—or had someone else joined him? Davis had to get out. He stooped down and slid along noiselessly between the pews until he reached the center aisle. He crouched and waited. His timing had to be perfect.

A split second after the next flash of lightning, he dropped to his stomach and shimmied across. With one hand he clutched the book that shifted constantly under his raincoat. He crossed the next row of pews and crawled to the side door. He reached up and felt for the handle. His hand grabbed a metal bolt slide. The bolt squeaked as he slid it back.

A beam of light instantly focused on him.

Davis leaped up and slammed into the door with his shoulder, but it didn't budge. Lack of use and rust had sealed it closed. Footsteps tore down the aisle toward him. He braced himself against a pillar and kicked out with both feet. He kicked again.

Grudgingly the door yielded. He pushed through it and dashed back out into the rain. Mud sucked at his stockinged foot as he splashed toward the car.

He threw the journal onto the front seat beside him, jumped in, and slammed the door. Through the rivers of water on the window he could see a blurred figure and bobbing flashlight closing on him fast.

"Damn!" His hand trembled as he fumbled for the key he'd left in the ignition. His stockinged foot slipped on the unfamiliar contours of the accelerator. The engine coughed once, then died. "Please, come on!"

Davis twisted the key again and the engine roared to life. A dark figure loomed near the window. Hands tore at the handle. He jammed the car into gear when he saw a gun come out of the coat, kicked down the accelerator, and spun away. Glancing in the rearview mirror he saw the figure and small beam of light disappear behind him in the driving rain.

He wrestled the Ford down the twisting muddy road at speeds that threatened disaster. His body was numb with fear. He glanced constantly back in the mirror, afraid of finding headlights behind him.

With one steel-wrenching bounce, the Ford careened onto the main highway, and he turned toward town. He punched at the steering wheel in disgust as his mind raced over what to do next.

37

MATT ARRIVED AT the small diner on the corner of 19th and
M Street, as arranged. He stood across the street and waited,
trying to convince himself that he had no other alternative.

The dark streets seemed particularly dismal. A cold rain
mixed with snow fell on the thinning traffic that splashed
by. Christmas shoppers were passing by, while others were
going home after another day of work. For them life was
routine and predictable. On the corner outside the diner a
gaunt-looking man was hunched inside his soaked Santa
Claus costume, ringing his brass bell as people rushed past
him with barely a glimpse.

A courier on a bicycle with a package strapped to his
back threaded his way through the traffic with a reckless
disregard for danger. He pulled his bike onto the sidewalk,
and leaned it against the building while he went inside to
make a delivery.

Matt crossed the street, walked past the Santa, and
stepped into the small diner, shook the water off his coat,
and walked to the booth beside the window.

Cahill stood up as he approached and made introductions.
"Matt, this is Lee Higgins, section chief of the Counter-
Intelligence Division of the FBI." Higgins was a short,
white-haired man who was smoking a pipe. Matt thought his
most striking feature were his piercing steel-gray eyes.

"Sit down," Higgins said and went about lighting his
pipe with slow deliberation.

Matt took a seat beside Cahill. "What's your interest in me? I haven't done anything except try to find out why people in Loudonville are dying."

"Two reasons. First, we're concerned for your own safety. Second, the security of the Niwot Project. The entire future of our country may hang in the balance."

"You fucking sons of bitches are letting an entire town die, then killing anyone who finds out that you made a mistake because you want to hide it."

"Are you done? You're quite right, you know. Everything you said is true, but only to a point." Higgins leaned across the table, his steel-gray eyes steady and trustworthy. "We don't want to kill anyone, but we can't do anything about saving the town until we get to the bottom of the cover-up and get the executive action order canceled."

Matt felt the blood drain from his head. He stared into the gray eyes, looking for some clue, trying to read the man. "You can start by calling off your agents and making sure nothing happens to Dr. Davis."

Higgins showed sudden concern. "You mean Dr. Walter Davis from the CDC? We don't know where he is. We've been trying to contact him to find out what he knows about the CDC's interest in the Niwot Project."

Matt sneezed and reached for a Kleenex. He was drenched in sweat and his body showed the strain and lack of sleep for the past week.

Higgins handed Matt a glass of water. "Son, you're not looking too good. I want you to see a doctor, then we'll keep you in protective custody." Higgins continued, "I have every reason to believe there is a high-level cover-up. I don't know yet who all is involved. We'll have to move cautiously."

"There's not time!" Matt shot back at him.

"I didn't say slowly, I said cautiously." Higgins addressed both Cahill and Matt. "With help from both of you, I think we can break this thing wide open."

Outside a car skidded to a halt. The doors flew open and

three men rushed into the diner. They ran over to the table and pulled Matt roughly out of his seat. "What's going on here?" Matt looked at Higgins.

Higgins started to stand but a powerful hand pushed him back into his seat. Higgins's face showed anger and confusion. "Leave him alone. He's in my custody now. I'm responsible for bringing him in."

"He's in our custody now. He's going with us. The DIA will handle it from here."

Matt turned and looked at Cahill, his eyes darting to another man sitting at a booth by himself. Cahill barely nodded. He caught Matt's signal, he understood what to do.

Outside the diner, Cahill rushed between the agents and the car and shoved a microphone in their faces while the other man moved up with a camera and snapped off three quick pictures. The agent with his hand on the door handle turned and bellowed out angrily, "Hey! No pictures. Get back out of the way."

"This is for *The Washington Post,*" Cahill said. "Does this have to do with the Niwot Project and a reported cover-up?"

The agent's face showed confusion and anger. "No pictures, you prick! Give me the camera. This matter is classified."

"Not anymore," Cahill said and stepped back out of reach as they grabbed for the microphone. The agents then lunged for the camera. At that moment, Matt drove a vicious kick into the shin of the agent holding him and broke free of the viselike grip on his arm. After sprinting across the street, he leaped onto the bicycle the courier had parked there and raced down the street into oncoming traffic.

The agents jumped into their car. Tires screeched in protest as the sedan spun around in pursuit of him. Matt pedaled furiously through traffic, swerving between buses and taxis, dodging pedestrians.

Matt glanced back and caught sight of the sedan weaving recklessly through traffic after him, but they were losing ground fast. While the bike cut and weaved like a snake between cars and taxis, and edged alongside buses, the black government Chevrolet slowed as traffic congested, then Matt lost sight of it.

At the next intersection, Matt ignored a red traffic light and turned south onto Connecticut Avenue. He pulled alongside a city bus, a dangerous maneuver because the driver didn't know he was there, making him harder to spot in traffic.

The bus turned onto 17th street, and after one block made a right turn, heading west on I Street. Matt was busy avoiding cars and staying with the bus and didn't notice the sedan swerve out of a side street and pull up beside him.

He caught sight of it out of the corner of his eye and squeezed the brakes desperately just as the car swerved into the bus in an attempt to crush him between the two vehicles. The sedan sideswiped the bus, sending sparks flying as metal ripped into metal with a screeching sound. The bus crumpled the side of the sedan, causing it to swerve wildly out of control into a car on the other side.

Matt was showered with broken glass. His front tire just missed the rear bumper of the car as the bike skidded to the pavement. Matt leaped to his feet again, righted the bike, and raced up Pennsylvania Avenue, risking death as he wove through traffic.

Two blocks later, he pulled up onto the sidewalk, jumped off, and left the bike leaning beside a parking garage. Matt ran through the parked cars and out the back into an alley, knowing he had escaped but had failed in his attempt to help Davis or Danielle.

38

Davis was not familiar with the area and had made a wrong turn. Glancing at the map, he tried to figure out where he was. The hilly, winding road should eventually lead him to Interstate 93, which would take him to Boston. The rain had stopped, but following the unfamiliar narrow road at night was difficult.

The next sharp turn brought him fact-to-face with flashing crossing lights and a long freight train. Davis stopped, turned on the overhead light inside the Ford, and took the opportunity to look at the material Strassman had left inside the journal.

He opened his pocketknife and ran the blade along the glued edge, and pulled a folder out of the back cover. He glanced through several pages. There were memos from both the Centers for Disease Control and the Department of Defense, and summary sheets of his own findings that he had telexed to Atlanta. Then he opened a large folded sheet.

He whistled under his breath. It was a detailed spec sheet and technical diagram of the monstrous Tokomak fusion reactor. The drawing showed the massive magnetic ring with laser guns aimed at its target in the center of hydrogen plasma. Strassman had risked everything—the project, his career—in order to save the town.

Davis was absorbed in the material. He didn't see the car that pulled up behind him. The loud *clack-clack* of steel wheels on rail blanketed all other sound.

The car banged the rear of the Ford. The sharp blow from behind startled him. Davis opened his door and jumped out.

He was instantly aware of his mistake.

Two men had already gotten out of the black sedan. In the headlights of their car, Davis could see them clearly. The man closest to him pulled a gun from his trench coat, and Davis stared into the barrel of a Bren 10mm automatic.

There was no hesitation, no waiting, no pleading. The gun kicked twice and spit fire in quick succession.

Davis felt himself slam against the open car door. There was no pain, just a crushing pressure, like a massive hand squeezing the life from his body. He opened his mouth, but his breath was gone.

In the last second of his life he realized he had failed. It was over for him; in the short space of one second of consciousness, his mind raced over the things he had wanted to do, things he would not get the chance to do. It made him angry. His vision dimmed and narrowed to a small dark, blurred spot. His face clouded as his paralyzed mind seemed unable to visualize the inevitable.

When the back of his head hit the pavement, he was already dead.

39

DANIELLE ADJUSTED THE temperature of the water and stepped into the shower. She shampooed her hair, then lathered her body. The steaming spray felt good, and for the moment she pushed all the problems from her mind.

She had wanted to tell Matt, but she couldn't. He had too much to worry about now. And it was not something she wanted to tell him over the phone.

Danielle cocked her head and listened, aware of something different, a sound or a draft, but after a few seconds of listening decided it was nothing. She finished by rinsing her hair with Clairol conditioner, then turned off the water. She stood dripping in the shower, listening, but heard nothing. The apartment was quiet.

She stepped out, took a towel from the rack, and started drying herself. A cold draft raised goose bumps on her wet skin and made her shiver. She noticed the bathroom door was halfway open. She thought she had closed it. She always closed the bathroom door before she showered. It was a ritual she faithfully performed even when she was alone, ever since she had seen *Psycho*.

She wrapped the towel around her hair and walked into the bedroom.

She stiffened and her breath caught in her throat. Two men stood back in the shadows of the dark corner of her bedroom, watching her. Their presence was an evil that moved over her and a gut-wrenching fear grew within her as she felt her head go faint.

They stepped toward her, into the light.

"Who are you?" Danielle demanded, suddenly very aware of her nakedness.

Their eyes widened as they looked at her. Beads of water sparkled from the light of the bathroom, clinging to her skin and running down her breasts in little rivulets.

She took a step back, pulled the towel from her head, and wrapped it around her body saronglike. The stares of the two men never faltered. "Who are you?" she asked again. She cupped her hands across her chest. "I'm expecting a friend any minute, so you'd better get out."

One man stepped up to her. "Miss Carter, we're agents with the DIA," and he pulled a wallet from his pocket and flipped his ID at her. "We have some important questions to ask you."

Danielle felt her knees go weak. Her mind was numb with fear as she tried to size up the situation. "How did you get in here? What do you want?"

The man held her robe out for her. "Get dressed. We've got a lot to talk about."

She reached out for the robe. She felt the tension of their maleness, of her nakedness, of her own vulnerability as prey. "Do you have a search warrant for being here?"

"Joe, go down and lock the front door and turn off the lights downstairs. This may take some time," and he smiled as he turned back to Danielle. "You may leave your robe on—for now." He pushed a chair toward her. "Sit down," he said. The tone of his voice carried a threat that didn't escape her.

She took a step back. "Just give me a second. I have to use the bathroom," and she closed the door matter-of-factly and snapped the lock. Her whole body began to shake with fear. She turned on the water in the sink, then turned and slammed the heel of her hand against the tiny window above the shower, forcing it open. She knew it was more than twenty feet to the ground outside.

Fortunately there wasn't time to worry about it. She knew that within seconds the door would be kicked open and they would be on her. Only her flexibility and strength as a dancer allowed her to jump up and slither through the opening. She hung by her fingers for a second, then dropped to the ground.

She hit with a force that shocked her, and left her fighting for her breath. She had heard a snap when she hit, and when she tried to stand, her right ankle gave way with a pain that left her numbed, nauseated; she fell onto her back. It was the same ankle she had injured once in ballet, and she knew she had broken it.

Danielle rolled over, got up onto one leg, and, with great effort and determination, limped away toward the alley.

Back at the cheap hotel Matt stretched out slowly onto the sagging bed, exhausted. The bruise over his chest had split open when the bike went down and now it was bleeding, soaking through the bandages and staining his shirt. The pain in his chest was excruciating and each breath sent a searing jolt through his rib cage. His mind swam with fear, and his leg muscles twitched involuntarily. He got up and put a cold compress over the cut, then stretched out on the bed again and fell asleep.

Four hours later he woke up sweating profusely, shaking, burning up and freezing at the same time. It was more than a bad cold. Matt knew he was dying.

He lay in the dark and stared at the ceiling. They had won. He was out of water and out of time. He could only hope that Davis had somehow managed to get away.

He couldn't reach Danielle, and didn't know what they had done to her. He wanted to touch her face, feel her hair, and smell the freshness of her skin. He wanted to hold her close, protect her. But he couldn't do that now. He couldn't go back to her, not until he finished what he had started. If he failed, if he made any mistake, she would die and he would never see or touch her again.

His thoughts turned to Jeff. There had been an accident and they wanted to cover it up, even if it meant more lives. The power-hungry, greedy bastards. He'd stop them. His fists were clenched so tightly his arms began to ache.

The next morning Matt went out to the newsstand on the curb and bought a copy of *The Washington Post*. He'd already decided what his next move would be. If he failed this time it would be final. He knew that in less than twelve hours, everything would be over. No more second-guessing. He circled the place and time and threw the paper on the bed.

At 8:30 that evening the President would be making an important announcement at the National Press Club. Also expected to speak were the secretary of energy and— unusually enough, if one didn't know what Matt knew— Undersecretary of Defense James Reintraub.

Good, Matt thought, that meant Reintraub thought he had won. Now Matt intended to prove him wrong.

He had to be careful. There was no room for error, not even with the smallest detail or he would fail. Even then, they'd probably stop him. He knew he had little chance of succeeding but it was his last shot.

From his hotel window he stared at the bone-white dome of the Capitol that rose above the trees in the distance, but he didn't feel very patriotic at the moment. It was a big gamble, and it would be his last. He knew it. He had been without water for four days, and his own life had started decaying. He was consumed with grief, that he would never get back, that he would never see Danielle again.

Matt looked at his watch, then left the room and slammed the door with a sense of finality.

Higgins knew what had happened. A mistake, a simple, unforeseen complication that had already killed a dozen people and threatened an entire town. It was almost forgivable, considering the importance of the project. But the lies, the cover-up, the order to "sterilize" it—those were all unforgivable. And now they must be held accountable for their actions.

Higgins had sent for Parker and nervously bit on his pipe while he waited for him. He knew it was time to make a decision and put his own neck on the line if he intended to get to the bottom of this. He replayed the scenario over again in his head. If Reintraub stood to gain, who else?

Higgins kept coming up to the same conclusion. *Nobody!* Reintraub alone formed the Special Operations Interagency Group and probably had given the executive action order. Higgins was certain Reintraub had acted alone.

He hoped his conclusions were right. There was a knock at the door. "Come in."

Parker entered and closed the door behind him.

"Frank, it's time." Higgins handed his agent a handwritten two-page report of the SOIG, sealed and stamped "EYES ONLY." "Can you get it to him?"

"Tonight?" Parker asked a little hesitantly.

"Immediately."

"I'll try."

"You have to."

40

THE SITUATION WAS getting out of hand, and Reintraub was visibly tense as he drummed his fingers on the latest SOIG report. The six members of the SOIG seated around the table watched him. "What the hell were you doing at a diner with Strong, while we're combing the entire fucking city looking for him?"

Higgins stared at him with quiet contempt. "He was going to turn himself in when your guys came storming in. You know, I get the feeling that you don't even care about finding the truth. You just want him out of the way."

Reintraub stiffened, his voice was low, like a growl. "We are trying to protect this country's most important undertaking since the Manhattan Project. That's my prime objective—and it is supposed to be yours as well. Your handling of this has been inexcusable."

Higgins didn't answer right away and a malignant silence dampened the room. Higgins lit his pipe, then put it down and turned his full attention on Reintraub. "Mr. Secretary, there are some of us on this SOIG who have concerns about just what your priorities are."

Reintraub pounded the report with his fist. "The Niwot Project is my priority, and it damn well better be for everyone here. OPEC meets in less than four weeks and there can't be the slightest glitch with Niwot between now and then. That teacher is a threat to this whole project. We will find him and eliminate him."

"Not anymore. The executive action order has been canceled," Higgins said.

"By whom?!" Reintraub screamed as he came out of his chair, his face twisted into a snarl.

Higgins drew from his pipe and sent a soft swirling cloud upward. "By me."

"Bullshit. You don't have the authority to do that."

The door to the conference room opened and everyone turned. The President walked in and went to the front of the room. "He didn't do it on his own authority," the President said. "He was following my instructions." The President glanced around the room. "This teacher should be given a medal of honor, but we know that can't happen. We intend to keep this project secure, but I don't think we have to kill the rest of the town to accomplish that, do you?"

He turned to Reintraub and stared at him, eyes unblinking as if trying to see inside, to see what made him tick. "You have too myopic a view of things, Jim, a rigid, self-serving attitude that serves to protect your own narrow-minded interests."

The President opened the SOIG file and slowly turned the pages. The room grew deathly still. He closed the file and addressed the group. "It seems that Dr. Davis, the head of the field division of the CDC, finally figured out what killed the people, and you had him killed for his efforts. But the teacher was more clever. He has outfoxed all of you and now you've jeopardized the security of our highest priority project. And he's turned your SOIG project on its ears. We've got to try to find him, if your agents haven't already killed him."

Reintraub didn't say anything, but his glare never left the President.

The President stood up and turned his back to Reintraub and addressed Higgins. "Lee, you're in charge of cleaning up this mess. I don't want any of this leaked out. I'll see that you get full cooperation from both the CDC and the staff at the Niwot Project. I want a complete, detailed report. Leave nothing out. I want to know just what the hell happened.''

The President turned to Reintraub again and shook his head. ''You know, the irony is that it was easier to save the town than it was to hunt them down and kill them.''

The President stormed out and the military guards closed the door behind him.

The members of the SOIG turned to Higgins, who was calmly trying to relight his pipe. After he was satisfied, he shook out the match and dropped it in an ashtray. Higgins turned and stared into the hard, cold eyes of Reintraub, and he knew that even now, Reintraub would dodge any retribution.

It wasn't supposed to work that way. He should be accountable for his actions but there would be no punishment, no censure for what had happened. The deputy secretary had done what was asked of him—had definitely overstepped his authority to do it, but he had carried out their wishes, nevertheless. No, the President would not fire Reintraub. It would stay within their own strange secret little world.

Higgins spoke. ''Mr. Reintraub, you're excused from the SOIG. Leave your report here.'' His eyes went to the door. ''You may go now.'' Reintraub's eyes burned into him, piercing with rage as he stormed out.

Higgins went to the window and looked out over the city. ''Matt Strong is out there somewhere. And we can't help him since we don't know where he is. If we can't find him he'll die anyway.''

He turned and looked back at the other intelligence directors. ''The question is—what's he going to do next?''

41

"YOU ARE NOW in the Air Force Corridor," said the Navy
J.V. addressing the tour group. "The Pentagon is the largest
office building in the world, covering thirty-four acres. It
has seventeen miles of corridors, yet its efficient design
allows one to walk from one end to the other in six minutes
or less."

Matt wasn't listening to the guide's canned spiel. He had
taken the tour earlier that morning and collected all the
maps and brochures he could find. He was busy keeping
track of which wing they were heading to next.

The J.V. continued, "There are over 3,700,000 square
feet of floor space in this structure, serviced by more then
30,000 people, both military and civilian. The building was
begun in 1941 during World War II, in order to bring under
on roof all the war department offices."

According to the pamphlet, there were a dozen different
ways of getting to the Pentagon. It was built in Arlington,
separated from the rest of the government buildings in
Washington, D.C., by the Potomac River. Located just
northwest of it was the Arlington National Cemetery.
Visible across the river from the superstructure's grassy
slopes was the Washington Monument and the Lincoln
Memorial.

Armed with notes and sketches in his pockets, Matt had
fallen in with his second tour group outside while it was
forming adjacent to the large colonnaded East Portal en-

trance. Like the morning tour, the afternoon group then moved into the large main concourse that was lined with shops and restaurants that served both tourists and personnel.

All tours took the same predictable route, and the first stop had been the Air Force Corridor with its imposing gallery of presidential portraits lining the halls. Then it was on to the Bradley Corridor and the large, impressive War Room, during peacetime used only for occasional press conferences. Adjacent to this was Room 2E-294, the Chiefs' Room, a "tank room" that resembled, both in looks and function, a corporation boardroom. There was an awesome hexagonal walnut table about ten feet wide and three times as long surrounded by plush chairs. Tall wooden panels on the wall were covered with detailed maps of the world.

Matt had made himself very familiar with the layout of the corridors and systematic numbering of rooms to match rings and floors. There were five wings that formed the pentagonal design. Each wing had five rings, labeled E on the outside to A on the inside. The inner A wall looked out onto a courtyard laced with walkways. The top brass and most important conference rooms had large windows on the top floor of E ring with views of the Potomac River and the Capitol dome in the distance. The wings were divided by large spokelike corridors that connected all five rings to each other.

Matt stopped at a drinking fountain beside the stairs leading down to the first sublevel. From the map he knew he was just above the custodial locker room for C wing. He slipped into the stairwell and raced down to the first sublevel.

To his right was a large metal door with a sign overhead: CUSTODIAL-MAINTENANCE AREA LOWER LEVEL C. Matt looked at the locking device on the door. There was a slot for a magnetic card, and a push-button panel requiring a numeric code. A camera mounted on the wall scanned the hallway.

Staying close to the wall to avoid the viewing angle of the overhead monitor, he slipped down the hall and stepped up to the door. He glanced back at the monitor to watch the path of the camera as it swept back and forth to make sure that he wasn't in the viewing angle, then pulled his school parking card from his wallet and inserted it into the slot, keenly aware of the monitor behind him. As he fully expected, nothing happened. He just stood there waiting, holding his card in the slot.

He waited five minutes with his card in the slot before the door opened and an overweight man shuffled out. Matt kept his body between the man and his card, pulled the card out, and grabbed the door while it was still open and nodded a quick greeting as he went in. The man barely acknowledged him.

Matt found himself in a massive room filled with rows of lockers. A handful of people were there, but no one close by. He quickly pulled off his jacket and tie and tossed them in a laundry cart, covering them with dirty uniforms.

He rolled up his sleeves and went over to a long row of washbasins lining the wall. He turned the water on and kept his head down, glancing occasionally in the mirror to check behind him.

Off in a corner at the end of one row of lockers, somebody was changing back into street clothes. When the worker slammed the locker closed and walked past him toward the door, Matt looked around. That was the locker he wanted. Remote enough, and it would not be needed until the man returned tomorrow.

He walked toward it while drying his hands on a towel, stalling for time to look around. He pulled out his pocket-knife, leaned close to the locker, and kept the towel over his hands. He quickly inserted a long slender blade into the hole and twisted back and forth. He had helped enough students who had forgotten combinations that he did it with ease.

The lock released and he opened the door. Matt went through the jacket hanging there and found a card. It was a combination identification card with photograph and magnetic code for the lock. He put on the jacket, attached the ID card to the front pocket, found the shower and restroom area, went into a stall, and sat down to review his plan.

The name on the ID was "Jenson." The photo looked absolutely nothing like Matt, the face fat, the head starting to bald. Matt pulled out his map and studied it again. He doubted if he could go from one wing to another, but he was betting that he could slip from the middle C ring where he now was to the outer E ring of C wing.

The timing was critical if he had any chance at all of succeeding. He would have to wait until evening when most of the office staff had left. But the press conference was scheduled for 8:30 P.M. He sat waiting, heard voices and the slamming of lockers, but he was perfectly safe in his unappealing little spot. His legs were cramped and his left foot kept going to sleep. His stomach growled, and he felt the pang of hunger. He'd grabbed a cup of coffee and a roll when he left the hotel, but that was ten hours ago.

He'd already accomplished the first part of his plan early this morning. When Cahill told him he would be attending a press conference with Reintraub, Matt had already decided on his next move. He'd called Cahill at the *Post* the first thing this morning and arranged to meet with him and provide him with new information. Matt took Cahill the results of the water test and a portion of Vicki's autopsy report. Nothing new or important, but when Cahill went to the copy machine, Matt had quickly gone through his desk, found the press pass, and slipped it into his pocket. Luck was with him—Matt also came across a signed authorization from the *Post* admitting Cahill to the press conference.

"Got to go. I'll call you tomorrow with some very important news," Matt said and left, while Cahill stood staring at his back as he left.

He rubbed his leg and shook his foot occasionally to restore circulation. He looked at his watch again. 6:15 P.M. It would be dark outside now, and he was certain most of the Pentagon offices would be empty. It was time for the next part of his plan, but he was cutting it close. He had little more than two hours to finish here and still get to the press conference downtown at the Press Club.

He stood up and almost fell over onto his useless numbed leg. Catching himself, he opened the stall door, his leg full of needlelike pain as feeling came back. After steadying himself, he walked around the massive room until he found what he needed: a maintenance cart with light bulbs, tape, wire, tools.

He grabbed the cart and pushed it out into the hall and up to the elevator. He was aware of the monitor above him, but he kept his back to it. He took a clipboard from the cart and held it against his chest to cover the ID. The elevator opened, and a man stepped off. Another man stayed and Matt pushed his cart in.

"Three, please," Matt said as he stood behind his cart.

"I'm not cleared for three," the other man said. "Take me down to lower level two and it's all yours."

The man got out and it started back up. Alone in the elevator Matt felt the icy grip of terror. "There are some corridors in the Pentagon you just can't amble into without a special pass," the guide had told the tour group. And the man who just got off wasn't cleared for three. Fear twisted Matt's gut into a tight knot and his heart beat furiously.

The elevator door opened and Matt stepped off, pushing the cart down the long corridor to the outer E ring. He approached a uniformed military guard and started to walk past him.

"Hold it. Wait a minute."

42

MATT STOPPED. HE kept the cart between himself and the guard, a tall, stout-looking warrant officer.

"Your ID and pass."

Matt handed the guard Jenson's identification card. "I've got a work order for E-31004." His mouth was dry as he waited while the warrant officer jotted down the information. He handed him the ID and nodded for him to go on.

When he was out of sight, Matt pulled out his map and notes. He was looking for E-31004, the office of Deputy Secretary of Defense James Reintraub. To the end of the huge hall, turn right at the E ring corridor, and follow it until he came to the office on the left.

He found the number, opened the door, and stepped into the front office for the secretary and receptionist; the office was empty, the lights off. Matt pushed the cart through the inner door and found himself inside the office of Deputy Secretary Reintraub, a large office with a great view of Washington.

Matt flipped the lights on, took the small stepladder from the cart, climbed up, and took out one of the bulbs from the overhead light. He stayed on the ladder and scanned the room. His best bet would be Reintraub's desk or the bank of locked file cabinets that lined one wall.

He jumped off the ladder, raced through the papers on top of the desk but found nothing. He didn't really expect to. He pulled out his pocketknife, and after several nervous minutes finally slid his blade over the latch and pulled open the drawers.

The drawers were filled with hanging files, jammed tight with hundreds of official documents. Matt fingered through them as fast as he could. He had gone through two drawers on the right and was halfway through the first drawer on the left when he stopped. He pulled out the file labeled "TOPAZ-THE NIWOT PROJECT" and laid it on the desk.

He froze. There was somebody in the front office.

The door opened and a guard, a marine sergeant, walked in. Matt was on the ladder diligently reinstalling the bulb he'd just taken out. The TOPAZ folder was in plain sight on top of the desk and the file drawer was still open.

"Turn the lights off, would you, Sarge?" Matt asked while seemingly focusing his full attention to the light fixture.

The lights flicked off, then back on. "Thanks. That's the third bulb I've had to install this week." He took his time screwing the cover back in place.

The marine looked at him, glanced around the room, then slowly closed the door and left. Matt climbed down and thumbed through the papers in the file. There was a letter from Evans, a memo to Strassman, a memo detailing the need for total secrecy, and a note regarding Dr. Evans at the CDC. Reintraub knew what had happened in Loudonville; he had known from the very beginning. Matt took the entire folder and put it inside the cart under a stack of paper towels and left.

Matt pushed the cart down the hall and approached the security warrant officer again. This time the guard stopped in front of him.

"I want to see your pass or work order."

"My supervisor still has it. He got a rush order to fix the light in E-31004 and he called and sent me right away. He has the work order."

"The name of your supervisor?"

"Johnson. Ralph Johnson."

"Stay right here and don't move. I've got to call and check this thing out. Johnson could get us both in trouble for this. First the security slip, then you do the job, understand? Why did you even come up here without a pass or work order?'' Without waiting for an answer, the security officer spun on his heels and went to a phone.

Matt knew he was in serious trouble. As soon as someone checked the photo on his identification card, he was finished. He grabbed the folder from the cart, then turned and bolted down the corridor, back the way he had just come. A police whistle shrilled behind him.

He turned left, down one of the connecting halls, toward the inner B ring, then on to A. When he turned, he saw two military policemen closing in on him.

He stopped by a large door and tried it, opened it, and ducked inside. He turned around and scanned the dark room. He had entered one of the large tactical war rooms. He could make out a massive oval table surrounded by as many as twenty or thirty chairs. The wall to the left was lined by tall map panels. The maps were several deep and slid on tracks to reveal new maps as needed.

There was a door on the opposite side of the room and Matt was halfway across the room when he heard the door behind him open. He slipped behind a section of panel, then slowly moved a map across in front of him. A wooden pointer propped against the panel fell backward and he grabbed it just before it hit the wall. Somebody turned on the overhead lights, and three military policemen ran into the room.

Matt tried to press himself back flat against the wall, only inches away from the panels. His vision was limited to a narrow slit between maps, but he caught a glimpse of an army lieutenant move past him inches away. Matt held his breath and froze every muscle.

"Well, he's not in here. Lock the doors and meet us at corridor B-5, Sergeant," the lieutenant bellowed out. The door slammed shut and Matt heard someone lock the double doors from the far end of the room.

There was no more than ten inches between the wall and the panel in front of him. Suddenly, the map directly in front of him slammed aside and Matt stared into the face of a startled marine sergeant who was built like a bull with a thick, powerful neck. The marine's eyes were wide with surprise, and his jaw fell open. His right hand moved to the handle of his Colt .45 automatic.

In that split second Matt reacted. He swung the heavy weighted end of the pointer with all the force he could muster down into the marine's face. The marine, unprepared for the blow, reacted too slowly. He jerked back, but the handle caught the middle of his forehead with a loud, sickening crack. The skin burst open and blood streamed down over his startled face.

But he didn't move, and Matt struck again, this time driving the handle into his stomach. But it was unnecessary. Even as the pointer rammed into his gut, his legs buckled, and the marine slumped to the floor, bleeding profusely.

Matt stepped from behind the maps. He ran across the room and turned off the lights. He silently opened the door and moved into the shadows of the dimmed hallway. He realized he could easily get lost in the maze of crisscrossing halls and rings, but he had no choice. It was his only way out.

He ran down the hall, almost passing another elevator. He ran back, pressed his card into the slot, and signaled for the elevator. Matt was shaken. He had nearly killed a man and was moving deeper into an entangling complicated maze, past the point of no return. There was no turning back now, his options were gone.

The wait seemed forever as he looked up and down the hall. When the elevator opened, he leaped in and scanned the panel. There was no lobby button. He nervously pushed the lower button and the doors closed.

He didn't know what to expect at sublevel one. He glanced at his watch. He had only twenty-five minutes to get to the National Press Club. When the elevator doors finally opened, he sprang out, ready to run if necessary.

An iron gate blocked the corridor to the right, so he turned and ran down the hall to the left. The layout of this corridor was similar to the first one he had entered, and he took the first stairwell back up to the first floor.

At the top of the stairs, he found himself back on the large main concourse, the expansive hall dimly lit with only indirect lights, and the shops lining it closed for the night. The place was virtually deserted with only a dozen or so people scattered along the great hall. He started back down toward the large glass alcove that marked the main entrance, trying to cover the distance quickly with long strides. As he approached the entrance, he saw several guards at the door. Even at a distance, it was obvious that they were checking everybody that was leaving. They were looking for him!

Matt spun on his heels and started back the other way. He would have to use the other entrance, by the Potomac River. He now had to cover the entire distance across the great structure, over a quarter of a mile away.

There would be more guards looking for him at the other entrance. They had him trapped. He ducked behind a corner and pulled out his visitor's diagram and skimmed over it. He could feel the bulk of papers beneath his jacket. His hands trembled. There were no other entrances shown, but he knew that there had to be another way out. If he took the wrong door, he would be trapped in the inner courtyard, completely enclosed by five stories of building.

He stopped. Beside him was a door with a red sign overhead: EMERGENCY—FIRE EXIT ONLY. There was an alarm tripping bar across the door. He ran across the hall, threw his body against the bar, and flung the door open. An earsplitting alarm started ringing, and he nearly fell as the door gave way, but he caught himself and ran across the brightly lit parking lot as fast as he could, toward the safety of darkness.

Behind him, the alarm continued to blare out. He crossed a grassy strip on the boulevard and ran into the small park beside the river. Off in the distance he could hear sirens across the river in the city, but they appeared to be going away from him. He knelt down on the damp ground to catch his breath, pulled out the folder from under his coat, and gripped it tightly. He had never felt worse in his life; he was weak and nauseated, his chest was bleeding, he had chills and fever. But he was going to get to the conference or die trying.

The lights of the Washington Monument and Lincoln Memorial reflected on the calm water of the Potomac River. To the left a row of lights identified the Arlington Bridge. His only chance was to get across the river and back into the city.

He had twenty minutes to get to the Press Club.

He glanced back and saw a dozen men racing across the parking lot. Matt scrambled down the grassy slope toward the river, decided against the Arlington Bridge, and raced toward the bridge just ahead that would take him over the river and into East Potomac Park. He ran up the steep bank, jumped over the railing onto the sidewalk, and continued running at full speed across the empty bridge toward the city lights ahead.

Matt flagged down a taxi that had just crossed the bridge. He opened the door and leaned in. "Twenty dollars if you can get me to the National Press Club on 14th Street in five minutes."

"You got it, fella," and tires squealed as the cab shot forward into traffic.

Higgins was reviewing the situation with Parker and three members of the SOIG when his phone rang. "Hello. This is Higgins."

"This is Dick Cahill. My press pass is missing," he said.

"Why is that important to me now?" Higgins asked.

"The President and Reintraub are giving a press conference in less than thirty minutes to announce the United States's new policy toward dealing with OPEC," Cahill explained. "I think Matt Strong is going to try to get in, using my press pass."

"The crazy fool!" Higgins said. "He's going to get himself killed. Meet me there. I'm on my way." Higgins slammed the receiver down and turned to Parker. "Get a car out front now!"

43

MATT ARRIVED AT the National Press Club on 14th Street and stepped behind a line of cars while he tried to make himself more presentable. He pushed his hair back, and tucked in his shirt. He wiped the sweat from his face with a tissue, then got into line with more than one hundred and fifty members of the press corps.

Security was tight. Secret Service agents were going through camera bags, checking microphones and recorders, then running hand-held scanners over everyone before they were cleared to enter.

Matt stepped up to the entrance and handed over his press pass and clearance sheet. His name was checked against the list. A man took his pass and handed it to another agent who reviewed it while the scanner was passed over him.

"Step over here please." A stout-looking man with short-cropped hair holding his pass motioned for him to step aside.

Matt felt a cold grip of fear as his heart pounded. He hadn't seen anyone else pulled out of line. What did they want? He was beat after his trip to the Pentagon, soaked with a drenching sweat, and had chills and fever. If anything happened, he was too weak to even fight or run anymore.

He had one shot.

The rest of the press members had already been cleared and were inside. The agent holding his press card checked something off on a clipboard, turned, and handed his pass back to him. "All right, Mr. Cahill, go ahead. You're cleared."

Matt was the last one to squeeze into the back of the crowded press room. The national TV network reporters were at the front, near the microphones and in sight of the President. The rest were jammed in the back to listen, observe, record, and photograph. Matt was behind everyone, in back of the cameras.

The room was jammed with rows of folding chairs to accommodate as many press members as possible. A thick tangled network of cables and wires stretched down the center of the room to a bank of bright lights at the rear. There was a great deal of noise and scrambling as technicians shouted instructions to cameramen, soundmen tested microphones, and people jockeyed for position.

Sam Richman, the President's press secretary, entered the room and walked to the podium. All conversation died. Cameras started flashing away as he looked out over the room. He was a man of slight build, dressed in traditional dark suit, white shirt, red tie. He held the podium and leaned toward the cluster of microphones in front of him.

"We want to welcome all of you to the Washington Press Club."

Matt looked out over the room. There was not a vacant seat anywhere, and the back of the room was standing room only with cameramen, reporters, and technicians crowded together along the wall.

"The President will introduce Deputy Secretary of Defense Reintraub, who will then make a brief statement on our new energy policy. He will then take twenty questions and afterward the secretary of energy will make a brief statement. We will follow our usual procedure and protocol."

Matt was almost amused by the political tap dance the press secretary was performing. Sure, TOPAZ was a top-secret DARPA project, and Reintraub would get his chance to stand in the limelight, but in the end the lethal realities of the Niwot Project would be hidden beneath the bureaucratic trappings of the DoE. Matt waited for the event to begin.

In the center of the back row were live television cameras

from all the major networks as well as two local Washington, D.C., stations. The cameramen were adjusting lenses and lighting on the press secretary as he spoke, waiting for the President and Reintraub to start. Several security men had moved along both sides of the room and looked nervously over the audience.

Matt presumed the security men were Secret Service and not with the DIA, so he ignored them for the time being and concentrated on what he had to do.

In the center aisle, halfway to the front of the room was a microphone on a stand, presumably for any press toward the rear of the room who wanted to ask a question. Matt focused his attention on that microphone.

The President entered a side door with Reintraub and the energy secretary beside him and walked confidently to the podium, while the press rose and applauded. The President smiled, acknowledging their welcome, and waved them to be seated. Matt was in awe at being so close to the President in person, as well as seeing all the national TV news personalities that he recognized.

The President adjusted his notes and looked out at the press. "As you know, the OPEC ministers are meeting in four weeks to discuss quotas and prices of crude oil. We all remember long gas lines, rationing, shortages, and high fuel costs. We are on the brink of a new era, one in which we will no longer be dependent on foreign imported oil. We have undertaken a project bigger and of more global importance than the Manhattan Project that introduced nuclear warfare. The United States is now prepared to become the leader in energy."

Reintraub moved to the podium. "We are caught in the greatest struggle of all time. The race for energy. Developed industrialized nations are running out of fuel. The old fossil fuels of coal, gas, and shale are limited resources and are nearly depleted. Newer forms of energy like solar, geothermal, wind, and nuclear power have all been tried, but they are costly and can supply only a fraction of the growing demand for energy. Our dependence on other nations to supply our needs makes us vulnerable. I am proud to announce that we are on the verge of harnessing the power of thermonuclear fusion.

"I want to tell you about the Niwot Project. This project was started at the Plasma Fusion Lab in Princeton in 1982 after Congress passed the Magnetic Fusion Act. The first prototype Tokomak Fusion Reactor will soon be able to produce one million watts of electricity from a cup of water."

The room was deathly still as the press tried to absorb what they were hearing.

Reintraub gestured with his hands for dramatic effect, like a television evangelist pointing the way to salvation. "Cheap. No radioactive waste. Magnetic thermonuclear fusion. It's our new sun for tomorrow. America will be the leader in this newest technology and we will never again be dependent on foreign oil."

There was a sudden murmur throughout the room as the press tried to digest what they had just heard. The first question was from Peter Jordan of NBC, asking for more details about the Niwot Project.

Matt shoved past the reporters in the back and moved into the aisle. He crouched and moved down the aisle, staying beside the chairs on the left side. He moved to within fifteen feet of the microphone and squatted down to wait. He had a clear shot at the microphone.

Matt glanced at the security men at the side of the room. One of the men had locked his eyes on Matt, never blinking, his gaze never leaving him for a second. Did Matt's appearance in the aisle seem threatening? Or worse, had he been recognized? Matt tried to look to his left and behind him, but the lights blazing out from the dark room blinded him. If they came up behind him, he wouldn't be able to spot them until they were on him.

Matt stayed low on his haunches, but shifted to keep the kinks out and the blood flowing. He stole a quick glance over at the agent on the side. He had moved toward the rear.

Matt had counted sixteen questions—or was it seventeen? He looked to the side. Where was the agent? Two more questions. Arlene Doddson from Monitor Radio stood and in a very precise and stately manner said, "Mr. Reintraub, it seems I get the privilege of the last question."

Matt never heard the rest of her question. The door to the side opened, and four men moved in quickly. Two of them looked directly at Matt as he squatted by the aisle, then they moved toward the rear of the room. He had just run out of time.

"Ladies and gentlemen, thank you—"

Matt leaped to his feet and covered the short distance to grab the microphone. "Mr. Reintraub, what about the investigation of several deaths by the Centers for Disease Control that were related to the Niwot Project, and a reported cover-up by your department?" He held up Reintraub's personal memo book and the Niwot folder with a list of names. "These are your notes. What about this list of people who died?"

Cameras clicked away, spotlights swooped down on him. Security men had Matt by the arms and the mike had gone dead. The plug lay on the floor at his feet. The papers were ripped out of his hands and he was yanked to the back of the room.

There was an eruption of noise as reporters scrambled to find out what was going on and the place became chaos. The four men who had just entered moved in.

"Let him go," Higgins demanded. His agents took the papers from the secret service and pulled Matt free.

Reintraub's face blanched, then turned red as the realization of what was happening began to sink in. At the moment of his greatest triumph he'd been beaten, defeated by the teacher. Reintraub stared out over the crowd to catch a glimpse of the man who had destroyed him, but could see nothing behind the glaring lights.

Reporters caved in on Matt, but the agents pushed through them as they guided Matt from the press club.

Matt felt a sudden sharp pain in his chest, his knees buckled, and everything went black.

44

MATT FELT A sudden stab in his arm and opened his eyes. His mind was groggy and he was confused as he tried to focus on the room. He was in a strange place, white ceiling, electrical monitors around him. Matt forced himself to concentrate, and with a great deal of effort turned his neck and looked around.

A young female lab technologist was taking a blood sample from his elbow. Matt looked at his chest where a large tube disappeared into his left side.

"Pneumothorax," someone said. Matt looked over to see Cahill's friend, Dr. Tom Grant, standing beside him. "The broken ribs punctured your lung and it collapsed, so we had to put a chest tube in to re-expand it. Nasty-looking hematoma over your ribs, too."

The lab technologist pulled the needle out and put a Band-Aid over the vein. Matt looked up and saw several bottles hanging from an IV pole, with a tangled network of plastic tubing going into his other arm that was taped to an arm board.

"This is Georgetown University Hospital. You've been unconscious for four days. We thoughts we were going to lose you once, but you're just too stubborn to die."

"What's all that?" Matt asked, his throat parched and his voice barely audible.

"You're getting three antibiotics and packed white blood cells. You owe your life to Dr. Davis. His notes told us what to do to save you." Grant jotted a few progress notes in Matt's chart, then flipped it closed. "Your throat is going to be sore for a day or two. We had to put in an endotracheal tube when you were on the ventilator."

The door opened and Higgins walked in, followed by Danielle on crutches. Matt grabbed her with his only free arm and pulled her down to him. They kissed and held each other in a long embrace, crying.

"I thought you were dead," Matt whispered as they sobbed and hugged. "What happened to your leg?"

"I broke it. How do you feel? You know, you almost didn't make it."

"You said you had something important to tell me," he said, stroking her hair. "What was it?"

She looked over at Dr. Grant and he nodded to her. Danielle took his hand and leaned over him. She smiled as she brushed away her tears with the back of her hand and said, "We're going to have a baby."

It was the end of a bitter winter, a bright sunny day that would reach sixty degrees. Patches of snow melted and slowly soaked the bottom of a bundled pile of the thick Sunday edition of *The Boston Globe* that was stacked on the sidewalk. The blue Nova, burdened with luggage tied on top and a black Cinelli bicycle strapped to the trunk, pulled to the curb and stopped.

Matt broke the string and took a paper. There was a picture of James Reintraub on the front page. Reintraub had resigned.

On the same page Matt read that the Celtics had beaten the Lakers in overtime. Interest rates had stabilized and analysts predicted that the stock market was poised for another record high.

The paper mentioned nothing about a plan that went sour, nor anything about the deaths of fifteen people, or about the murder of four people who had tried to save them, no mention of a cover-up, the people responsible, or the calloused way the government chose to put the whole issue behind it.

Reintraub was like all the other ambitious, ruthless morons out there, Matt thought. They always won because they had no limits or morals, only uncontrolled greed. Matt smiled when he looked at Reintraub's picture. He hadn't stopped them, but he sure as hell had gotten their attention.

Jeff would have been proud.

Danielle opened the door. "Let's go, Matt. We've got a long trip ahead of us."

Matt nodded and dropped the paper in the melting snow. He was leaving, going back to Colorado to build a new life, and put the past behind him. He had a family to take care of now.

The overburdened Nova pulled away without protest, as if it sensed this trip was to be its noble swan song.